Love on the Horizon

Love on the Horizon

PENNY ZELLER

Love on the Horizon
Copyright ©2025 by Penny Zeller
www.pennyzeller.com
www.pennyzeller.wordpress.com
All rights reserved.
Published by Maplebrook Publishing, LLC

No part of this publication may be reproduced, distributed, or transmitted in any form or by any means, including photocopying, recording, or other electronic or mechanical methods, without the prior written permission of the publisher, except as permitted by U.S. copyright law. For permission requests, contact Penny Zeller at www.pennyzeller.com.

The story, all names, characters, and incidents portrayed in this production are fictitious. No identification with actual persons (living or deceased), places, buildings, and products is intended or should be inferred. Any brand names or trademarks mentioned throughout are owned by the respective companies.

This book may not be used for AI training, data collection, or anything else pertaining to AI.

Cover Design by EDH Professionals
Developmental Editing by Mountain Peak Edits & Design
Proofreading by Amy Petrowich

All scripture quotations are taken from the King James Version of the Bible.

All hymn lyrics as found in the public domain.

Print ISBN: 978-1-957847-52-8

Dedicated to everyone who's ever
yearned for a place to belong.

I will praise thee; for I am fearfully and wonderfully made: marvellous are thy works; and that my soul knoweth right well.
Psalm 139:14

Chapter One
Chicago, 1897

THE BEST DREAMS WERE the ones that came true.

And Magnolia "Mags" Davenport's dreams were about to come true. She could feel it in her bones, as old Mrs. Fryman used to say.

She took a step back and scanned the bustling city. Hadn't she read in a discarded newspaper that Chicago had reached over a million people? Yes, her decision to travel West would be a good one.

The train depot beckoned her, and she entered the stately brick Dearborn Station with its enormous clock tower. Folks hurried in every direction. Hopefully, with twenty-some railroad lines and countless departures, one of those departures would surely lead her to the new life that awaited her.

No one would be the wiser that a twenty-three-year-old woman would be boarding for free.

For what could she do? The two dollars she'd saved would only be for absolute necessities.

The lines to purchase tickets meandered through the building. Mags stood on tiptoe to see the departure signs when she noticed a wealthy couple in front of her in deep conversation.

"I anxiously anticipate seeing our grandchildren again," the woman, who wore an elegant dress of the latest fashion, said.

"Yes, well, I'm never fond of visiting Horizon, but I know how much it means to you, and it's been all of two months since we saw the grandchildren."

"Indeed, Bertram. I missed them the second we boarded the train for Denver, and this time, having been in Maryland, I miss them all the more. Besides, Horizon is such a lovely place, and the people are so kind. I've actually made a few friends there."

The man named Bertram, in the finest of silk hats, grunted. "Yes, Gladys, we all know you've made friends in Horizon."

The topic that Bertram and Gladys spoke about intrigued Mags, and she stepped closer. Horizon sounded like just the place she'd like to live, especially if people were kind. Goodness knows she'd had her share of spiteful and cruel people in Chicago—many of whom were related.

Gladys leaned her head back, the purple lilacs and other foliage atop her extravagant hat nearly poking Mags in the eye.

"Oh, dear me. I'm so sorry." The woman nodded in her direction, then returned her attention straight ahead.

Feeling suddenly tattered and disheveled in her dress, Mags resisted the urge to lower her head and stare at her worn and holey shoes. But not this time. Her curiosity had been piqued about this Horizon place. She tapped on Gladys's shoulder. "Ma'am, if you don't mind..."

"What is it?" The woman's voice wasn't unkind, but it was clipped, and wariness filled her countenance. Perhaps she thought Mags would be asking for funds like so many beggars did—like Mags had a time or two.

"Might I ask about this place known as Horizon?"

A smile lit Gladys's face, and the starch in her frame dissolved. "Our son, his wife, and our grandchildren live there." She handed her leather reticule to Bertram and opened the golden locket at her neck. "If you look closely, you can see our four grandchildren. The older ones are Polly and Hosea. The two little ones are Pansy and L.J."

Mags squinted to see the tintypes of the four children. Their smiles lit up the frames. Such happiness! What would that have been like?

"Oh, yes. They are lovely children."

"Indeed. So that is why we visit. What else would you like to know?"

"Is Horizon in Montana? California? Colorado?"

"Idaho."

That wasn't the answer she'd expected. "Idaho?"

"Yes, it really is a bit backward and primitive in my opinion, but it is improving. They now have a hotel, although we don't stay there. We stay with our son and his wife when we visit."

Bertram cleared his throat. "Must you make friends with everyone you meet, Gladys?"

Gladys's perfectly shaped brows dipped. "Yes, I must."

"Thank you for the information. Horizon sounds delightful."

And that was just the place Mags would go, provided her plan worked. And provided the conductor failed to realize she hadn't purchased a ticket.

It wasn't the most ideal of situations, but when had she ever let that stop her?

3

Mags raised her chin and took a deep breath. Yes, she would go to Horizon. Find a fresh start, escape her past, and maybe, just maybe, find a place where she belonged.

Mags examined the route posted on the board with the words *Chicago, Union Pacific and North-Western Line, Bennick Railways* along the bottom. The trip to Horizon, Idaho, would not be an expedient one. Had she ever really known how far Illinois was from Idaho?

Not likely, because Idaho was not something she'd ever given thought to. Sure, she'd heard about the Wild West and the at-times frightening happenings there. She'd read in a newspaper once about a train robbery in Montana and a shootout in Wyoming.

She tapped Gladys on the shoulder. "Begging your pardon, ma'am."

"Yes?"

"Might I inquire as to whether Idaho has cities?"

Bertram didn't allow his wife to speak, but instead answered the question. "Trust me, young lady, when I say that if there weren't cities in Idaho, we'd never visit there."

She dispelled a breath of relief. "Thank you."

"Although there aren't many," added Gladys.

Mags needn't go where there were *many* cities, just one where she could secure an honorable job. She turned back to the route and traced the solid black line with her finger. From Chicago to Omaha, then to Denver, back up to a place called Green River, then Pocatello, Boise City, and Cornwall, then smaller print with the word *Horizon*.

Honestly, it didn't seem *that* far. Besides, travel by rail, while there would be several legs of the trip and many stops, shouldn't take too terribly long.

The price of a ticket to such a place momentarily deterred her.

Momentarily.

For how could she afford such a cost? She bit her bottom lip. She knew that such a ticket was really a series of tear-off coupons for each leg of the trip. If Mags failed to secure the "main" ticket, she'd have no tickets for any of the stops.

A conundrum if there ever was one.

Ma was fond of quoting that nothing was impossible with God, and for a minute, that thought entered her mind and lingered. But Mags shoved it aside. How could God have allowed her to lose her parents, be separated from her sister, and be forced to live with her despicable aunts?

Another thought came to her then. Mags didn't need to afford a ticket. She just needed to be persuasive.

The train whistle blew. Someone bellowed, "All aboard!" The odor of smoke filled her nostrils, but it wasn't offensive; rather, Mags welcomed the scent of impending freedom. Folks waved to their loved ones, and she pretended some of those people were seeing her off as well. With her free hand, she waved and smiled, ignoring the perpetual pinch in her heart.

Then she removed from her carpetbag a tattered piece of paper that she'd found discarded on the floor of the depot.

As luck would have it, it was exactly three minutes before the conductor found her in line.

"Miss, I'll need to see your ticket."

At just the opportune time, she released the scrap of paper, and it swirled and fluttered in the air. "Oh, no! Dear me, sir, did you see that?"

"See what?"

Mags forced the tears to sprout in her eyes. "My—my ticket. It just blew away in the breeze. Might I have a moment to search for it?" She covered her mouth with a hand and forced the choked sobs.

The man, an older and portly sort in a uniform accentuating his generous middle, stared in the direction where she'd released the paper. "My sincere apologies, but we can't go back and get the ticket as we haven't the time. I'm sorry."

"But—but how will I ever embark on the trip to see my ill grandmother if I don't have a ticket?" She lowered her head and squeezed her eyes shut, eliciting more tears. After wailing for a good several seconds, Mags covertly peered through one eye at the conductor. He tended to other passengers all the while answering inquiries. Had he forgotten about her?

Another cloud of smoke rose from the train. The line to board all but disappeared, save for her and two others standing on the steps awaiting entrance. Mags hiccupped and purposely shook her shoulders for effect while she again covered her face in her hands.

"I'm sorry about the ticket, miss."

"My grandmother..." she ensured her shoulders quaked all the more with exaggeration, but not too much fanfare, for then the man would know she wasn't being forthright.

However, she was desperate.

Seconds ticked by, and the breeze blew her skirt from covering her threadbare shoes, and she shifted so her feet would remain covered. A faded dress was acceptable, but shoes barely held together, and her big toe exposed would not earn her the free ride on the train. It would indicate the vagabond that she was.

"Now, now, miss. Please don't cry."

"But Grandmother hasn't much time to live. She called for me, and I..." Mags sniffed and dabbed at her nose with her sleeve. If only she had a handkerchief.

The conductor said nothing. A passenger peered through the window at her with a scowl, likely because she was impeding the train's departure. She pulled in a breath and held it. Had the conductor seen through her schemes? If so, she'd need a secondary plan. Just as she was conjuring up an idea, the man again spoke.

"Why don't you go inside, since there's nothing we can do about your ticket?"

Mags raised her head and blinked rapidly. She placed a hand on the man's arm. "God bless you, sir." It was a phrase she'd heard the blind man on the corner asking for money say time and time again when someone dropped a coin in his battered, upturned hat.

The conductor offered her a compassionate smile before opening the door and ushering her inside the train.

As she plunked into the seat, Mags exhaled a sigh of contentment. She had no idea the outcome of this escapade, only that she'd successfully completed the first portion of the trip for a chance to start a new life.

Chapter Two

"Hey, mister. Want a paper?"

Timothy rarely purchased the newspaper. There were plenty of other ways to find out about the latest Horizon scuttlebutt. But when the young boy peered up at him, Timothy reconsidered. The lad wore dirty trousers with holes, and he was too thin for his age.

"How much for a paper?"

"Ten cents."

Timothy reached into his pocket. All he had was a nickel or a quarter. "Do your parents live here in Horizon?" he asked. He returned the nickel to his pocket.

The boy's attention focused solely on the quarter in Timothy's hand. Without looking up, he answered, "Yes, sir. They do. Pa's real sick, but I'm the man of the house 'til he gets well. Got me a ma and two sisters I have to provide for." He straightened his narrow shoulders. "You gonna buy the paper, mister?" Hope filled his features. "I only got two of 'em left."

"I am. Under one condition."

The boy's shoulders slumped. "Why's there gotta be a condition?"

"What's your name?"

"Ozias."

"And your last name?"

"That's what I gotta do? Answer a bunch o' questions before you'll buy a paper?"

Timothy had an ulterior motive. If he could find out about the boy's family, perhaps he could help them. "It is."

Ozias shrugged. "Last name is Agnew."

Timothy traded the quarter for the newspaper. While he couldn't afford to lose that much money on an unnecessary purchase, his heart broke for the poverty-stricken boy.

"Pleasure doing business with you, sir." The boy pocketed the quarter without so much as offering change. Then he scampered off and zipped around the corner before Timothy heard him shout, "Newspaper! Get your *Horizon Herald* here. Only five cents!"

Five cents? But Ozias had told him ten cents. Had the boy innocently erred?

Timothy would like nothing more than to perch on the bench in front of the mercantile and sit a spell while perusing the newspaper, but there was work to be done. And feed to be bought. He tucked it under his arm and continued on his way to conduct the errands he had come to town for, but he couldn't get Ozias out of his mind. Why hadn't he seen him in church? Was his family new to town? Was Ozias telling the truth? Timothy had grown up in a loving home with three sisters and a brother, and while they struggled a time or two during droughts or when hail destroyed the crops, he'd never had to scrounge for money the way it appeared Ozias did.

He threw a bag of feed into the back of the wagon, then started toward the church. Maybe Albert, his brother, knew the Agnew family. As a pastor, Albert seemed to know just about everyone in Horizon.

Albert stood behind the lectern when Timothy entered. He stopped speaking and waved. "Hello, Timothy. Just working on this Sunday's sermon about pride. Always a convicting topic. So, what brings you to the church?"

"Do you know a family by the name of Agnew?"

His older, but much shorter and skinnier brother, stroked his beard. "I don't recognize that name. Why?"

Timothy explained about his interaction with the young boy. He omitted the part about the dishonest exchange of money. Albert would never let him hear the end of it.

"There are a lot of new families moving in, so maybe they've recently arrived in Horizon. I'll see what I can find out."

"Thanks, I'd like to see if there's a way we can help them."

"Have you asked at *The Horizon Herald*?"

"I haven't yet, but that's a good idea."

"Have you purchased a pair of spectacles yet?" Leave it to Albert to change the topic of discussion to something unpleasant.

"Not yet."

"Well, besides the ones you purchased from the peddler?" Albert smirked. Who said pastors couldn't have an ornery streak? Of course, while Timothy was about a decade younger, he *did* recall Albert's mischievous antics when they were children.

Albert raised his eyebrows. "How did it go with the peddler, anyway?"

Timothy would rather *not* discuss the money he wasted on the eyeglasses from the vendor—more like a swindler—who'd traveled through town hawking his wares. He'd attempted to con Timothy into buying more than a useless pair of spectacles. A packet of crop seeds hadn't really been what the con advertised them to be. Upon closer examination, Timothy discovered the packet contained miniature woodchips instead. While peddler wagons had grown rare in Horizon due to the railroad and folks being able to secure just about anything they needed through the *Montgomery Ward Catalogue* at the mercantile, of those who did visit, some were legitimate. Others, not so much.

His family had discussed many times his need for spectacles because he couldn't see clearly, especially at far distances. He figured that by purchasing the eyeglasses, it would appease them. It may have appeased them, but the eyeglasses hadn't worked for Timothy. "I'm not so sure I really need them. It's primarily things in the distance that are blurry."

"I do recall you used to be a sure shot, almost as good as Pa. That last time we went out for target practice..."

"I know, I know, I couldn't even hit one of those cans."

Albert chuckled. "It's not so bad to have to wear spectacles, is it? A lot of people wear them, including the Lieutenant and Reverend Marshall."

"The Lieutenant and Reverend Marshall are both old."

His brother shrugged. "True. But I don't think you have to be elderly to wear them."

Timothy harumphed. "They get in the way of my work, and they'll fog up in the winter. I don't think eyeglasses are for me."

"Maybe you can travel to Cornwall and pay a visit to the optician."

"There's no time to be taking trips to Cornwall. I've got a farm to manage." It was the rationale he used whenever he didn't really want to do something, but in most cases, it was true.

"You're just full of excuses, aren't you?"

The way Albert cocked his head to one side, pressed his lips into a firm line, and folded his arms across his slim chest reminded Timothy of the way a father would scold his son. Likely, Albert used that same stance and expression with his sons, Simon and Sherman.

"Well, I'll let you get back to your sermon. Let me know if you find out anything about the Agnew family, and I'll stop by the newspaper office on my way home."

"Speaking of *The Horizon Herald*, I'm surprised, with all of these people moving in, that no one has wanted to rent that vacant building beside it. Landon's parents own it, but it sure would be nice to see a business in there rather than it remaining empty."

Timothy shrugged. "Could have something to do with the fact that some folks still believe there's loot still hidden in the attic or the walls somewhere and that ne'er-do-wells might attempt to break in and find it."

"After all this time? Not likely. Or at least, it wouldn't be likely for anyone who has lived in Horizon for any length of time. But you're right. That could be the case for those who don't know there is no plunder in the walls. On the other hand, I'm surprised someone wouldn't want to rent it, so maybe they can locate the plunder, although they would have to return it to its rightful owner."

They chatted for a few more minutes before Timothy exited the church. When he stepped through the doors, he noticed his three sisters and sister-in-law walking to the church, all of their children in tow. Maybe he could ask some of his nieces and nephews if they knew Ozias.

"Uncle Timothy, Uncle Timothy!" His nieces and nephews charged toward him, all seeing who could reach him first. In this case, it was Little Hans, and Timothy reached down and swung the young boy around, eliciting a giggle and a, "One more round, Uncle Timothy!" To which he obliged before the dizziness set in.

Sure, he would like to have a family someday and have his own children, but God blessed him with so many nieces and nephews that it was all right by him if he was just an uncle.

The children all talked at once, and when they were finished, Timothy asked his question as well as signing it at the same time for Polly and Hosea, his deaf niece and nephew. "Do any of you know a boy by the name of Ozias Agnew?"

"I've never heard of him," said Sherman.

"Me neither," said Becky.

Carrie shook her head. "No. How old is he?"

"He's probably around six, I would say."

Carrie focused her gaze up at the sky. "I don't think he goes to our school. I would surely know of him if he did."

Gus pretended to stroke his chin. "Can't say as I have."

Little Pansy tapped Timothy on the arm. "Uncle Timothy?"

"Yes?"

"I haven't ever known him my whole life."

Timothy chuckled at the petite girl who was a smaller replica of her mother, Mae.

The children bounded off for a game of tag, and Timothy's sisters approached him. Both Ruby and Velma pushed prams with their daughters, Evelyn and Gloria, respectively, in them. He forgot at times that Albert's wife, Velma, wasn't his sister because everyone in his family was so close.

"What are you up to today?" asked Ruby, always the nosy one. Her youngest child, a little girl with the same red hair as her ma, smiled up at him and babbled. He lifted her from the pram and she snuggled against him. Velma's daughter, an energetic two-year-old who did her best to keep up with her older brothers, wiggled from Velma's grasp as she hoisted her from the pram, and toddled off toward the older children.

"Excuse me, I'd better grab her," said Velma just as her daughter turned, giggled, and ran as fast as her stubby legs would carry her in the direction of the others.

"I was asking Albert if he knew the Agnew family. Have any of you heard of them?" He handed Evelyn back to Ruby.

"I haven't," said Mae, "but I could ask Landon. He's had some new workers at the business."

Lucy, his eldest sister, chewed on her lip. "The name doesn't sound familiar. Why do you ask?"

Timothy relayed the story about the boy in tattered clothing, but again omitted his shady business practices. "I'm going to stop by *The Horizon Herald* and ask there as well."

"It's much better there now that the evil Mr. O'Kane is no longer the editor," said Ruby.

He was about to escape to the newspaper office before Mae asked one of the two questions he loathed. "Did those eyeglasses you purchased from the peddler work well?"

"Oh, yes," chimed in Lucy. "You didn't wear them to church last week."

"And he sure should have," giggled Ruby. Evelyn copied her ma and laughed too, her button nose scrunching.

Timothy groaned. "We're not bringing that up again, are we?"

All three sisters laughed, and Ruby released an unladylike snort at his expense. He was the closest to Ruby, but she was also the most annoying.

"That was so hilarious when you thought it was someone it wasn't at the church potluck. Remember that?"

"You don't have to bring it up every time I see you, Rubes."

"Well, where's the fun in that? Besides, it's just a testament that you truly need spectacles."

"I honestly thought it was Wilhelmina." How many times did he have to justify his error? His sisters were relentless.

"I'm sure we can all see how Timothy could mistake Alma for Wilhelmina." Lucy rolled her eyes.

"What's going to happen when there's a lovely young lady and you miss seeing her altogether?" asked Mae in her sweet, demure voice.

"It won't matter. As I mentioned before, I prefer to remain unmarried. A man whose mission is to farm the land would have no need for a wife."

"Pa has a wife, as do many farmers." Lucy arched an eyebrow, daring him to disagree. He wouldn't, as he'd never once in all his years won an argument against Lucy.

His sisters cast furtive glances at each other. "Or so he says," said Ruby. "Just wait until the perfect woman comes along, and then you will have to renege on your words."

"Nope. I've seen the women in this town, and I'm not interested."

"Not even in Mary Lou?" asked Mae.

"Not even Mary Lou. I've never been interested in her for more than a friend."

"Well, Mary Lou sure likes you," teased Velma, who'd returned to the conversation with a squirming Gloria in her arms.

"Down, Mama?"

Lucy set her down just as Becky ran up to the group. "We'll keep a close eye on her, Aunt Velma."

"Close eye," repeated Gloria, reaching for Becky's hand.

"Thank you, Becky. Now, where were we?"

Timothy could go all day without having to revisit the topic of discussion.

"We were discussing how Timothy should ask Mary Lou for her hand in courtship." Lucy's comment started another round of laughter.

Ruby leaned forward, her eyes large. "You're going to ask for her hand in courtship?"

"Absolutely not." Timothy folded his arms across his chest. "As I was saying, I'd never ask her because we're only friends and have been all our lives."

"Friendship is a delightful way to start a marriage," quipped Mae.

"And it's unfortunate you'll not take interest in her since she hails from such a lovely family," added Lucy.

"Lovely family or not, I'm not interested in Mary Lou. Never have been and never will be."

Ruby jabbed Timothy in the side. "What about Alma?"

"Definitely not Alma." Timothy suddenly experienced a foul taste in his mouth. He could only imagine what life with Alma would be like. The woman had a penchant for theatrics. "I have known these ladies since I was in school with them. They are best suited to be friends. Besides, Alma is just plain annoying."

They listed off two other women who'd set their caps for Timothy, and he shook his head. "Not interested in those two either."

"Look at the positive aspect of marrying Alma," began Ruby. But from the glint in her eye, he knew her next words would be anything but a positive aspect. "You could have all the charred cookies your stomach could hold."

Timothy scowled. "That's the truth. The woman can't bake."

His sisters' obnoxious gales of laughter likely sounded all the way to the mercantile.

"But you don't have to fear because Ma was once like that, and look at her now. Ma makes scrumptious meals," assured Lucy when she'd finally taken a breath.

Mae bobbed her head. "Yes. Don't give up on Alma. There's hope for everyone if there was hope for Ma. Remember those pancakes?"

"Those were the worst." Lucy pretended to retch.

"I thought the rubber eggs were awful." Mae shivered. "Rubes, you and Timothy are fortunate that by the time you were born, Ma had learned how to cook."

Lucy patted him on the stomach. "You'll never grow plump if you marry Alma."

He'd never grow plump anyway, not with the way he worked in the fields. He'd gone from being a scrawny boy to a strong and muscled man in the past several years.

Ruby pretended to be serious. "But honestly, Timothy, don't give up on any of those four who currently believe you to be a ripsnorter."

"A real humdinger, for sure," added Lucy.

Mae tapped her chin. "Or perhaps the most eligible bachelor in Horizon."

"I must make a contrary statement," said Velma. "Timothy is only one of the most eligible bachelors. What about old Mr. Gaw?"

"Old Mr. Gaw is as cantankerous as they come. He'll never find a wife," Timothy muttered. "And he's a hundred and two. Besides, I plan to be a doting uncle instead of a husband."

The looks on his sisters' and sister-in-law's faces indicated they didn't believe him.

"Mm-hmm," came a chorus of naysayers.

He'd hoped the finality in his voice would cause them to cease their teasing, but instead they laughed again. Timothy tipped his hat. "I best get along, seeing as how I have more errands."

"We'll discuss this matter further at a later date."

"No, Lucy, we will not. The matter is closed."

Timothy planted a kiss on Baby Evelyn's forehead, and she patted his cheek with her slobbery fist. Then, casting a glower at his sisters, he turned on his heel and stalked to the newspaper office.

Chapter Three

Mags settled into the comfortable seat on the standard passenger coach near the window. No, it hadn't been the elaborate Pullman car she'd anticipated, but it was still unlike anything she'd seen. Several round, white glass lights that reminded her of oversized pearls hung perfectly spaced along the ceiling. Green shades, matching the green seats, were opened, allowing passengers to see beyond the train, but could be pulled down during the evening or to prevent the sun from glaring into riders' eyes. Round curly-cue hooks above the shades provided a place to hang hats. In all, the double seats held sixty passengers total in the railcar, with toilet rooms—one for men and one for women—at either end. Excitement stirred inside her. Within days, she would be starting her new life somewhere else, away from the confines of the crowded Chicago streets. Away from family members who'd never hidden their disdain for her. Away from memories, both good and bad. At the thought of the former, she swallowed the lump in her throat.

You will always have your fond memories, no matter where you go. The words she said to herself were meant to appease the longing to go back in time, just for a minute, and relive those brief days of happiness.

Would she make new happy memories in Horizon, Idaho? Yes, she had to believe that she would. And if she didn't cotton much to Horizon, then she would just move on. Nothing said she had to stay.

She stretched her legs as far as she could in front of her. She knew days of travel awaited her, and the distance was lengthy, but at least the seats weren't without the faded green covering, and there was an armrest. Things could be worse. She could be walking to her new destination.

A niggle of concern caught her unawares. She didn't have a ticket for the removal of a coupon for each stop during her trip. How could she continue to travel?

No. She wouldn't worry about that now. But the thought persisted until she focused her attention on the crows converging about the passenger car as the train proceeded to move slowly on the tracks.

A harried young woman about the same age as Mags prompted her little boy onto the seat, then plopped beside him, carrying a baby in a wicker basket.

For the briefest of moments, Mags wished the woman and her children would choose another location. But as soon as the thought entered her mind, she chastised herself. The seats filled quickly, leaving nary an empty one, and a woman and her young children were far more preferable seatmates than a grouchy older woman or, even worse, an immoral man with a roving eye. Mags knew all about those types of men, and she did not want to be trapped beside one.

The little boy, clutching a book and squished between Mags and his mother, peered up at her, and Mags once again rebuked herself for wishing the family had sat elsewhere. She returned his smile. He had to be all of three, and the sleeping infant girl in the basket was no more than three or four months old. The train gained speed, and folks on the boardwalk beside it waved at the passengers. Mags waved back, pretending that someone was here to see her off, although nothing could be further from the truth. Not even Phoebe had come to bid her farewell, although Mags couldn't fault her for that.

Phoebe. Her dear sister. They'd embraced with tears streaming down both of their faces last night when Mags informed Phoebe she was off to find them a better life.

"I don't mind Chicago too awfully," said Phoebe. "You could just stay here. The baby will be born soon."

Mags could stay in Chicago, but where? Her landlord had let her apartment to a renter who could afford to pay more for the dank, rat-infested tenement than she could. She couldn't stay with Phoebe in the one room she and her husband, Larry, rented from a sourpuss of a woman.

It wasn't the first time there had been nowhere for Mags to go.

But it was the last time.

Tears brimmed in her eyes as she recalled hugging her sister and promising she'd send for Phoebe, Larry, and the baby once she settled in her new home.

At the time, Mags hadn't known that new home would be in Horizon, Idaho. She and Phoebe had discussed all sorts of places where Mags might find them a place to live. California, perhaps? She'd heard there were jobs to be had and many affluent cities. Maybe Denver? Or would Omaha, Nebraska, be their new home?

"What if Larry doesn't agree for us to move?" Phoebe had asked, tears streaking her face.

"He will. I'll find a good job for him so he'll have no option but to agree. And I'll send you all tickets."

"But how will you afford such a feat? And how will you procure a job for him?"

Phoebe worried too much. "Please don't worry. I'll take care of every last detail."

"I've been praying you'll arrive at just the destination God has planned for you."

Easy for Phoebe to say. She retained her faith after their parents passed. Had clung to it. Relied on Jesus for her comfort. Or so she'd told Mags when they'd reunited all those years later. But she wouldn't disappoint her sister in her response. "Thank you for your prayers."

"Are you sure a woman in her early twenties ought to travel by herself?"

"It's nearly the 1900s. I'm not concerned."

"You've always been the brave one, Mags."

The compliment offered the reassurance Mags needed.

Mags reluctantly returned her attention to her fellow passengers on the train. All sorts of people crowded into their seats, commotion ensuing as some tucked their carpetbags on the shelf, others hung their hats on the hooks, a wailing baby in the far back let her opinions be known, and a man in a business suit and velvet hat attempted to speak over the child.

"I'm just so glad we made it on time," the woman was saying as she patted her little boy on the head.

"Yes, Mama," said the little boy, although Mags doubted he fully understood the full impact of what his mother was saying.

"Your children are adorable," said Mags.

"Thank you," said the woman. "We're meeting my husband in Denver, and I dare say it hasn't been as easy as one would think traveling with two young children. Where is your destination?"

"Horizon, Idaho." Even as the words rolled off her tongue, anticipation trilled through her. What would this city called Horizon be like? What job opportunities would there be for her? Would the people be kind? Would they accept her?

"I must admit I've never heard of it. I've been to Boise before. Is it close to that city?"

Mags knew nothing about Boise or whether it was in close proximity to Horizon. As a matter of fact, she knew nothing about Idaho other than that it was in the United States. She struggled to recall if she had learned anything about it in school. But history hadn't really been her forte.

The woman awaited Mags's answer, and she didn't want to sound inept, so instead Mags did what she always did when she needed to weave a story to fit the circumstance. "Yes, it is near Boise. I will be taking a short wagon ride to Horizon once I reach the depot." Or maybe a stagecoach. She'd heard of those and wondered what that must be like, rushing across the plains.

"Do you have family there?"

"Oh, yes, my grandparents hail from Horizon." She recalled the older couple in the depot and the woman who had discussed her grandchildren. Perhaps she could pretend for a moment that the woman was her grandma. After all, the only woman who even bore a semblance to being her grandmother had rejected her.

"Well, that will be wonderful to be able to see them again. I honestly can't wait to be reunited with my husband. The children and I traveled to Chicago to visit my parents. My husband was unable to take time off due to work. I have truly enjoyed the trip to see my family, but Mother planned so many activities that I now feel I need a vacation."

Mags knew nothing about mothers who planned too many activities, and she knew even less about vacations. But she wouldn't let the woman know that. "Well, I'm sure that the train ride will be restful now that the commotion has ceased."

The woman nodded, "Yes, I've been on trains many times, and it's always a bit chaotic when we're all boarding. I'm just grateful to have found this seat."

The woman leaned back, took a deep breath, and closed her eyes.

"Are you going to sleep?" the little boy asked his mother.

"Just for a few minutes, yes." Her hushed and exhausted tone preceded a few soft snores before the woman's soft snores filled the air.

The little boy, in his crisp white shirt and knickers with suspenders, seemed satisfied with his mother's answer. He opened the book, moved his stubby finger along the words, and pretended to read.

"Would you like me to read that to you?"

The little boy nodded. Mags loved to read, and even more than that, she loved to read to children. That had been one of the delights of having to work for her Aunt Mikelanna, perhaps the only delight. Mags would *not* miss that horrid woman, not one bit.

Mags proceeded to read the story, adjusting her voice for the characters as needed. The little boy beside her giggled. Her cousins had laughed at her reading antics once upon a time as well. If only Mags could have secured the position of nanny with the wealthy family she'd met three years ago in Chicago. But they hadn't been impressed when they discovered she hadn't been completely forthright about her past experience as a governess. Mags shook off the disappointment and focused on reading the book, one that she had never read before. When she finished, the boy asked her to read it again, and so she did, four more times.

Such hope she'd held for her young cousins during those times of caring for them. Until Aunt Mikelanna determined that Mags was no longer needed.

When Mags finished reading the final time, the child leaned his head on his mother's shoulder and fell asleep, leaving Mags with a pit of loneliness.

She shoved that thought aside. After she turned twelve, loneliness was part of her everyday life. She should be accustomed to it by now.

Mags averted her attention out the window at the passing scenery. They'd long left the city behind, and expansive fields of green replaced looming buildings. A wagon in the distance caught Mags's eye, stirring a memory.

It had been just her and Ma for the first nearly six years of her life. Mags hadn't known anything about her father. Who he was, or where he was. And Ma never spoke of him. So, it came to be after Mags had just turned six, Ma decided to marry a man named Cassius Davenport. Mags knew, even at her tender age, that her life would be changed forever.

Cassius brought with him a daughter named Phoebe, who was a year older than Mags. It had taken some time for Mags to acclimate to Phoebe, and even longer for Phoebe to acclimate to Mags.

Ma worked hard at her job at the factory—a job she'd unfortunately had to retain even after she'd married Cassius due to owing the hospital an enormous amount of money from Mags's illness several months before. Ma would sometimes arrive home past dinnertime. Cassius's job as a milkman required him to begin his duties earlier in the day than Ma's, but Ma worked later in the evenings. Between the two of them, they worked it out so that Mags no longer had to stay with crotchety Mrs. Garcia in the neighboring apartment.

That alone was cause for celebration.

Mags recalled one afternoon in particular when Cassius had arrived at school and picked up her and Phoebe in the milk wagon. Children stood outside the doors, gaping. "*Your pa is a milkman?*"

Phoebe had puffed out her chest. "*Yes, he is. And the best milkman in Chicago.*"

Because Cassius wasn't Mags's pa, she couldn't agree with the girl's question, but she was still proud that the man her mother married had such a prominent position.

Cassius assisted Phoebe into the milk wagon, twirling her a bit before lifting her onto the seat. He did the same with Mags, and she giggled with joy before he set her next to Phoebe. Phoebe's dark eyebrows knitted together in a scowl. Mags attempted to ignore her as Phoebe was forever scowling when Cassius made the situation fun for Mags as well.

It wouldn't be until years later that Mags realized being a milkman wasn't quite as important as the children made it seem that day, but whether it was a distinguished position or not, the fact that the man who filled such a void in her life was employed as one made it prominent to her.

Cassius had to deliver a few more pints and quarts of milk and retrieve some empty bottles before he was able to take them home. Mags hadn't minded. She could stay in the milk wagon all day as they rumbled through town, delivering the delicious liquid. Cassius told them stories, including how sometimes folks didn't return the empty bottles or other times, milk was stolen right off the porches of the people's houses. Mags couldn't imagine someone being so dishonest.

When they had finally arrived home, Cassius withdrew three flat, skinny taffy candies from the cupboard.

Mags's mouth watered when he handed her one, and she could barely wait to eat it. *"I never knew those were in there."*

"It's because they are for today. It's a special day. "

"Why is it special?" asked Phoebe

"Because I received a raise in pay today."

Mags hadn't been surprised that Cassius received a raise in pay. He was a hard worker and the smartest man she had ever known. Maybe it would mean that Ma wouldn't have to work at the factory anymore and could be home with them.

More than almost anything, that's what Mags hoped because the guilt of the hospital bill was never far from her thoughts, although Ma had never insinuated it was her fault.

Phoebe bit a bite of taffy, licked her lips, and climbed into Cassius's lap on the worn sofa. *"Thank you for the taffy, Pa. It's delicious."*

Mags watched as Cassius and Phoebe spent time together laughing, talking about their day, and eating the candy. A feeling of sadness overcame her, and a heaviness settled into her chest. Why was it that she didn't have a pa like Cassius?

She sat at the table and ate her candy, attempting not to let the dismal thought of not being Cassius's daughter ruin the thrill of having taffy—a treat she'd only had one other time in her life.

"Magnolia?" Cassius's voice interrupted her thoughts. Only Ma and Cassius called her by her real name, unless one

counted the times one of her aunts was angry and referred to her as *"That child, Magnolia"*.

"Yes, sir?"

Cassius wiggled his finger at her. *"Would you care to join us?"*

Phoebe narrowed her eyes and pooched her bottom lip. She shook her head ever so slightly just so that Mags could see her, but her pa probably hadn't even noticed.

Mags took the hint. Easier that way than having Phoebe angry with her.

"No, thank you." Mags attempted to make her voice sound the same as it always did, but even in her own ears, it sounded sad.

"You're welcome to join us if you'd like."

Mags lifted her head and studied Cassius and Phoebe. They both had dark hair and hazel eyes. So opposite of Mags and Ma with their blonde hair and blue eyes.

Oh, how she wanted to join them. How she wanted to be Cassius's daughter like Phoebe was. She had the best ma in the world, and if only she had a pa, her life would be perfect.

Perfect indeed!

But it wasn't to be. And even if she did try to be Cassius's daughter, Phoebe would have something to say about it. Or she would take Mags's only doll from her in retaliation. Mags stared down at her taffy. Suddenly, it had lost its flavor. If only she were fortunate like Phoebe, and Cassius were her father, too. He was kind. Thoughtful. And Ma loved him. Mags knew that because Ma repeatedly told him so. And Cassius would tell Ma what a blessing she was in his life.

It was because of Cassius, too, that they had begun to attend church every Sunday. Mags didn't know much about God at first and why they sang songs to Him, but when she saw the pure joy on both Ma's and Cassius's faces as they sang from the hymnals, Mags figured that whoever God was, He must be someone special to have folks sing about Him and pray to Him.

"*Magnolia? How about you come over here and tell me all about your day at school?*"

"*She doesn't have anything to tell unless she wants to tell you about how she got in trouble at recess.*" Phoebe inclined her head toward Mags. "*Do you want to tell him about what you did, or should I tell him?*"

"*I don't think we're going to talk about what Magnolia did at recess today. Maybe we can talk about it later, but for now, we're going to enjoy our taffies and talk about the good things of the day.*"

That had made Mags smile. Perhaps in a prideful way because she'd won the most recent battle with Phoebe, but even more so because that's how Cassius was. He didn't focus on the sorrow-filled parts of life.

Mags had slid out of her chair and run to Cassius. She plopped on the couch beside him and Phoebe. "I did get a good mark on my math paper today."

"That's my girl," Cassius patted her on the head. He had just called her *his girl*. Did that mean she was important to him?

"Excuse me. I need to get a drink of water." Phoebe slid off of Cassius's lap and bounded to the adjacent kitchen area.

Even all these years later, Mags would determine that her legs had a mind of their own that day as she leaped from her place beside Cassius and onto his lap. She'd nestled her head against his chest. He smelled like milk and taffy. She rested there listening to his heartbeat and pretending that for just a minute, he was her pa too.

Cassius put an arm on her shoulder and planted a kiss on her head.

Mags closed her eyes and smiled.

Of course, Phoebe had to ruin the moment. *"That's my place, Mags!"*

Cassius opened his other arm, and Phoebe climbed onto his lap, all the while attempting to shove Mags off the other side.

"I dare say you're a feisty one today, Phoebe." Cassius had laughed.

Phoebe slipped off his lap and folded her arms across her chest. Then she'd stomped off into the room she shared with Mags. Not entirely a room exactly, but instead a tiny area portioned off from the kitchen by a curtain and holding only a bed and a wooden crate for their meager belongings.

Mags peered up at Cassius. She loved that she looked like Ma with her long, pretty blonde hair, but in just that moment, she wished that she had brown hair like Cassius and Phoebe. Then maybe she could be his daughter. He was thin, but she'd seen the way he carried the milk jugs and bottles to the people's porches. Cassius was a strong man, but even more than that, she felt safe when he was around.

Like the mean stray dogs in the alley couldn't pester her when he was there.

She reached up and put a finger on his chin where dark hairs had begun to sprout. Ma would tease him about forgetting to take a razor to his face. Small lines crinkled around his kind eyes.

"Cassius?"

"Yes, Magnolia?"

Mags shrugged her shoulders. *"Do you think maybe someday you could be my pa too?"* The words had tumbled from her mouth before she could stop them. *"I mean, never mind that I asked that."*

Phoebe would have her hide and then some for sure for trying to take her pa away.

"I would be honored to be your pa, too."

"You would?"

Had she heard him correctly?

"Of course. I always tell everyone at work I have two daughters anyway." A smile had lit Cassius's face.

And Mags had patted his shoulder. *"Do you think I could even call you pa?*

"I reckon that would be just fine."

Things were difficult to understand when you were six. Things like the fact that Mags had a different last name than Ma, Cassius, and Phoebe. She had wondered that day how she could change her last name to the same last name as the rest of her family. *"Do you know how I could have my last name be Davenport, too?"*

"As a matter of fact, I do."

At Cassius's comment, Mags's eyes widened. *"How?"*

"I could adopt you, and since I'm now your pa, your last name would be Davenport."

Mags wasn't familiar with adoption in those days. She had never even heard the word.

"Why don't I talk to your ma about this, and we'll see what we can do about you becoming Magnolia Davenport?"

The joy that swelled in Mags's heart could barely be contained. She had wrapped her arms around Cassius's neck. *"Do you mean it?"*

"Yes, I do."

"And do you think Ma would agree?"

"I'm pretty sure she would. We've already discussed it."

Phoebe had stormed back into the room. She stomped her foot once before raising her voice. *"You can't be my pa's little girl because I'm my pa's little girl."*

Cassius had opened his arms to Phoebe and pulled her into them. Mags didn't really appreciate having to share him with Phoebe at that moment, especially because he had just become her pa. He'd already been Phoebe's pa for all those years, and this was Mags's first day. But she did her best to be kind and scooted over a minuscule bit so Phoebe would have room too.

"My sweet daughter, Phoebe. You are so precious to me, and I love you so much."

Now that Cassius was Mags's father, would he say something like that to her someday? Would he tell her she was precious and that he loved her?

A tear slipped from Phoebe's eye. *"I love you too, Pa."*

Cassius planted a kiss on Phoebe's forehead. *"I am reminded of something about God."*

Phoebe knew more about God than Mags did, so Phoebe nodded. Mags just shrugged. Cassius and Ma spoke about God a lot in those days. Ma never used to until Cassius started taking them to church on Sundays. Now they even prayed all the time before meals.

"I'm reminded that God is full of love. He doesn't just love one of His children, but He loves them all."

"And now that I'm your child, you love me just like you love Phoebe?" Mags recalled the desperation in her heart at what Cassius might say.

"He doesn't love you as much as he loves me." Phoebe's dark brows had furrowed, and she nuzzled deeper into Cassius's chest.

Mags recalled staring at Cassius as the seconds ticked by. What would he say? How would he answer Phoebe's question? She couldn't very well expect him to love her as much as he loved his own child.

"*I love you both very much.*" Before Mags or Phoebe could say anything else, Cassius drew them both into a hug. "*I am a blessed man.*"

Mags hadn't wanted the moment to end. Oh, but to have a father's love! But when it had, she angled back, wanting to memorize every feature of her new pa's face. That's when she'd seen a lone tear slide down his cheek.

"*And just like God, I have enough love in my heart to love both of you.*"

"But you're my pa, not hers."

Phoebe's spiteful tone had knifed its way into Mags's heart. Would Cassius change his mind and say he didn't really want to be Mags's pa?

"*Yes, Phoebe, I am your pa. But I have also agreed to become Mags's pa.*"

"But how?"

"*I'm also reminded of how God adopts us into His family after we surrender our lives to Christ.*"

Phoebe may have understood what those words meant, but Mags did not. She had no idea how to be in God's family. And she'd never asked.

"*I want to grow to be like the Lord as much as I can, with His help. Just as He adopts us into His family, I would like us to adopt Mags and her ma into our family.*"

"Mags's ma is already in our family, and I even call her Ma." Phoebe's clipped voice meshed with her scowl that dared Mags to say otherwise.

Mags remembered that day. It was the second day after Ma and Cassius had married. Phoebe had taken it upon herself to call Ma, Ma. Mags hadn't told her she couldn't share with her or that Ma wasn't really Phoebe's mother. Even though Phoebe deserved it, Mags wouldn't do that because Ma had told her that Phoebe's ma died when Phoebe was just a baby. So Mags decided early that she would share Ma with her new sister. And now she wondered why Phoebe couldn't be just as generous back.

"Just because we are adopting Ma and Mags into our family does not make me love you any less. I could never love you any less, Phoebe. You are my precious daughter. Just like God could never love us any less than He does."

That seemed to settle Phoebe's apprehension a bit. "You are sure you won't love me less, Pa?"

"Absolutely not. Nothing could ever make me love you any less. But wouldn't it be nice if I could be Mags's pa too? I know you have a generous heart, Phoebe. Wouldn't you consider sharing me with her since she doesn't have a father?"

Phoebe had regarded Mags, and for the longest time, Mags held her breath, scared to breathe or even make the slightest movement. What if Phoebe said no? Would that make Cassius change his mind?

Finally, Phoebe had agreed that she would share.

The baby in the basket started to whimper before launching into an all-out cry, interrupting Mags's musings of the past. The woman in the seat beside Mags swooped her from the basket and began to comfort her.

Just like Ma had comforted Mags. Never would a day go by that she wouldn't miss her mother and the man who adopted her as his own. But now, years later, there wasn't much left for Mags in Chicago.

She would miss Phoebe, but that would be the only person she would miss.

Chapter Four

Timothy sauntered to the newspaper office. Mr. Meldrum, the new editor, looked up from the printing press. "Mr. Shepherdson, what brings you to *The Horizon Herald* today?"

"Do you have a newspaper boy working for you by the name of Ozias Agnew?"

"I'm afraid I don't have anyone by that name working for me."

"He was selling papers today."

"Could be one of the two newspaper boys passed on the papers to him. I've been having that problem on occasion."

"Strange. Well, he sold me this one today."

Mr. Meldrum offered a pointed glance at the paper. "That's only half of the newspaper. You didn't get the entire thing."

"I didn't?"

"Unfortunately, not. Something tells me this Ozias is selling used papers. This edition is from two days ago."

Timothy hadn't even noticed the date when he purchased it. No wonder Ozias had slid the quarter into his pocket instead of a collection pouch.

"Here," said Mr. Meldrum. "I have an extra of this issue, and it's the entire thing."

"Thank you, sir. I appreciate that."

"You're welcome. Your sister has a story in it this week about that vacant building."

Ever since a new editor had been hired at *The Horizon Herald,* it had improved greatly from the days when evil Mr. O'Kane was managing editor. Timothy should know. He'd helped Ruby garner an article just to keep her job at the fledgling paper.

Now Ruby wrote an article approximately once a week or whenever there was a significant news story. She'd also authored a book about the happenings in Horizon. Timothy doubted she could stay away from her trusty typewriter for long, even with a family and a farm that she helped manage.

Timothy left *The Horizon Herald* and strode past the vacant building. He stopped, reversed course, and peered into the dirty windows. Ruby had been working on the story about the supposed loot hidden somewhere inside.

If there was loot concealed in the attic or walls, wouldn't someone have found it by now?

Timothy continued down the boardwalk, waving at townsfolk as he did so. He climbed onto the buckboard of his wagon and started for home; the newspaper tucked safely in the back beneath a bag of feed so it wouldn't blow away.

He contemplated the day's events.

A little boy had duped him. But it was obvious Ozias Agnew did it with a different motive, and Timothy aimed to find out who he was and how Timothy could best help the family if they were, in fact, hungry.

When he arrived home, Timothy finished his chores and sat on the porch with his dog, Goose, beside him. He read Ruby's column on the front page.

After Thirty Years, Mystery of Hidden Loot Continues to Baffle Residents and Visitors Alike by Ruby Lynton

Next month marks the thirtieth anniversary of the supposed stolen loot being hidden in the vacant building between *The Horizon Herald* and the bank.

In the summer of 1867, highwaymen robbed the stagecoach on its route between Ingleville and Horizon. One of the robbers disguised himself as an elderly man on the way to visit his family in Horizon. His plan was effective, and the strongbox was easily stolen. The driver and a passenger both lost their lives, and the robbers fled with $26,000 in gold and silver from the treasure box. The heist drew lawmen from around the Territory seeking to locate the bandits, who largely evaded capture.

The four bandits escaped into the nearby mountains after a brief stop in Horizon. Unbeknownst to the townsfolk, these highwaymen stopped first at the vacant building, which then housed the former barbershop. The men then visited the saloon. When the posse, who had been searching for them near the robbery location, returned to Horizon, the highwaymen left town and headed to the mountains. One bandit, an outlaw by the name of LeSage, was killed in a gun battle by the sheriff. Two were later found dead near the Snake

River, supposedly from a late-summer storm that raged through the area. After thoroughly scouring the area, one was captured two months later in Boise City. The loot was never found.

To this day, the scuttlebutt is that the stolen treasure remains hidden in the vacant building. However, extensive searches have indicated no such silver or gold in the walls or the attic. Such a rumor is thought to be just that—a rumor.

Since that time, the vacant building has undergone extensive rummaging. Treasure hunters seeking to find something will be woefully disappointed. There is nothing there. "We've ferreted the place from top to bottom. If it were there, it would have been found long ago. It is rumored that the loot was instead taken to the mountains and buried somewhere only known to the highwaymen," said Mr. Clouse, who assisted in riding with the posse and later examining the vacant building.

What would happen if someone were to stumble upon the treasure after all these years? "They would need to return it to the rightful owner," said Sheriff Zemboldt. "Although I would surmise that there would be a reward."

Still, the chances of unearthing the silver and gold remains slim.

Today, the building, while owned by Bennick Enterprises, is abandoned.

"Good article, Rubes," Timothy said aloud. He opened to the second page, and an advertisement for a traveling optician caught his eye. "Huh. Wonder what this is."

Goose jumped up and rested her paws on Timothy's leg. Timothy patted her. "I know, Goose. The spectacles I purchased from the peddler aren't needed to see things up close, but maybe they'll clear my vision for seeing things in the distance."

His dog tilted her head to one side.

"Probably not, but if there's any likelihood they do, I won't have to even contemplate visiting a traveling optician."

He placed the spectacles he purchased from the peddler on his face. He lifted his gaze, the eyeglasses distorting the crops in the distance. The beginnings of a headache throbbed at his temples. He removed the wire-rimmed glasses and set them on the chair beside him.

It wasn't that he even needed spectacles to read, because he didn't. The problem was that things far away caused him to squint in an attempt to see them more clearly. He grasped the edges of the newspaper, one in each hand, and perused the advertisements. A journeying eye doctor could provide him the opportunity to purchase some spectacles without having to take much time away from the farm to travel to Cornwall.

An illustration of a man using an odd device to look at someone's eyes, punctuated by several words written in large typeset, covered a quarter of the page. He read the words.

How are your eyes? This is your opportunity to consult with Dr. L.F. Tudor, a traveling optician who will be in Horizon to see patients for three days only.

Dr. Tudor has 27 years of experience, having fitted over 53,000 eyes with spectacles. Your thorough examination and consultation are both free. Dr. Tudor has the latest equipment and advanced methods and is a prominent optician who permanently sees patients in Boise City. He is not a traveling optician who will disappear after selling you spectacles, never to be seen again. Do not trust your eyes to anyone else. Plan to schedule your appointment on Wednesday afternoon, Thursday, or Friday at The Horizon Hotel. Spaces are limited, so schedule your appointment soon.

Timothy read the advert a second time. The traveling optician was only going to be in Horizon tomorrow through Friday. Would there be any spots left for an appointment?

While the consultation and examination were free, what would be the charge for the spectacles, should he need them? He did have some funds saved from last year's crops, but most of that would be needed to purchase seed and feed next spring. Perhaps he should forego considering the purchase. He scanned the area beyond the porch. The crops and trees in the distance and even his dog, who chased after a rabbit, were blurred, as was the barn to the right. There was no doubt his eyes needed some serious assistance.

The following day, Timothy rode his horse into town to secure an appointment. "You're very fortunate," said the woman behind the hotel counter, "to have secured the last spot. Dr. Tudor will see you on Friday at 8:30 a.m."

"Do you know the prices of the spectacles?"

"I regret that I do not. But I am sure Mr. Tudor will have a list when he arrives this afternoon. Would you like to stop by then?"

Unfortunately, Timothy didn't have time to stop by that afternoon, so he ensured he had funds when he arrived at his appointment on Friday just in case.

Timothy would never consider himself one prone to nerves, but in this situation, he was a little apprehensive.

A short, plump young woman of about his age greeted him when he entered the hotel on Friday. She patted the sides of her blonde hair, which had been pulled into a bun atop her head, and adjusted her skirt. "May I help you?"

"Yes. I have an appointment with Dr. Tudor."

She blinked several times and leaned closer, bridging the space between them. "What is your name, kind sir?"

"Timothy Shepherdson, ma'am."

"Timothy Shepherdson." She held his gaze. "Just one moment." The woman tossed him a broad smile, then disappeared into an adjacent room, looking over her shoulder at him twice as she did so. Timothy sauntered around the foyer area. With the exception of previously making his appointment, he'd not visited The Horizon Hotel. Expensive furniture surrounding a rock fireplace adjoined a counter where the woman who'd spoken with him two days ago checked in new guests.

"Mr. Shepherdson?"

"Yes, sir?"

"I'm Dr. Tudor. Pleasure to meet you." The optician was a thickset man in a pinstriped suit. He had more hair on his face than on his head and wore spectacles himself. He offered a hand, and Timothy shook it. Timothy dwarfed the man by a good foot, but Dr. Tudor won the contest of width.

The young woman returned and dipped her head. "Mr. Shepherdson, this is my lovely daughter, Miss Tudor."

"Pleasure, ma'am."

Miss Tudor blinked so rapidly that Timothy figured she had an eye condition. Good thing her pa was an optician.

"Will your wife and children be joining you for appointments?" asked Dr. Tudor, leading Timothy into a bordering room where several items had been placed atop a wooden table with two chairs.

"I'm not married."

"Did you hear that?" the optician whispered to his daughter.

Red stained her cheeks. "Yes, Father." She batted her eyelashes at Timothy and gestured for him to sit in a chair in front of a peculiar-looking machine. She then stood against the wall.

"Are you having problems with your eyes?" Dr. Tudor asked.

"I am."

"Although you are having issues with your sight, I'm sure you can see how beautiful my daughter is."

"Oh!" tittered Miss Tudor. She held a hand to her heart.

How was Timothy supposed to answer that?

Dr. Tudor came to the rescue before Timothy had to say a word. "I imagine you find her to be a handsome woman, just like all the young men who arrive for appointments."

"Uh..."

"Oh, Father," chirped Miss Tudor.

"Now, now, my daughter, you know it's true." Dr. Tudor returned his attention to Timothy. "Are you a farmhand?"

"No, sir. I own my own farm."

"I see. Did you hear that, my daughter?"

"I did."

Dr. Tudor returned his attention to Timothy. "Now, Mr. Shepherdson, do describe your symptoms."

Timothy set the eyeglasses from the peddler on the table next to the machine. He noticed a yellowed paper affixed to the wall in front of him. "I struggle with seeing things in the distance clearly."

Dr. Tudor stroked his bearded chin. "Are those objects blurry?"

"They are."

"Do you find yourself having to squint?"

"I do, but it doesn't seem to help much."

"Do you feel like your eyes are strained, and do you rub them often?"

"Yes, I do." Timothy released the breath he had been holding. Perhaps this had been a good idea. Dr. Tudor seemed to know just what Timothy was experiencing. Much better than the peddler who'd been more interested in parting Timothy from his hard-earned dollars than listening to his symptoms. If Dr. Tudor were able to help him, Timothy's sisters would certainly be happy when he didn't engage in a case of mistaken identity at the next church potluck. And Albert would be thrilled when Timothy was back to his accurate self as a sure shot, hitting the tin cans when he, Pa, and Albert practiced shooting at targets.

"I'm going to do a few tests, but first, pray tell, where did you get those spectacles?" Dr. Tudor lifted the eyeglasses Timothy purchased from the peddler and held them at arm's length. "These are detestable. Not of good quality at all. Please tell me you haven't been wearing them."

Timothy cringed. Did he have to admit he purchased them from a traveling peddler? Truth was always best, but... "From a salesman," he said.

Dr. Tudor arched a bushy eyebrow. "Please don't tell me it was a peddler in one of those snake oil wagons, determined to sell all matters of quackery."

"I regret to inform you, sir, that it was, but I have learned my lesson."

"That's the problem with purchasing eyeglasses from those types of individuals. There are no prescriptions. They just sell you whatever they have."

"Prescriptions? As in medicine?"

Dr. Tudor chuckled, his ample girth shaking as he did so. "No, my friend, you'll need no medicines, just a prescription for eyeglasses if my suspicions are correct. Have a seat in that chair. The paper in front of you is what's referred to as a Snellen chart. First, I'd like you to hold one hand over your right eye and read to me the letters on the paper secured to the wall, beginning with the first line."

Timothy did as he was told. *"H."*

"Good. Now the second and third lines."

"O, M, N, G, Z."

"Excellent. Continue to the next line."

That line was slightly blurry, so Timothy squinted. *"A, E, R, K."* The next lines were impossible to ascertain. Was that a *b*? An *f*? "I can't read the lines below that."

"All right. Change eyes."

The other eye was about the same. Dr. Tudor said nothing when Timothy finished, only nodded at Miss Tudor, who wrote information on a sheet of paper.

"This will assist me in determining what lens prescription you will need. Now lean forward and place your chin on the little holder. I will ask you some questions about which letters and numbers are the clearest."

Dr. Tudor asked Timothy numerous times which letter was clear between a couple of different choices. Some of the letters were blurry, and some were clear. Some were as though he looked into the distance, while others were right in front of his face. Timothy had never seen such a machine before. He thought again about the article that indicated Dr. Tudor had an optician's office in Boise City. Surely he wasn't a snake oil salesman himself. Not with all this fancy equipment.

"You may sit back in the chair and give your eyes a rest."

Dr. Tudor shook his head, his own round spectacles sliding down the bridge of his nose. "I regret to inform you that you have myopia."

"Myopia? Is it serious?"

Miss Tudor giggled and tucked a stray hair behind her ear. "Please don't worry, sir."

"Indeed," added her father. "Myopia is a common condition. It just means that your site is limited to items that are close. For instance, you can easily read the Bible or the newspaper, but to see a house or a wagon in the distance is somewhat of a struggle. Would you concur that's an accurate assessment?"

"Yes, I would. I have no trouble at all reading from my Bible or the newspaper."

Dr Tudor reached for the spectacles Timothy had purchased from the peddler, removed his own, and placed the spectacles on his face. "Oh dear. I can see why these were not effective for you, Mr. Shepherdson. These eyeglasses, although I cannot presume to know exactly the strength of prescription, are for someone with hyperopia."

Good. At least he *didn't* suffer from that. "Hyperopia?"

"Yes, that would be an individual who can see better far away but struggles with close objects being blurry."

"So, I was using something opposite of the prescription I need?"

"Indeed. But I have good news for you. Today, I can sell you a pair of the finest Brazilian pebble lenses on the market today. They're superior, made especially for defective eyes, will serve you well for at least a year, and no longer will you struggle to see things in the distance."

"Brazilian pebble lenses?"

"Yes. Termed as such because the glass is made from quartz pebbles, and they are straight temples as well. Or perhaps a pair of lorgnettes."

Miss Tudor's titter echoed in the small room. "Oh, Father, you know a man such as Timothy Shepherdson would not cotton to a pair of lorgnettes."

Timothy had no idea what he was talking about. "I'm afraid I'm unfamiliar with that type."

Dr. Tudor, who had joined his daughter in her amusement, temporarily sobered. "You may be aware of opera glasses."

"I'm afraid I've never been to an opera."

"Lorgnette spectacles possess a handle, and you hold them up to your face."

Timothy could do nothing to hide his shock. He tugged on his collar, wishing it were looser around his neck. "My apologies, sir, but that will never do. I work long hours on my farm, and I need both of my arms."

Dr Tudor laughed, his mirth undulating his abdomen, and his roaring chuckle ceasing only when he gasped for a breath. Finally, he settled. "My dear friend, it was merely a joke. I wouldn't sell you lorgnettes. While men did wear them years ago, they seem to be favored more by women in the current age. And suffice it to say, many times they are more for style than for practicality."

Timothy released a strangled breath. "That's good to hear, sir."

"The type I will sell you will serve you well, of that I am confident. I have a reputation for selling only the finest of spectacles."

It would be nice to be able to see well again. "How much would they cost?"

"I'm aware that eyeglasses are an extravagance and not one easily afforded by most. That is why I have a special offer for you today."

Timothy had heard something similar from the peddler.

Dr. Tudor continued. "My goal is to achieve complete customer satisfaction. And if you are ever in Boise City, you may stop by at any time to purchase a new pair, should you break these or need a stronger lens."

"Break them?" Visions of him laboring on the farm equipment, riding his horse, or mending fences flashed through Timothy's mind. "Sir, I mean no offense when I say this, but I would be unable to purchase them if they are delicate."

"Not delicate, however, they will be breakable. But they will be on your face, and you won't be carrying them around."

"On my face only on occasion, correct?"

"Unfortunately, probably on your face more often than not."

"I have to wear them all day?"

"If you want to see clearly."

Timothy did want to see clearly, but he had his pride. "I reckon I acquaint spectacles with older folks or those in ill health."

"At one time in our history, that was the case. But times have changed in our modern world. More and more folks rely on spectacles, and they are no longer seen as something for ancient, sickly people. Take me, for example."

Dr. Tudor had to be at least sixty.

"Now I don't want you to worry about the cost, because anyone who has made an appointment when I am here in Horizon will receive the special discount."

He would welcome a cost reduction. "Special discount?"

"Yes. The fourteen-karat gold eyeglasses are $4.50 to $8 per pair."

Timothy knew his eyes bulged. It would take him more than a sufficient amount of time to earn enough to pay for the spectacles. "I reckon I don't need fourteen-karat gold spectacles." No sense in having spectacles that were worth more than his boots.

"That is why I have a second option. You can get a pair of Brazilian pebbles for $2.50."

That was still expensive but doable. "That would be acceptable," he heard himself say.

"Very well. Stop back by on Monday. It will take me a few days to make the glasses, as it is a labor-intensive project."

"Are you still seeing customers on those days?"

"No, I'm only seeing customers through the end of today and constructing the glasses Saturday and Monday. Yours should be available by Monday afternoon. You will have to pay in advance, however."

Timothy didn't want to be skeptical, but he figured someone could pay for their spectacles in advance and never see them. He'd already been taken for a fool once with the peddler.

"I know what you're thinking," said Dr. Tudor. "You have no worries. I don't aim to skip town as I am not a typical traveling optician whom you may never see again. I have a stellar reputation and have been in business many, many years in Boise City. I don't plan to destroy my good name by not following through with providing spectacles for someone who has already paid for them."

"Do you have a lot of pairs to make?"

"I do. This is my first year visiting Horizon, and I plan to visit each year henceforth. That way, if folks don't want to travel to Cornwall or Boise City, they can wait until I return. Do you know the Lieutenant?"

"I do."

"He ordered a new pair since he accidentally broke his a few days ago. He opted for the fourteen-karat gold variety, and his will be available tomorrow afternoon. Should you have any questions after he retrieves his pair, do feel free to consult with him."

Timothy withdrew two wadded dollar bills from his pocket, along with two quarters, and handed them to Dr. Tudor.

"My lovely young assistant will tend to the payment and will also make a notation that you have paid for your spectacles." Dr. Tudor steepled his chubby fingers." I would be remiss if I didn't mention my daughter will also be here until late Monday. She is unmarried but quite marriageable."

Timothy avoided Miss Tudor's constant gaze. Poor woman. Did Dr. Tudor express hints to every available gentleman who sought an eye appointment?

"Well, I best be on my way." Timothy stood and pushed in the chair. "I'll plan to retrieve my spectacles on Monday afternoon. Dr Tudor, Miss Tudor." He slapped his cowboy hat back on his head and made his escape.

As he climbed on his horse, Timothy marveled at how he had it all planned out. He would wear his new spectacles while at home and shooting at tin cans with Pa and Albert.

And those were the only times.

Chapter Five

Boarding the train on the second leg proved to be a problem. Mags no more had a ticket to Omaha than a fancy frilly parasol.

Think, Mags, think. She hadn't come this far to not have a plan.

The passengers disembarked, and Mags checked the schedule. She hadn't much time if she wished to board the next train.

Standing nearby was a stylish woman in a traveling outfit, complete with a skirt, a jacket with leg-o'-mutton sleeves, and a red velvet Victorian hat with a sprig of flowers. A crowd was drawn to her, and Mags slipped in behind a woman with a fluffy pompadour and stood on tiptoe to see.

"Who is she?" Mags whispered to the pompadour woman.

"She's an editor for a highly respected New York newspaper."

"An editor?"

The woman held a finger to her lips. "Shh."

Mags had never met a woman newspaper editor before. From what she knew, the job was one limited to men.

"It is so nice to meet you all," gushed the editor.

"Are you working on a story?" a man from the crowd asked.

"I'm an editor, not a reporter." She paused to allow the distinction to sink in.

The onlookers gasped and chatted amongst themselves.

"As such, I am responsible for polishing the articles prior to publication."

The woman was lovely, and Mags fought the nip of envy, wishing she owned such elegant clothing. The woman calmly answered some of the numerous questions directed at her.

"Do you ride for free on the train?"

She waved the inquiry aside with a delicate hand. "Yes, but of course."

That was all Mags needed to hear.

Yes, she would relish a chance to listen to more of what the woman had to say, but time was of the essence. She must somehow, someway, convince the conductor that she ought to ride free since she was an editor for a prestigious paper in Chicago.

But she looked nothing like the editor woman. The total opposite, really. Mags wore a tattered dress, and even if she were to change into her best dress in her carpetbag, she'd still look ragged compared to the editor. Especially Mags's shoes, which could hardly be considered exquisite button-up boots.

The editor carried a silk beaded reticule, not a dingy carpetbag. And Mags had no notebook in her hands like the woman did.

A discarded piece of stationery on a nearby bench caught Mags's eye. That was a start. Not quite a notebook, but better than nothing. The top half appeared to be some sort of a list, perhaps someone hoping to remember to bring the necessities for their trip. The bottom half was blank. Perfect.

Now she just needed a pencil. But first, she'd change into her other dress.

After exiting the privy, Mags searched the area for someone, *anyone*, who might have a pencil she could borrow. If the next train was on time, she only had a mere thirty minutes to do so.

Finally, she observed an older gent with a black fedora carrying a physician's bag. Might the doctor own a writing utensil she could use?

Mags smoothed her skirt and approached him. "Kind sir. Might you by chance have a pencil I could use?"

"I do, but I daresay it's my best cedar pencil, so I would expect it back."

"Not a concern. I shall return it to you posthaste."

"Very well." The man retrieved the writing utensil from his bag and handed it to her. She thanked him, then set about her scheme, regretting that she may have lied to the gracious lender.

Or perhaps not.

If he rode the same train she did, Mags could surely return the pencil. She'd never cottoned to lying, but sometimes desperation caused such actions.

Or at least that's what she would tell herself, even though her conscience batted at her something fierce.

She thanked the man and scurried toward the conductor just as the "All aboard!" announcement echoed through the commotion. Taking a deep breath, standing straighter, and putting on her best earnest expression, Mags waited in line.

"Ticket stub, please."

"Hello, kind sir."

"Ticket please, miss," he repeated.

This might be slightly trickier than she'd anticipated.

"Did you see my colleague?"

"Your colleague?"

"Yes, she's my boss and the editor of a prestigious New York newspaper."

The conductor narrowed his eyes, but Mags refused to be deterred. "What's your profession?"

Good. She had his curiosity piqued. "I'm a reporter."

"You don't say?"

A thickset man with a full beard and a crabby countenance raised his voice. "What's the delay? Are we or are we not boarding?"

Mags pivoted to face the interrupting man, careful not to allow the toes of her worn boots to be exposed beneath her skirts. "Please, sir, do go ahead of me."

"I will," the man growled, nearly toppling Mags off her feet.

She righted herself and did her best to retain her calm persona.

The conductor looked at the tip of her head down to her feet, and Mags scrunched her toes in her shoes. Would he see through her façade? Determine she was no more a reporter than she was the Queen of England?

"What exactly is the topic of your article?"

The words popped from her mouth before she gave them thought. "How today's trains couldn't function without conductors."

"You don't say?" This time, the conductor tugged at the bill of his cap.

"Yes. You see, without conductors, our trains would fail to operate properly. You collect the tickets, manage the cars, and oversee other employees."

"That's true." The older man with a rotund center squared his posture.

"Yes, and thus, I must be on my way." She lowered her voice. "I must say I'm thrilled to be visiting Sacramento for the story of my career."

"Go ahead." The conductor gestured for her to enter the train. "Thank you for acknowledging the hard work of conductors."

"Indeed. And thank you." Mags didn't wait a second longer. She scuttled up the stairs and into the train, thankful the conductor had believed her. Even if she had been a trifle dishonest.

Mags lounged in the seat, exhilaration coursing through her veins. She'd made it this far all on resourcefulness and ingenuity. She leaned back and closed her eyes. Maybe this would be easier than she'd anticipated.

The train chugged along at a constant speed. Mags must have fallen asleep because a tap on her shoulder startled her. She turned to see the physician from the depot standing beside her in the aisle, tapping his toe.

"My cedar pencil, please?"

"Oh, yes. Indeed. Here it is." She withdrew it from her carpetbag.

The doctor narrowed one eye and opened his mouth as if to say something before clamping it shut and retreating to his seat.

"Honesty is always best." Ma's words revisited her.

"*The Lord expects us to be honest in all things.*" Cassius's words followed Ma's.

Well, sometimes one had to be dishonest in order to achieve what was necessary.

But dishonest in claiming your ticket blew away, claiming you are a newspaper reporter, and stealing another's pencil?

Mags attempted to hush the contrary words. *It's only temporary. Once I reach Horizon, no more lies.*

A woman in her twenties ought not partake in the sharing of fibs.

As I said, it is only a momentary habit.

Arguing with herself must surely indicate either a lack of sleep or a guilty conscience. Lest lying become a habit she couldn't break, Mags would need to reconsider how she coaxed her way to Horizon. She'd had to lie a time or two in her life after Ma and Pa died. She wasn't proud of it. Wasn't overjoyed that she'd chosen to do something that would disappoint her parents.

A child in the seat two rows ahead of her referred to a woman as her aunt. Mags stared out the window as Omaha passed her by.

❦

No one had come to see her off when she left Chicago. Mags wouldn't fault Phoebe, and she'd said her goodbyes the day before. And truthfully, she hadn't expected her aunts to bid her farewell. Not when they despised her as they did, and Mags hadn't seen them in years.

Mags unfolded the piece of stationery with Phoebe's address. She committed it to memory just in case she lost the scrap of paper. Immediately upon arrival in Horizon, Mags planned to write to her sister. Would Larry agree to move his family to the new city?

Every now and again, Mags thought about her aunts. Aunt Mikelanna, Aunt Thirza, and Aunt Darla, and the painful memories of servitude, disrespect, and hatred from the women who were supposed to have loved and cared for her.

The day of the funeral, the pastor spoke of peace, and he and his wife did the best they could to offer their condolences. But they hadn't offered Mags and Phoebe a home. She couldn't know their reasoning, but the pang of it still struck her heart at odd moments.

"Who will care for us now that our parents are gone?" Mags had asked.

"I'm sure you have relatives that would take you in, and if not, we would find somewhere else for you," the pastor's wife answered.

"I have a grandma whom I've met a couple of times. She lives over on 15th Avenue," said Phoebe.

Mags had only met her extended family once. Would they come for her? She thought Ma had mentioned that Aunt Thirza worked at the soap factory as they'd passed the enormous building one day. But that was all Ma had said, for she never spoke of her sisters.

They had stayed with the pastor and his wife in the parsonage that first night. Mags wanted to stay there permanently and didn't mind that it was tiny and uncomfortable on the floor. But such was not an option.

The following day, a woman arrived. She was short and squatty with a permanent frown. Phoebe recognized her grandmother right away. *"Have you come to take me to live with you?"* she'd asked.

"I have."

Mags watched with a mixture of amusement, hope, and trepidation. The woman cast her several glances, none of which included so much as a smile.

"Gather your belongings, Phoebe. I haven't much time."

Phoebe's face lit up for the first time since Ma and Pa's death. She looped her arm through Mags's elbow. *"Get your things, Mags. This will be a new adventure for us."*

"Surely you don't think this girl is coming with us?"

"Why would she not?" asked the pastor's wife. *"She was Cassius's daughter as well."*

"Not really. Besides, I only have room for one. You'll have to secure other accommodations."

Even now, a tear slipped from Mags's eye as she recalled that day. She swiped it away lest the other passengers see her dolefulness.

She'd begged for several minutes, pleading with Phoebe's grandmother. *"Phoebe is my sister, and I promise to be no trouble at all."*

Mags had clutched the woman's arm and implored for the opportunity to stay with her sister, the only family she had left. Phoebe's grandmother's words replayed in her mind as if they'd occurred only yesterday, rather than a decade ago.

"Surely you don't believe groveling will do you any good in this instance? It's very unbecoming of a young lady. Now, please remove your clutch from my arm."

The tears hadn't really stopped since Ma and Pa had passed, but at the woman's words, they erupted in full force.

"But please, I promise..."

"*You're not a Davenport. Your father is someone else, and we don't need any scandal in our family. Tongues will wag. Now hush, child. Back away, and, Phoebe, it is time to go.*"

The pastor's wife also attempted to intervene to no avail. Phoebe left with her grandmother, and Mags ran and hid behind the church, where she sat down and curled her knees to her chest while she sobbed.

She recalled wondering about something that still entered her mind even all these years later. If God was such a wonderful God, why had He taken her family away from her? And why did no one want her?

Chapter Six

In Denver, Mags disembarked, hoping to use the same tactic again for reboarding at the next stop. Unfortunately, after meals, she hadn't enough money in her coin purse for even one stage of the trip.

The depot reminded Mags of a castle. She perched on a bench outside the middle section with the tall tower and waited until the conductor announced for passengers to board a different train. The area surrounding the depot was agog with activity. Everyone seemed to be going every which way. Folks arriving, folks leaving, folks waiting, and folks jabbering on with each other.

Two women, one older and one who appeared to be a few years younger than Mags, strolled along the front of the buildings. Their dresses, boots, and hats clearly indicated wealth, as did the way they held their heads high. "I am just not keen on it, Mother."

"You needn't keep it then."

"I do find it rather drab."

Mags watched the interaction between the two women.

"If you find it so drab," said the mother, "Discard it."

"I shall." The woman threw something in the nearby garbage bin.

When the women disappeared, Mags walked to the bin, watching to see if the women would return. Inside, a wadded piece of bright-pink fabric rested among the refuse. Mags lifted and unfolded it. The colorful dress boasted a white collar, white puffy lower sleeves, and black etchings across the bodice and the waistband.

In short, it was lovely.

Too lovely to be stuffed into a garbage bin.

Mags held it against herself. Might it fit? The younger woman appeared to be about Mags's same size. Surely with slight alterations, she could wear the garment.

A line formed near the train traveling to Horizon, and Mags hastily stuffed the dress into her carpetbag and scrambled to seek a place in line.

"Ticket or stub, please," said the conductor.

Mags attempted to use the very same ruse as she used at the previous stop.

The dour-faced, rail-thin man scowled. "I don't care if you are the President of the United States. If you don't have a ticket or a stub, you won't be boarding the train."

"But, sir..."

"Next, please."

The other passengers nearly shoved Mags out of the way, and she stumbled to the left. Her chest tightened in panic. What now? She couldn't very well be stranded in Denver. Not that she couldn't procure employment in the city, for she likely could. But Denver was *not* her destination.

Horizon, Idaho, was.

She stood for a moment and wrapped her arms around herself, her carpetbag bumping against her. For a second, she figured she ought to surrender to such an outlandish notion of traveling for free. But then thought better of it. She would not—*could not*—allow this to deter her.

There had to be a way. Mags just had to devise a plan.

Hitching a ride on a railcar was not her first choice. But it was her only choice. Especially after the conductor refused to allow her to board without a ticket. She hadn't come this far only to be stranded. It was just her luck that this was a mixed train with passenger cars toward the back, a caboose, freight cars, and…alas, just as she'd hoped. A cattle car.

She'd need to hide before executing her plan. Mags had seen bums run alongside the train and hop on at the last minute. She would have to do the same. Two men lurked behind a tree by the furthest of the two cattle cars. Were they planning the same thing?

The train whistled, and she was reminded she hadn't much time. Mags glanced both ways, then darted in the direction of the trees. She clutched her carpetbag in her left hand. She'd need her right hand to grab onto the train.

She could do this. She had to.

"All aboard!"

Mags's trepidation heightened.

The two men rose from their hidden positions, and Mags did the same. They'd undoubtedly partaken in such an escapade before. As for her?

She took a visual sweep of the area once more, even as her heart pounded in her chest. One of the men hopped on the train, and the other, with the grace of a doe, did the same.

Her pulse quickened. Oh, how she wished she didn't have to wear a dress! Her skirts would be such an impediment.

But there was no time to search for a pair of men's trousers. No time to ponder any longer, for if she did, Mags would miss the train entirely, and who knew when the next one headed for Horizon would leave the station.

She stumbled and nearly tripped, barely righting herself as the train increased its speed. Mags threw her carpetbag through the open door, then ran alongside the boxcar. Would anyone see her? Attempt to thwart her mission? For a second, she regretted tossing her only possessions onto a train she may never board.

Mags reached for the edge of the open door and missed. She urged her legs faster and stretched her arm again toward something to clasp onto. She wrapped her fingers around the opening and prepared to propel herself inside when the train whistled and sped up. Her legs went out from beneath her, and she dragged through the weeds adjacent to the tracks. Her arm muscles groaned, arguing with the weight of her body. "Please, please help me," she said to no one in particular, for no one could even hear her over the train wheels. Desperation overtook her, and tears spilled from her eyes. What if she let go and was sucked beneath the train?

She looked up to see one of the men inside the boxcar staring at her. "Sir, please..." she stuttered as fear stormed through her veins. Mags lost her grip with one hand, and the momentum threw her sideways against the boxcar. She clasped the opening with both hands once again as the pain rippled through her shoulders, neck, and upper arms.

Her right foot smacked against a boulder, and she winced in pain. Her fingers slipped, and she thought she saw her life flash before her eyes. Finally, when she was about to give up, two strong arms heaved her into the boxcar.

Mags lay face down, fear, relief, and uncertainty all trundling through her. She gasped, attempting to catch her breath before slowly rolling to one side, scooting farther into the train so her legs were hanging off the edge, and finally, scurrying to the corner. She closed her eyes and attempted to catch her breath.

The train careened, causing her to slide to one side as the mode of transport accelerated.

She took two deep breaths, willing the intensity of her heartbeat to slow. Every part of her ached, especially her arms. A sizable rip from her shoulder to her elbow on the left side reminded her of how very close she'd been to losing her life.

Mags scanned the boxcar, the odor of manure stinging her nostrils. A short, balding man crouched in the opposite corner, gripping her carpetbag. Another man of about forty with an abundance of greasy black hair sat three feet away. She recognized them both as the ones who'd lurked behind the trees and caught their ride just before she had. "Thank you," she gasped.

"You're welcome," said the thick-haired man.

"What are you doing here?" The balding man narrowed his eyes at her and bunched his mouth in a bitter pucker.

"I'm doing the same thing you're doing."

The other man's voice caused Mags to jump. "Just give it to her. What would you want with a woman's carpetbag anyway?"

"Might be that it has some money or jewelry in it."

Mags could only wish she owned other jewelry besides Ma's ring, carefully sewn to the inside of the bag, and she kept the only coins to her name in the bodice of her dress. "You'll find no money or jewelry in there."

"Right, and I'm the engineer of this here train."

"If you're the engineer, what are you doing riding in a cattle car?" quipped the thick-haired man.

"Shut up, Yates." The bald man stared at her with beady eyes. "How can it be that you're travelin' with no money and no jewelry?"

"A thief stole it." Why was it that fibbing rolled off her tongue so easily as of late? Although this time she felt no guilt, for she needed her carpetbag.

"Give it to her, Haswell."

"Ain't none of your business what I do and don't do. 'Sides, don't be tellin' folks my name."

When Mr. Yates said nothing, Mr. Haswell jerked his gaze from Mags to the other man, then back to Mags.

The clicking of the wheels on the tracks, the air whistling through the railcar, and the pungent smell of damp hay reminded Mags of her poor decision. She scooted closer to the wall and studied the open door. Until the train stopped, there would be no escaping.

Each man had a checkered bindle, and they wore worn coats, Mr. Haswell's with threadbare patches on the elbows. Mr. Yates's droopy pants, held up with suspenders on his lanky frame, partially covered his scuffed brown boots.

"Please, sir, my carpetbag."

Mr. Haswell curled his upper lip and clenched his teeth. His left eye twitched.

Mags crouched further into the corner, her breathing shallow as a case of the nerves consumed her. If not for Ma's ring…

Mr. Haswell threw the carpetbag at her, and it hit her smack-dab in the shoulder. "Thank-thank you." Her voice quivered, and she hugged the possession to her chest. There were many things she could live without, but Ma's wedding ring was not one of them. Someday, she'd see if someone could size it specially for her finger, which was much larger than Ma's petite one.

"Just watch your back," the man sneered.

"That'll be enough of that, Haswell."

"Ain't the boss of me, Yates. Never was." He muttered a slew of curse words.

"If you want to reach your destination without being arrested, you'll mind yourself."

"You ain't one to be threatenin' nobody." Haswell extracted a whiskey bottle from an inner pocket in his dingy brown coat and took a long swallow. The smell of alcohol, mixed with manure and now body odor, drifted Mags's way and she nearly gagged.

Finally, the men quieted, and the only sound was the roaring of the train and the swishing of the air through the open door.

Mags inspected her grimy hands. They reminded her of all of those days working hard for Aunt Mikelanna for little reward. Not that she needed a reward for helping someone, but there hadn't been even so much as a thank you from her aunt or uncle.

The pastor had located her Aunt Thirza, who worked at the soap factory. She, Aunt Mikelanna, and Aunt Darla arrived at the parsonage that evening, scowls on their pinched faces. Aunt Thirza had requested privacy.

Mags had wanted to beg the pastor and his wife to stay while her aunts, whom she'd only met once, discussed her future. But she hadn't been able to find any words with the lump in her throat.

"Well, I'm not taking her in," Aunt Thirza sneered.

"Nor am I," agreed Aunt Darla.

"It's our sister's own fault this happened, anyway." Aunt Mikelanna added.

"It's not her fault," said Mags. She would always defend Ma. Besides, how could it be her fault?

"And she's belligerent as well." Aunt Darla and Aunt Mikelanna nodded in agreement with Aunt Thirza's statement.

"What an awful child."

"But it wasn't Ma's fault. How could it be Ma's fault that she got cholera?"

Aunt Mikelanna brushed her words away. "You know nothing of what I speak. Can you cook?"

"Yes."

"Can you clean?"

Mags bobbed her head in answer to Aunt Mikelanna's questions.

"Can you tend to children?"

"I don't have much experience with children, but I would be happy to learn. My own ma was a wonderful mother, and she taught me how to care for others."

"Yes, we're sure she did," Aunt Darla snapped.

"How old are you?" asked Aunt Thirza.

"Twelve."

"Cici was always our mother's favorite," Aunt Mikelanna muttered beneath her breath. Mags could see why Ma was Grandmother's favorite.

"Yes, well, our mother's judgment of character was never her strong suit." Aunt Thirza flicked a piece of lint from her skirt.

"I have an idea. Why don't we each take her for two years? By then she'll be eighteen."

"I'm not taking her in at all," declared Aunt Darla.

"She's probably a thief," added Aunt Mikelanna, "and I don't want anything stolen."

"Oh, no, I'm not a thief. I know stealing is wrong."

Today, Mags reflected on the irony of that statement and how she had once stolen and ended up behind bars. But back then, after her parents died, she never would have imagined taking what wasn't hers. She never would have dreamed of lying and having to survive by telling untruths. Guilt gnawed at her heart. What had she become? She might not have stolen since the day that landed her in the city jail, but she had lied to secure her trip to Horizon, Idaho. She pushed the thoughts aside as they served no real purpose other than to discourage her. Ma, and later with Cassius's help, had raised her to be honest and forthright. The painful years living with her aunts hadn't changed her into someone like them. In fact, although she was a survivor, she knew right from wrong even more strongly than before.

Mags just needed to begin a new life, and she'd toss everything from the past far behind her. No one in Horizon would ever know that she had lied or stolen.

But when you lied about the train tickets, you did steal from the railroad company. The annoying contrary voice settled like a lump in her stomach. She'd make no excuses for what she'd done to get this far, and someday she vowed to pay back every cent of the cost of the tickets.

The faces of her aunts again loomed in her memory.

"I'll take her for the first two years," said Aunt Mikelanna. "Until she's fourteen."

"I'll take her until she's sixteen," added Aunt Thirza.

At first, Mags was elated that they wanted her. She would do whatever it took to please them and to be accepted by them.

"Well, I'm not taking her at all," repeated Aunt Darla. "You two can do whatever you wish."

"But where will I go after I'm sixteen?" Mags had asked, a peculiar panic creeping into her soul.

"That is not our concern."

No wonder Ma hadn't wanted anything to do with her sisters. They were dreadful.

Chapter Seven

MAGS'S THOUGHTS RETURNED TO the present. She opened her carpetbag, thankful none of her meager belongings had been stolen, then brushed off her soiled skirt. Her dress would not only need mending, but a good washing as well. At least there weren't any livestock to contend with.

She glanced at the men in the railcar. Mr. Haswell nodded off, his head lolling to one side. Mr. Yates clasped his hands behind his head and crossed his legs at the ankles.

What if Mr. Yates hadn't pulled her aboard? She shuddered at the thought of being run over by the train. "Thank you, sir, for saving me."

Mr. Yates regarded her. "How old are you? Twenty or so?"

"Twenty-three." Why was she sharing this information? She closed her mouth tightly. It wasn't any of Mr. Yates's concern how old she was, even if he had saved her life.

"Figured as much. What's a young woman your age doing all alone, hitching rides on trains?"

She didn't have an answer for that, and for some reason, her mind failed to conjure up something that sounded better than the truth, so she shrugged.

"Running from someone?"

"No." Or was she? Her aunts hadn't paid her any mind in years, and she'd never run from Phoebe. Running from *something,* maybe?

"Where are you headed?"

The man was full of questions, none of which Mags wanted to answer. "Horizon, Idaho," she babbled before she could stop herself. She bit her tongue. What if Mr. Yates and Mr. Haswell were wanted criminals? She certainly shouldn't be sharing with them her plans. But why would Mr. Yates rescue her if he were a lawbreaker?

"Never heard of it."

Mr. Haswell blinked his eyes open and muttered, "You ain't heard of a lot of places." He chugged more whiskey before wiping his mouth with the back of his hand and falling back asleep.

"Do you have family in Horizon?"

"I do."

That wasn't the complete and utter truth. Not even an ounce of truth. But maybe, just maybe, if she presented herself well in Horizon, she'd find a community that accepted her. A place where she belonged.

One thing was certain—a change in attire proved necessary.

"Why didn't they just send for you? Why are you train-hopping?"

Mags contemplated how different the two men were. Mr. Haswell appeared to be the perfect definition of a drunk vagabond, while Mr. Yates appeared to be a man just down on his luck. And Mr. Yates's voice was inquisitive, but calm. Mr. Haswell's was loud and brash.

"My ticket was stolen." A nudge from her conscience reminded her this was not true, but it must seem peculiar that she was a stowaway.

"I'm sorry to hear that. Seems like some freeloaders pride themselves on taking what doesn't belong to them." Mr. Yates's gaze shifted briefly to Mr. Haswell, who was now snoring obnoxious, thundering snores with his mouth wide open, and drool trickling down his chin. Mr. Yates returned his attention to her. "I have a daughter who would be about your age."

Curiosity bested her. "If you don't mind me asking, what happened to her?"

"Nothing happened to her. I just haven't seen her in a good five years."

"I'm so sorry." Mags thought of how not seeing her and Phoebe would have devastated her pa.

Mr. Yates rubbed the back of his neck. "Her ma decided being married to a drunk wasn't the kind of life she wanted. Can't say as I blame her. In hindsight, I wish I could take it all back. That I could have left the bottle alone." He stared off into the distance. "Sure would like to have my family back."

"Maybe they'll give you a second chance."

"No, there'll be no second chance. My wife got sick of bailing me out of jail after I'd spent all of our money at the saloon. One day, she'd had enough. She filed something called a divorce, it was granted, and she and our children went to live with her parents in Idaho."

"Idaho? Whereabouts?"

"Cornwall area, last I heard."

"Is that why you're headed there?"

Mr. Yates shrugged. "I've been all over to the East Coast, to the South, and now back this way."

"But if you went back to this Cornwall place, you could probably see them and tell your wife you're trying to get your life back."

"I appreciate your suggestion on the matter, but I've been without a job for several years. I already tried to go back once, and it did no good."

"So now you ride the rails?"

"I do, since I don't have a place to call home, I go from place to place. Sometimes I find someone temporarily needing help, and when I'm finished, I move on."

His story saddened her. One thing she longed for was a permanent home, something it sounded like Mr. Yates hadn't had in several years. "I'm sorry."

"Don't be sorry. Every decision I made was of my own choosing. This happened because of the choices that I made. I once had a well-paying job, a comfortable home, and a family I loved more than anything. Now I have the clothes on my back, a few coins in my pocket, and that's about it."

A thought occurred to her that she could end up homeless just like Mr. Yates. Moving from place to place with nowhere to put down roots. Trepidation niggled at her. She should have stayed in Chicago. While she didn't have a home, at least it was familiar, and she wasn't floating along with no destination.

"Do you have yourself a name?"

"Mags." He needn't know her last name.

She leaned back against the railcar wall. "Do you know how far it is to the next station?"

Mr. Yates shrugged. "I'm not sure. I believe Boise City. If memory serves me, we stop there before Cornwall."

"Will you be stopping in Cornwall to see your family?"

"I will be attempting to secure a job there, but as far as hoping to see my family..." a pained expression lined Mr. Yates's tanned face. "Not sure about that yet. I've been praying about it." He wiped the moisture from his forehead with the back of his hand. Not even the rushing of air through the open door could alleviate the stifling heat. "Do you believe in God?" he asked.

"I know He exists, and my parents had a strong faith. But as for me, I'm not sure He's that fond of me."

Mr. Yates's brow furrowed, and he seemed to be considering her statement. Would he launch into a lecture? Ask her why she felt as she did?

"I'm sorry to hear about your parents."

"Thank you." Even the thought of Ma and Pa and how much she missed them caused emotion to burn her throat.

"So, you're visiting family in Horizon?"

"Yes," she squeaked, wishing she hadn't told that untruth since now she had to maintain that falsehood. Phoebe's image popped into her mind. How was she faring? Sadly, Mags hadn't seen much of Phoebe until recently, when Mags stumbled upon her at the grocery store. She hadn't even known where her sister lived after she moved into her grandmother's home.

It had been that long.

The hurt stung. So many lost years between them. But when they'd reunited, it was as though they'd never been apart.

"Why do you think the Lord isn't fond of you?" Mr. Yates's words brought Mags back to the present.

"He's been absent."

Mr. Yates searched her face. "Absent?"

Mags didn't really want to discuss this matter with anyone, let alone a stranger. Even if the stranger saved her life. "Yes. Every time I've prayed, He hasn't been there."

"I didn't even believe in God until I met a preacher man who spent time talking to me and answering some questions. I credit him for helping me get off the bottle." Mr. Yates fished a scrap of paper from his pocket. "He gave me a Bible, too, but that was stolen from me a few train rides back. Thankfully, I have this sheet of paper he gave me that has some verses on it."

"What kind of verses?"

"Verses reminding me about God's love. Verses of comfort." Mr. Yates handed the soiled paper to her, and Mags scanned the meticulously written words. One verse in particular caught her eye.

"Have not I commanded thee? Be strong and of a good courage; be not afraid, neither be thou dismayed: for the Lord thy God is with thee whithersoever thou goest."

If only the words were true. If only God had stayed with her through the turmoil, through the pain, and through the loss. But alas.

"The one from Joshua, chapter one, is my favorite," Mr. Yates was saying. "The Lord told Joshua those words, but the preacher man told me it applies to us, too. That God never leaves us and is with us always."

"Always? I mean no offense when I say this, but I highly doubt He is always with us. In my way of thinking, with all the people He has to tend to, He oftentimes forgets about us."

"No, I don't think so. The preacher man told me it doesn't matter what predicament we find ourselves in. God's love is never failing. Him walking through everything with us is a constant."

Mags wasn't convinced. Where was God when she'd prayed her parents would recover? Where was He when she prayed to be able to go with Phoebe and be raised by Phoebe's grandmother? Where was He when she prayed all those nights living with Aunt Mikelanna and rendered to a tiny corner of the cold apartment with only a holey blanket to lay her head upon? Where was He when she lived with Aunt Thirza and gave her entire earnings to her aunt and uncle, and in return, was given a place to sleep in the squalor-ridden back room and a crust of bread for supper? Where was He when she had lost track of Phoebe?

But you later found Phoebe, Mags's contrary voice reminded her. A voice she needed to adamantly shush.

"He loves us very much, so much He gave His Son for us."

"With all respect, Mr. Yates, I'm not of the mind to listen to a sermon." She handed him the scrap of paper.

"It was the preacher man's prayers that got me off the bottle. God heard those prayers and answered them."

Mags's heart pinched. If only God had heard *her* prayers. "If the preacher man helped you so much, why aren't you staying with him and his family?"

Likely for the same reason the pastor and his wife didn't invite Mags to live with them instead of her horrid aunts.

They hadn't wanted her.

"Their house was too small, and it was at that point that I realized I should return to Cornwall. Still praying about what to do once I arrive there."

A sliver of her wished she had the faith this man did. Would his family reject him even though he no longer imbibed in excess?

The train rolled along the prairie, and at some point, Mags fell asleep. The train's whistle and subsequent slowing jolted her awake. How long had she slept? She stretched her arms overhead and yawned.

Through the slats in the boxcar, she could see buildings and people walking along a boardwalk and wagons in the distance. Was this Horizon?

The train slowed to a stop, and both of the men stood. A loud clanging noise that sounded like someone banging on the side of the train jostled her. "What is that noise?"

In response, Mr. Haswell dug his fingernails into the tender flesh on her arm. She cried out. "Shut up or they'll find us," he hissed.

"Who?"

Mr. Haswell ignored her, and Mr. Yates stood, his back to the open door. He shot her a pointed look. "You'll need to run when I say so," he whispered.

"Run?"

He nodded. "But where will I run?"

"Anywhere. Just get away, or they'll catch you."

Panic rose within her. "Will you be running too?"

The banging sounded again. "On three." Mr. Yates turned around, grabbed her elbow, and nearly pulled her off the train. "Run!"

"But..." she had so many questions.

"Run!" Mr. Haswell sneered, pushing her aside.

Mags clutched her carpetbag and dashed along the worn path adjacent to the tracks, whipping her head around twice to see if anyone followed. She saw a depot ahead and folks disembarking from the train. A familiar voice sounded. Mr. Yates?

Through a crack between the train cars, she watched as two officers arrested Mr. Yates and Mr. Haswell. Her stomach knotted. Would they come after her next?

"Miss?"

She jumped when a man dressed in a train employee's uniform tapped her on the arm.

"Yes?" she asked, breathless. Would he turn her in to the officers? A shudder throttled her spine. She absolutely, positively never wanted to go to jail again.

"Are you lost?"

"Lost? Oh, yes, as a matter of fact, yes, I am. I alighted from the train and was going for a walk. I must have lost my wits about me." Could he tell she was fibbing?

"I will accompany you to the depot."

"Thank you, sir."

His eyes darted to her dirty dress and the rip in her sleeve. Would he change his mind and speculate that she was not, in fact, lost, but had train-hopped without so much as purchasing a ticket?

The officers with Mr. Yates and Mr. Haswell in their custody stormed past Mags.

"Hey, she's one of us," barked Mr. Haswell.

Mags gasped. The railroad employee looked at her as if waiting for her to expound on Mr. Haswell's insinuation.

"How utterly atrocious," she uttered as her hand flew to her chest. "Who was that appalling man?"

"A bum, Miss."

"A bum?"

"Yes, a stowaway. A vagrant who wants a free ride."

Mr. Haswell was grumbling to the officer. "That woman is one of us. She was on the train with us."

"How very frightening," said Mags. For a second, the officers fixed their gazes on her. Could they see the guilt written on her face? Her heart raced in her chest. What would become of her if they believed Mr. Haswell?

"You would do well to stay away from the likes of those kinds of people. They'll learn someday that crime never pays."

Mags offered a thin smile in response. What would have happened if she'd been caught as well?

Chapter Eight

FAITH, FAMILY, AND FOOD, in that order. Timothy reclined in the chair on his porch, clasping his hands behind his head. "Oh, and you too, Goose."

Goose yipped and propped her paws on Timothy's leg. Timothy unfolded his hands and patted her on the head. "We're blessed, Goose. Reckon that's the truth."

Timothy scanned the land in front of his humble cabin. How could God have blessed him so richly? He was a young man in his early twenties, but already owned a home and land. Pa and Ma had helped him secure it, and Albert and brothers-in-law, Jake, Landon, and Hans, had been instrumental in assisting him with building the cabin.

But all in all, it was God's doing. At times, Timothy felt right undeserving of the gifts the Lord had so graciously bestowed on him. Some folks didn't have the loving family he had, and some lacked enough sustenance to properly fill their bellies. But not Timothy. When he wasn't eating at Ma and Pa's or invited over to his sisters' homes for supper, he was feasting on plentiful food from his garden in the summer and from his cellar in the winter.

He drained the coffee in his cup and peered at the sunrise. He best get to work before heading into town to retrieve his spectacles.

Three hours later, Miss Tudor, the optician's daughter, gleefully greeted him the second he walked into the rented room adjacent to the foyer at The Horizon Hotel.

"I'm here to pick up my spectacles."

"Oh, Mr. Shepherdson." She tittered and held a hand to her bosom. "How have you been since we last spoke?"

"I'm fine, thank you, and you?" Even if the woman was extremely dramatic, he needed to ensure that he was always a gentleman.

"I'm fine." She fluttered her lashes at him. "And how is your farm?"

"The farm is fine. Just busy tending to the crops."

"Oh, yes. Father said you have a sizable farm."

"Not as big as some, but just right for what I need."

She stared at him, her cheeks rosy. She dipped her head. Awkward seconds passed before Dr. Tudor piddled through the doorway, a box in his hands. "Good to see you, Mr. Shepherdson. I have your spectacles right here."

The doctor handed him his eyeglasses. Timothy was not impressed. He no more wanted to wear them than move to a city.

"Try them on, and see how they fit."

"Oh, yes, do," chirped Miss Tudor.

Timothy did as the optician asked.

"Mr. Shepherdson, I must say the spectacles are very becoming on you," Miss Tudor twirled a strand of blonde hair around her finger.

Timothy was astonished at the woman's brazen behavior. He felt his own face redden, and he was about to remove his extra set of eyes when Dr. Tudor asked, "Can you see better now?"

"Sure." He really didn't want to admit that he could see better because he wanted nothing to do with the spectacles, but it was true—things were clearer, especially across the room. The floral wallpaper was now more than just a blur.

"Good, well, if you have any questions at all, I'm here for the rest of the day, and then I will be traveling back to Boise City on tomorrow's train. You're welcome to make an appointment there at any time."

Miss Tudor chose that moment to interject. "Oh, yes, Mr. Shepherdson, you most absolutely must visit Boise City at your earliest opportunity."

Timothy had been *through* Boise City on the train once, but had never stopped to peruse the city. Doubtful he'd do it anytime soon. Not with chores beckoning and his desire to stay as far from cities as possible.

Miss Tudor inclined toward him, expecting an answer.

He couldn't very well be rude. "I will keep that in mind, Miss Tudor."

"Oh, yes, lovely."

Dr. Tudor cleared his throat. "I don't want to interrupt the congenial conversation between the two of you, but I must add that I will also be back in Horizon next year. I'd like to see you then for a follow-up just to be sure your eyes haven't changed."

"Couldn't they get better over time?"

The optician chuckled. "Not likely. If only it worked that way. But alas, it typically does not. "

"How often do I have to wear them?"

Dr. Tudor gave him a pointed look as if preparing to reprimand him. "As we discussed at your previous appointment, if you wish to be able to see, you'll need to wear them most of the time. Of course, up close, you shouldn't need them if you're just reading your Bible and such, but as you are out driving the wagon, riding your horse, or even working in the fields, you will need them to clear things up."

Timothy withheld his protest. He wouldn't be wearing them during all of those occasions. "All right, well, thank you."

"So long, Mr. Shepherdson." Miss Tudor apparently saved her broadest smile for that moment.

He slapped his hat on his head and walked out of the hotel. As soon as he had taken about four steps, he hastily removed the glasses and stuck them in his shirt pocket lest anyone see him wearing them.

Timothy loaded up the items from the mercantile into the back of his wagon just as a young boy approached him. "Hey there, mister. Would you like to buy a newspaper?"

Timothy recognized him as the young lad who had sold him the used, overpriced newspaper that was missing a few pages. The boy must have recognized him, too, because his eyes widened. "Oh! Never mind, mister. Never mind!" He was about to dodge away when Timothy grabbed him by the arm.

"Not so fast, young man. Where are you getting these newspapers you're selling?"

The boy shrugged but didn't answer.

"I'm going to need to speak with your parents."

The boy shook his head so quickly, his too-long, dirty hair swung from side to side.

"No, sir, you can't be doing that."

Who were his parents? And where did they live? He mentioned before that he was helping to support his family, but had that been the truth?

Sheriff Zembrodt ambled toward them. The boy attempted to pull away from Timothy's grasp. When he realized he wouldn't succeed, he turned his face to Timothy. "If I take you to my parents, will you not tell the sheriff about what I done?"

The sheriff drew closer, and the boy's panic clearly rose.

"I think I can agree to that stipulation," said Timothy.

"All right, you can just follow me, then." The boy shrugged out of Timothy's grasp and started running down the boardwalk. Timothy followed him, but the boy was fast. Maybe Timothy ought to recruit him for the town's next baseball game. He struggled to keep up with him, but finally did so just as the young'un headed out of town and cut through a grove of trees behind a hill. Timothy followed him for about a half a mile, weaving through sagebrush, then finally a clearing housing a makeshift shelter built not far from the river.

The blurriness of the scene caused Timothy to squint. Perhaps he should wear the expensive eyeglasses he'd just purchased. He ho-hummed about it for several seconds before reaching into his pocket and winding the temple tips over his ears.

Miserable, uncomfortable apparatus!

The boy stopped, put his hands on his hips, and attempted to catch his breath. "This is where we live. My pa is sitting over there, and Ma's probably in the house."

There was no house, just a large faded quilt draped over a tree branch, creating somewhat of a tent-like structure. Two little girls peered at Timothy from behind one of the trees.

"Don't mind them. They're my sisters."

A woman a few years older than Timothy stepped away from the river with a bundle of clothing in her hands. "May I help you?"

"Yes. I need to talk to this young man's parents."

"Ozias, what have you done now?"

When Ozias only shrugged, the woman redirected her gaze to Timothy. "I'm his mother, and his father is right over there." She pointed at a man sitting in a chair with his foot propped up on a barrel. "You probably do best to talk to his pa. Ozias, I do hope you haven't gone and gotten yourself into trouble again."

"I ain't done nothing, Ma. I was just in town working like I always do every single day." He extracted a few coins from his trouser pocket and handed them to the woman.

She reached an arm around him, planted a kiss on his head, and said, "Thank you for your hard work today."

Ozias beamed and looked up at Timothy. "I'll take you to Pa," he said. When they were out of earshot of his mother, Ozias stopped. "Say, mister?"

"Yes?"

The boy fiddled with a small hole in his shirt. "Please, can you not tell my ma about the newspapers? I don't want her to cry because she's done enough crying lately."

The sentiment broke Timothy's heart, and he offered a quick prayer seeking God's wisdom regarding how to handle the matter.

Timothy had barely approached when the man sitting in his chair with his leg propped on a barrel and a rifle across his lap scowled. "Who are you?"

"My name is Timothy Shepherdson, sir." He extended a hand to the rawboned man who appeared to be about thirty years old with greasy red hair, a matching beard, and holey and tattered clothes.

"Name's Harvey Agnew, what do you want?"

"Do you and your family live here?"

"What's it to you?"

"I was just wondering." Timothy's gaze went to the man's bandaged foot covered by a soiled wrap. "What happened to your foot?"

"Don't see how that's any of your business."

Timothy wasn't sure how to respond to the irritable man.

"If you don't got any business being here, then you need to leave as you're trespassing."

"Is this your land?" As far as Timothy knew, the land was part of the Hilt farm. Did Mr. Hilt even know he had squatters on his property?

"You ask too many questions."

"I was wondering if I could speak to you about your son."

"What's that boy gone and done now?" Timothy noticed Ozias hadn't stuck around but was instead near the river with his mother and sisters.

"I know he's trying to help support you in your time of need."

The man spat to the side. "Who said we were in need?"

Even a blind fellow would be able to see that the family lived in poverty.

"We're doing just fine. Now what's my boy done?"

"Do you know he sells newspapers in town?"

"That's what he said. Comes home with a few coins every now and again."

"Unfortunately, sometimes he's dishonest about the newspapers he sells."

Agnew narrowed his eyes. "What do you mean by dishonest?"

"I think he's selling newspapers he finds as some of them don't have the entire issue contained within them. And he's overcharging and not giving the correct change."

The man pursed his lips. "Guess I'll be having me a talk with that boy."

"I wouldn't be too hard on him. He's trying to do the best he can to help your family."

"Do you have children, Mr. Shepherdson?"

"I do not."

"Then the way I see it, you ain't got no right to tell me how to raise mine."

"I didn't tell you so that he could get in trouble. I told you so that maybe you could have a talk with him about seeking honest employment."

Agnew snorted. "As if a seven-year-old could seek honest employment."

Timothy took pity on Ozias. While Timothy, as a youngster, worked alongside Pa on the farm, he also had an abundant amount of time for fun with his brother and sisters. It wasn't all work at the age of seven, nor should it be. But apparently Ozias didn't have that option.

"You can leave now that you've said your piece."

Timothy wondered at the man's hostility. Was it because the family had fallen on hard times, or was he always this cantankerous? "It was nice to meet you. Is there anything I can do to help your family before I go? Chop some firewood or—?"

"I don't take charity, and neither does my family. You best take your leave."

Timothy touched the brim of his hat and walked back the way he came. When he rounded the corner by the makeshift home, he caught a glimpse of Mrs. Agnew.

Her shoulders slumped, and black circles underlined her eyes. She looked far older than she likely was. "Ma'am, I know your husband says your family doesn't want or need charity, but I want you to know that if there's any way I can help you, I'd be happy to do so."

A single tear trailed down her face. "Harvey is really struggling with his injury."

The little girls clung to their mother's skirts.

"Who is that man?" the older one whispered.

"My name is Mr. Shepherdson."

Ozias wandered over then and looked at him, an unspoken question in his wide eyes. Timothy shook his head. He'd not betray the trust of the young boy, although he figured Ozias's pa would probably tell Mrs. Agnew what Timothy had told him.

"If you don't mind me asking, ma'am, what happened to your husband?"

"He crushed his foot when it was caught in the threshing machine at the farm where he formerly worked."

Timothy had heard about such injuries. Many people died from threshing machine injuries. "I'm sorry to hear that. Is there anything I can do to help?"

"My husband doesn't believe in charity."

"How long has he been out of work?"

She shrugged her narrow shoulders. "I've lost track of time. We moved here about two weeks ago."

"Do you have any other family?"

"We don't, it's just us. Girls, why don't you run off and play now, and be sure to stay away from the river." The girls scurried away, leaving Timothy with Mrs. Agnew and Ozias, who was still staring at him with a worried look in his eyes.

"We have a very generous town. I haven't lived in any other towns, so I'm sure they're just the same, but folks would be happy to help. I know you said your husband dislikes charity, but my brother is a pastor, and he could come and speak with Mr. Agnew."

"I doubt he would talk to a pastor. He's mighty angry with the Lord right now due to the accident."

"I understand." The woman's raised brows indicated she didn't believe him, and of course, how could he understand what the Agnew family was enduring? He couldn't, but he did care.

"We've been blessed that Ozias can bring home a few coins from time to time. I would like to take a job in town, but there's a lot to do here, and Harvey isn't fit to mind the children right now."

"I would like to see about getting Ozias a different job."

"Thank you, but he seems to be doing well selling newspapers."

Behind his mother, Ozias held the finger up to his mouth and shook his head again.

"I'll be on my way, but I will stop by in a few days to see if your husband has changed his mind about accepting help."

"I'm not sure that's such a good idea. Harvey doesn't like visitors."

Timothy lowered his voice. "If you don't mind me asking, he doesn't harm you and the children, does he?" Timothy would not be leaving until he knew if Agnew was abusive. That was something he refused to stand idly by and allow.

"No. As a matter of fact, before the accident, he was a godly man who cared deeply for his family, but after his foot was crushed...he has changed, but he would never lay a hand on me or the children."

"Do you want me to send the doctor to check his wound?"

Mrs. Agnew shook her head. "There's no way to pay the doctor."

"I would pay for it for you."

"No, that's fine, but thank you all the same. He did have an infection in it, but it's been doing a lot better as of late."

Mr. Agnew called to his wife, interrupting their conversation. The last thing Timothy wanted was for Agnew to take out his anger on his wife for Timothy being there.

"Ma'am," he said, tipping his hat.

"I'll walk you a short way," said Ozias. Timothy nodded, and Ozias fell in step beside him. When they were out of earshot, the young boy spoke. "Thanks for not telling Ma about the newspapers."

"I did have to tell your pa, so he may tell her."

The boy paled. "I don't want Pa to say I can't go into town and help the family."

"I do think you should help your family, but working at an honest job for honest wages." Timothy thought of his nephews, Hosea, Simon, Sherman, Gus, and Little Hans. Was there something Ozias could do to help them with their chores? And Timothy could pay him? One thing was for certain—he needed to talk to Pa and Albert about the next steps for the Agnew family. Timothy hated to see anyone do without the necessities.

"I better get back. Thank you again, mister."

"You're welcome, Ozias. When a man says he'll do something, it's best that he keeps his word."

"Why?"

Timothy figured even if Agnew hadn't spoken to his boy about the importance of honesty, Mrs. Agnew likely had on numerous occasions. "If you are dishonest then people won't believe anything you say."

"But I don't think I was dishonest about them newspapers. I found 'em in the trash bin or lying on a bench. They could be sold just the same as new ones can."

"However, they were missing some pages, and someone was expecting the entire newspaper, and they were expecting it to be new information, not news from a week ago. If you're going to sell an old newspaper with missing pages, then you ought to have been forthright in telling your customers. And you should always give the correct change."

"Yeah, I'm sorry about the change," said Ozias. He shoved his hands into his trouser pockets.

"And," added Timothy, "it's not only important to people but more importantly, God has a lot to say about honesty in His Word."

The boy's cheeks flamed red. "Ma's read to us from the Bible, and I think I might remember some things about honesty."

Timothy placed a hand on Ozias's shoulder. "Thank you for helping take care of your family. You're a hard worker. I just think we need to find you the right job." At least until school started again. Hopefully by then, Agnew would have recovered, and Ozias could return to book learning, especially at his young age.

"Yes, sir." Ozias turned on his heel then and ran back to his family's shelter. Timothy strode to town, his mind full of options. He'd been taught from the time he could remember that it was important to help those in need. While he didn't know the entire story, he also knew that Albert, Lucy, and

Mae, had been adopted from the orphan train and had come from difficult places. As had his nephews, Hosea and Gus, and his niece, Polly. Times were tough for a lot of folks. Pa's often said words rang through Timothy's mind. *"If we see a way we can make a difference, then the Lord expects us to step up and do so."*

What was God expecting Timothy to do to help the Agnew family? Especially a family that denied wanting and needing help? A man who refused charity? Timothy then chuckled to himself when he thought of the lecture he'd given Ozias. He had no ambition to marry and be a father himself, but he figured a little practice didn't hurt in case he needed it for his nephews.

The following day after church, the family met at Ma and Pa's house for a noonday meal. He met Pa and Albert in the barn.

"Your sermon on pride was a good one," Timothy told Albert.

"Thank you." Amusement lit Albert's eyes. "Did it assist you with deciding to wear your spectacles more often?"

Timothy hadn't worn his eyeglasses to church yesterday. He just couldn't bring himself to wear the uncomfortable eye pieces.

Pa chuckled. "You should know your brother better than that, Albert. It might take six or seven sermons on pride to get him to wear his spectacles anywhere but on his farm."

"I wouldn't say it's prideful, Pa," said Timothy.

Skepticism etched his father's face. "Really?"

Albert leaned against the door. "I think you might be the stubbornest Shepherdson of all of us, Timothy."

"I doubt that. That distinction would probably go to Rubes."

"I think you're both the most stubborn."

Timothy couldn't argue with Pa's words. Not really. He had to admit he could be slightly stubborn when the need arose. He ran his hand through his hair as he thought of the topic he needed to broach with his father and brother.

Pa sobered and cocked his head to one side. "Is something bothering you, son?"

"As a matter of fact, yes." Timothy told them all about Ozias and the subsequent visit to the Agnew family. "I don't understand why Mr. Agnew doesn't want help. It's obvious his family is hungry. Ozias can barely keep his trousers around his waist. If I were Agnew, I would want my family to be fed."

"It's hard on a man's ego when he can't work. So much of who he is is wrapped up in how he cares for his family. Mr. Agnew is unable to do that." Pa was always so wise, and Timothy hoped to have even a fraction of his wisdom when he was his father's age.

"I'd be happy to get a collection of food together and other basic necessities and deliver them," said Albert. "Perhaps he'll talk to me."

Albert was adept at meeting with people who needed help and making them feel comfortable around him, but Timothy doubted that would be the case with Agnew. "His wife didn't think so. She said before the accident, he was a godly man who took care of his family, but that he's angry with God now."

Pa removed his hat and held it against his leg. There was a peppering of gray around his temples that Timothy hadn't noticed before. The realization that Pa was getting older took him aback.

"The most important thing we can do is to pray for them," said Albert.

Timothy agreed. "What I'm also fixing to do is to see if Ozias could assist the other boys with picking rock on the farm, and then I would pay him. It would put him around good influences and off the streets and would be an opportunity for him to earn an honest wage."

Pa spun the rim of his hat in his hand. "I like that idea, under one condition."

"What's that?"

"That you allow us to donate to the fund."

"We can use some of the offering as well. It's a great idea, and it just might be the way we can covertly help this family." Albert and Pa awaited Timothy's response.

"Yes. I think so, too."

But would Ozias's parents allow their son to work with Timothy's nephews on his farm?

Chapter Nine

MAGS STEPPED OFF THE train at the most recent stop. The former conductor had taken pity on her when she shared a sad story of falling down a hill and losing most of her belongings, including her train ticket stubs, and allowed her to board.

Now, as she stood amongst the other travelers, she peered up at the sign and read the word *Cornwall*. Disappointment flooded her. She had so hoped it was Horizon. But likely, Horizon was much bigger than this dusty small town she found herself in.

"Please, sir, can you tell me how long until the train leaves for Horizon?"

The conductor nodded. "It'll be about ten minutes."

She was almost to her destination. Would she be able to convince the train employees to allow her to ride? Ought she stay in her soiled dress and relay the same story she'd used before? But a whiff of her sleeve revealed the strong odor of cow manure. Best she change and concoct another story.

Ten minutes was barely sufficient, so she needed to hurry. Mags practically ran to the outhouse, thankful it was unoccupied. She emerged in her only other dress, besides the lovely pink one she'd stumbled across in the trash bin, then stuffed her soiled one into her carpetbag.

An older couple walked past her. They looked familiar, and upon second glance, Mags recognized them from Chicago as the ones who were traveling to Horizon to see their grandchildren. "Hello."

The woman cocked her head to one side. "You look vaguely familiar, dear."

"Yes, we met in Chicago. We are both traveling to Horizon."

"Oh, yes, I remember now."

"I don't believe we've been formally introduced. I'm Mrs. Gladys Bennick, and the peevish one is my husband, Mr. Bertram Bennick."

"Magnolia Davenport."

"What a lovely name."

That always brought a smile to Mags's face. "Magnolias were my mother's favorite flower." The thought of Ma caused a deep pain to sear Mags's heart.

"Did I show you my grandchildren?" Mrs. Bennick opened her locket. "This is Polly, Hosea, Pansy, and L.J."

"You already showed her when we were in Chicago," growled her husband.

"I'm sure she wants to see them again, don't you, Magnolia?"

"Yes, I'd love to see the photographs again." And she would. The children appeared so happy in the tintypes.

"I just can't wait to get to Horizon. I've missed the grandchildren something fierce."

"You just saw them two months ago," said Mr. Bennick.

"Yes, and that's been two months too long."

"May I have your attention?" A man from the depot tapped on the wooden railing, and the crowd hushed. "If your destination is Horizon, please meet over there beneath that tree." He pointed to a sycamore tree.

"Oh! That would be us." Mrs. Bennick folded her arm through Mags's. "Come along, dear."

Perhaps if Mags stayed by Mrs. Bennick's side, she would have no problem securing a ride.

Once everyone was in place beneath the tree, the man continued. "I regret to inform you that a bridge was unfortunately washed out due to last night's rain. The railroad company is hard at work and in the process of fixing the bridge, but this will necessitate folks taking the stage to Horizon."

"It should be fixed posthaste," muttered Mr. Bennick. He sidled up alongside the employee. "My wife and I will absolutely not ride the stage."

"Sir, my apologies, but the tracks at that section are currently beneath water. I assure you, it's only temporary."

"Will the train be available tomorrow?" asked Mrs. Bennick.

"I'm afraid tomorrow will necessitate riding the stagecoach as well, Mrs. Bennick. It will take more than a few days to correct the situation."

"Well, I never. You do realize we are in a hurry to see our grandchildren."

Mags felt sorry for the railroad employee. It wasn't his fault that the rain had washed out the bridge.

Mr. Bennick took the man aside, spoke a few words, then returned to Mags and Mrs. Bennick, his arms folded across his chest, and a scowl on his face. "I do *not* cotton to the stagecoach one bit. You would think that, as the owner of Bennick Railways, I would have a say in what type of transportation I must board to arrive at my destination."

"Oh, Bertram, you are so fussy. You'll do just fine on the stage, and it's not all that far."

"I'm surprised you're so amenable to it since it'll delay our visit with the grandchildren."

Mrs. Bennick pursed her lips. "Well, there is no other choice now, is there? Either ride the stage or stay in Cornwall, and we all know how you dislike Cornwall."

The railroad employee's booming voice interrupted the conversation between the Bennicks. "Ladies and gentlemen, if you will follow me over to the stagecoach."

Mags followed the other passengers. Would anyone notice that she didn't have a ticket? She was so close today, arriving in Horizon. She couldn't allow anything to interfere. Besides, she had no funds to stay in a hotel in Cornwall until the tracks were fixed.

"That's right, you're traveling to Horizon as well," said Mrs. Bennick.

"Yes."

"Delightful!"

Mags was thrilled Mrs. Bennick thought so.

In total, there were three men and three women, including Mags, boarding the stage. Mags had never ridden on a stagecoach before, and excitement thrilled through her veins as she stepped inside and took a seat on the far left. Mrs. Bennick sat beside her, and Mr. Bennick beside her and across from the two men and the other woman. From their appearances, Mags inferred they were all wealthy folks. That and the fact that they seemed to know the Bennicks quite well. Anyone who owned a railway wasn't poverty-stricken. That much she knew.

"Ma'am, I can put your carpetbag on the top of the stagecoach," offered the driver.

"I'd rather keep it with me if it's all the same to you." After her experience with that despicable Mr. Haswell, she wouldn't allow her carpetbag out of her sight. She did not want to lose Ma's ring or Phoebe's address.

"Dear, you might as well allow him to put it on the top. There's limited room inside and the ride does get long and tiring."

"That is most certainly true," grumbled Mr. Bennick.

"Now, now, Bertram. Before nightfall, we will be in Horizon and then to see our darlings. Any amount of riding on this confined and distasteful stage is worth seeing them, is it not?"

"Thank you for the offer, but I do wish to keep my carpetbag with me," Mags repeated.

The driver opened his mouth to say something more, and Mrs. Bennick waved him away. "You heard the young lady. She'll keep her carpetbag with her."

Still worried someone might ask her for a ticket, Mags rehearsed in her mind what she might say. Would she say she lost it like she had before? Or…

Finally, when the stagecoach started moving, she released the breath she had been holding. No one asked her for her stub, and no one assumed she didn't belong there. She was again grateful she had changed into her other dress. If she hadn't, would Mrs. Bennick have wanted to walk with her? Stand beside her? Act as though Mags *belonged*? What would have been even better would be if she could have switched to the lovely pink one. Then she might have even appeared to belong with the other elegantly dressed passengers.

But as bumpy and uncomfortable as the ride already was within the first few minutes, it was just as well that she saved her very best dress for when she arrived in Horizon. She wanted to make a good impression, after all.

Horizon. Was it as wonderful a city as the Bennicks mentioned? Would Mags find acceptance there? More importantly, would she be able to find a job? A way to support herself? She had survived for years without acceptance, but she couldn't survive long without funds for necessities such as food and shelter. Perhaps the Bennicks would hire her.

Scenery flashed by, and plumes of dust filled the air as thundering hooves pounded the ground. The stagecoach wavered to and fro, jolting her. A much rougher ride than the train—even the ride in the boxcar was less tumultuous. The two other men engaged in conversation with Mr. Bennick about business matters, and Mrs. Bennick and the other woman, who introduced herself as Mrs. Washut, and was married to the older of the two other men, spoke about charity fundraisers. Mags had met folks like the Bennicks and Washuts a few times in her life. She wondered what it would be like not to have to worry about where your next meal came from.

She stared out the window again. Cornwall, from what she could see anyway, seemed a fraction of the size of Chicago. Would Horizon be about the same size? She could ask Mrs. Bennick, but she didn't want to appear uneducated about such matters.

"How is the railroad?" Mr. Washut asked.

"Doing well," said Mr. Bennick. "As one of the top railroads in the country, we certainly have been busy as far as transatlantic travel goes." A flicker of annoyance crossed his face. "Of course, I suppose even the top railroads have to contend with issues such as washed-out bridges on our more inconsequential spurs."

The other man, a younger, dour-faced one with a long oval face who'd introduced himself as Mr. Kellinghaus, added his opinion. "I'm surprised you hadn't heard of the washed-out bridge sooner. Don't you have employees to keep you apprised of such happenings?"

Mr. Bennick uttered a frustrated sigh and spoke slowly. "We do have employees to keep us apprised, and while our office in Denver and our home in Maryland have telephones, we have been traveling and wouldn't have received the message unless someone had notified the depots prior to our arrival."

"Still, one would think that a company as successful as Bennick Railways would do all they could to avoid inconveniencing upper-society travelers such as the Washuts."

"Surely, even you, Mr. Kellinghaus, know that a washed-out bridge is a weather-related event and is not the fault of a railway company."

"Be that as it may," argued Mr. Kellinghaus, "for every day the spur is inaccessible, your company loses money, am I correct?"

Mr. Bennick adjusted the lapels on his jacket and smoothed his sleeves. "I trust someone such as..." he paused and plastered on a smile that failed to reach his eyes. "Someone such as yourself, while lacking proficiency in business matters, understands that my employees are doing all they can to rectify the situation."

"But you can't know for sure since you didn't even know about the situation in the first place."

Mr. Bennick's face reddened at Mr. Kellinghaus's continued attempts to cause strife. Mrs. Bennick offered Mr. Kellinghaus a frosty look. "Now, now, Mr. Kellinghaus, might I ask why you are being such a bother? We have a fair distance to go, and yet only minutes into our trip, you've decided to take it upon yourself to exhibit your vexatious personality."

Mr. Washut, who up until this time had been a mere spectator of the conversation between the two other men, nodded. "Well said, Mrs. Bennick."

"Thank you. Now that we have addressed that matter, I must declare that Bertram and I have been away from this part of the country for far too long due to vacationing at our Maryland home. Mrs. Washut, have I shown you the tintypes of my grandchildren?"

"Gladys, everyone has seen the photographs of our grandchildren." Mr. Bennick's exasperated tone indicated he may have grown tired of hearing about the only reason Mrs. Bennick wanted to visit Horizon.

Mrs. Washut clapped her gloved hands together. "Actually, I would love to see the photographs."

"Thank you. As you'll recall, these are Hosea, Polly, Pansy, and L.J."

"They are such darlings. I recall the photographs you have of them in your Denver home." Mrs. Washut gazed admiringly at the locket. "Mr. Washut and I have yet to be blessed with grandchildren, although our daughter and her husband own two dogs and a cat."

Mrs. Bennick rolled her eyes and pursed her lips. "Hardly the same. But someday when you do have grandchildren, you'll want to see them all the time and spoil them silly."

"Oh, for certain!" Mrs. Washut beamed.

"Gladys, you coddle those children far too much."

"Bah humbug, Bertram. You don't coddle them enough."

All of the talk of the photographs caused a sadness to linger in Mags's heart. Oh, how she wished she owned a tintype of Ma. Even now, sometimes the memory of her image blurred in her mind. She swallowed hard.

If only things had been different.

If only God were in the business of answering prayers. Or, at the very least, hearing them.

Mr. Bennick withdrew an expensive timepiece like the one Mags had seen in the costly jewelry shops in downtown Chicago. He flicked open the cover. "We are already nearly an hour into the ride."

"Might as well sit back and relax, Bertram," chuckled Mr. Washut. He retrieved his own timepiece from his expensive suit pocket.

Mr. Kellinghaus scrutinized Mr. Washut's timepiece. "That's a nice pocket watch, Washut."

"Thank you. It's a Thiele and is fourteen-karat gold. I purchased it in New York during our last visit. Would you care to run an eye over it?"

"I would." Mr. Washut handed the timepiece to Mr. Kellinghaus, who opened it, examined it closely, then handed it back to its owner. "I'll have to purchase myself one of these at some juncture."

Mrs. Bennick fingered the locket around her neck. "Will you be staying in Horizon?"

Mrs. Washut bobbed her head. "Yes, our accommodations are in Horizon, but only for the night. We will then continue to Spokane to see my second cousin twice removed. Pray tell, is Horizon Hotel an acceptable place to lodge?"

"We roomed at the boardinghouse on our first visit, then The Horizon Hotel on a subsequent visit. We now stay at Landon and Mae's home. While The Horizon Hotel is nothing like the hotels in Denver or New York, it's bearable."

The topic of discussion returned to fundraisers and charities, and Mags had settled in for an uneventful ride when a man emerged from a grove of trees up ahead and waved his hands.

"Must be someone who needs a ride," commented Mrs. Washut.

The stage slowed, and Mags could hear voices outside the stagecoach window. She brushed away the fine layer of dust that had settled on the sleeve of her dress.

A red-bearded man stood to the side of the road. "Hello, there! I'm in a predicament. Got any room inside the stage? I need to get to Horizon to fetch the doctor since my pa fell ill."

"Where's your horse?" asked the driver.

"It threw a shoe. Can you help me?"

"Sorry, but there ain't no room on the stagecoach. This isn't one of them larger ones that can carry more passengers."

"What about on top?"

"No room there either. I'll send help when we reach Horizon."

The man lowered his head, and his shoulders slumped. "I'd be obliged if I could somehow hitch a ride."

Mags pondered whether they could scoot closer together to provide room for the desperate man, but with Mr. Washut's girth and a crate the shotgun messenger had placed inside at their feet, there really was no room.

"Reckon you could ride along on the side if you're of the mind to do so and you've got the balance to stand on the footboard."

"Much obliged." The man stepped on the yellow footboard, his right hand clutching the window area so he wouldn't fall off. Even so, when the driver beckoned the horses, the man would have to do a balancing act.

He turned his head just then, his face mere inches from Mags. "Well, hello there. Ain't you a pretty thing?"

Despite the heat of the crammed stagecoach, Mags shivered. Something about the man caused her consternation. She ignored his words and focused straight ahead since she was now precluded from taking in the view from the window.

Sudden movement caught her eye. Her breath hitched when she observed the man raise his revolver with his left hand and take aim in the driver's direction. A harsh warning flashed in his eyes as his gaze met hers. "Don't you say nothing at all, or I'll shoot you and everyone else too."

Mags's heart pounded wildly in her chest, and breath-pinching fear trundled through her. He lowered the gun, then raised it again. She couldn't allow him to shoot the driver. Couldn't allow him to take a life. Couldn't allow him to harm any of the passengers, should he choose to do so.

If only God answered prayers, then she'd pray for a way to stop the evil man.

Chapter Ten

At the unexpected idea, Mags folded at the waist and unbuttoned her boot. The man must have caught her movement because he jerked his head toward hers again. "What are you doing?"

"I have a pebble in my shoe, and I'm attempting to remove it." Would he believe her?

"Well, hurry up about it." When he whipped his head back to face the front, his beard blew off, exposing a clean-shaven chin, and he uttered several oaths.

Terror flashed in Mrs. Bennick's eyes. Had she noticed the gun as well? Mr. Bennick directed a hard stare toward the man. Mr. Washut clutched his wife's hand, and Mr. Kellinghaus busied himself with a button on his suit jacket.

Mags removed her boot and pretended to empty an imaginary pebble as the stagecoach rumbled down the road. The man pulled back the hammer on his revolver and extended the gun from his body. If she were to do something, Mags must do it now. In an act so hasty she knew she could never replicate it again, even if she tried, Mags rammed the heel of her brown lace-up boot as hard as she could against the man's hand. If the pain wasn't enough, the shock was. The man cried out and simultaneously shot a bullet to the left, thankfully missing the driver, before falling off the stagecoach and tumbling down the embankment.

"What just happened?" asked Mrs. Bennick.

Were they safe now, or would the man attempt to catch up with them again? Mags leaned her head out the window. Through the dust-filled haze, she saw the man in the far distance as the stagecoach increased its speed. She closed her eyes and willed her heartbeat to settle.

"I believe you just saved the driver's life," said Mr. Bennick.

Mags wanted to bask in the praise, but the sight of men emerging from a grove of trees just up ahead caused her heart to leap to her throat. "Who are those men?"

Mr. Bennick leaned forward and peered out the window. "Those would be stagecoach robbers."

"Highwaymen? Oh, dear! Whatever shall we do? First that odious cretin, and now this?" Mrs. Washut flung the back of her hand to her forehead. "I do believe this is the thing nightmares consist of."

Mrs. Bennick's eyes bulged. "I've never endured such an atrocity." She clutched Mr. Bennick's arm. "Please do something, Bertram."

"Maybe a shootout will solve the problem," he muttered.

"This is why we have the protection of the shotgun messenger," said Mr. Kellinghaus.

"Do they mean to rob us?" Mags asked, noting that her inquiry stated the obvious. She thought of Ma's ring in her carpetbag. She'd not part with it.

"Now I'm wishing I hadn't put my trunk on top of the stagecoach," whined Mrs. Washut.

Mr. Washut patted his frantic wife's arm. "There would have been no room in here for that oversized trunk. Besides, dear, if they're planning to rob us, they'll take whatever is available to them, whether it be from the top of the stage or in the coach."

Mags peered out the window again. One of the men's gazes caught hers. His dark eyes glared into her soul, and she shuddered. Suddenly, she had an idea. She managed to weasel her way out of unfortunate circumstances before, and this should be no different.

With a sudden burst of inspiration, she opened her carpetbag and withdrew both Phoebe's address and Ma's wedding ring. She tucked both into the pocket in her dress, protected should the robbers steal her carpetbag. "I have an idea," she said.

Mrs. Bennick's shoulders shook and her chin trembled. "Yes?" she whispered.

The stagecoach slowed as gunshots rang out. "We haven't much time. If you will all hand me your valuables, I will hide them in my dress's secret pocket."

"And why would we trust you?" asked Mr. Kellinghaus. "You could be a thief as well."

Mags could hardly deny that she had stolen a time or two in her life. "Well, you can take a chance on me, or you can take a chance on the highwaymen stealing your possessions. Which would you rather choose?"

"I'd hardly choose you." Mr. Kellinghaus's high forehead puckered. "I'll keep my valuables, thank you."

Mags flinched at the harsh tone of his sneer.

"The highwaymen will inevitably steal all that we own." Mrs. Bennick paled. "I feel as though I may faint dead away."

Mags rested a hand on her arm. "Mrs. Bennick, please give me your rings and necklaces, and I will hide them beneath my dress for safekeeping."

"All right, yes, I will." With a shaky hand, Mrs. Bennick removed her wedding ring, another ring she had on her right hand, a hairpin, and the locket, and handed them to Mags. "Bertram gave me that hairpin."

"And I'll buy you another if the highwaymen steal that one," her husband reassured her.

Mrs. Washut did the same, as did Mr. Washut and Mr. Bennick, who handed Mags their timepieces and stacks of cash, which consisted of more money than Mags had seen in her entire life.

Mags peeked out the window. Where had the robbers gone? "Now, if you'll afford me a semblance of privacy..." The men turned their faces from her, and Mrs. Bennick held up her shawl, somewhat blocking Mags from the rest of the passengers as she stuck the items in the pockets beneath her dress. "Do not breathe a word that I have these," Mags admonished the other passengers. Mrs. Washut pretended to button her lip, and her husband nodded in agreement. Mrs. Bennick blinked rapidly.

Mr. Kellinghaus rolled his eyes as his mustache twitched. Mr. Bennick merely stared at Mags with an unblinking gaze. Did he believe she would return his timepiece, cash, and his wife's jewelry? She hoped so. While she didn't know the Bennicks well, she wanted them to think favorably of her.

The stagecoach lurched to a stop, and one of the men opened the door. "Get out!" he snapped.

"Oh, please don't harm us." Mrs. Bennick clasped her husband's arm for security.

"Then do what we say." The man herded them to the side of the coach.

One of the other men directed the shotgun messenger and the driver to drop their guns while two more men pointed their own pistols directly at the messenger and driver, leaving them no choice but to obey. Another man scooped up the weapons.

"Throw down the strongbox," yelled a robber with long, thick blond hair peeking beneath his cowboy hat.

The driver tossed the strongbox, and it thudded to the ground. A tall, thin highwayman aimed his pistol at the box and shot the lock.

Mrs. Bennick cowered against Mr. Bennick. Mrs. Washut began to whimper. Mr. Kellinghaus offered a witty remark, which earned him a gun held to his temple. And Mags realized something for the first time.

All of the men wore the same bushy red beards. Were they fake like the man who'd fallen off the foothold? The answer to her question arrived a second later when the tall, thin outlaw turned so abruptly that his beard twisted crookedly to the side with the movement.

One of the men, a squatty and stout older fellow, reached in and yanked Mags's carpetbag and the crate from the stage.

"What's in here?" he asked.

When no one answered, he stomped to the driver and held the pistol to the man's chest. "What's in the crate?"

Instead of waiting, he pivoted and opened the lid to reveal a mailbag. "Just as I suspected." He removed it and set it to the side. "Looks to be our lucky day, men." He then unbuttoned Mags's carpetbag and dumped the contents on the ground. "Whose is this?"

Mr. Kellinghaus had the audacity to point to Mags.

The short, round fellow marched to Mags, the empty bag in his hand. "Is this all you got?"

"It is."

His stale breath wafted on the air, and Mags nearly wretched. He removed his hat, revealing thinning strands of greasy brown hair. "Everyone, put valuables in this hat. All coins, all dollars, all jewelry." He jabbed Mr. Washut in the side. "Empty your pockets, old man."

Mr. Washut dug a hand into his trouser pocket and turned it inside out. "I don't have any left. I gambled it all away in Cornwall."

The man spat to the side. "Why is it I don't believe you? Fellas, does he look like the gambling sort?"

The other highwaymen chuckled. "No, he don't," said the tall, thin one, never removing his attention from the driver and shotgun messenger.

"Empty the other pocket," he directed.

Mr. Washut did as he asked. The short, round man glared at him before moving to Mrs. Bennick, who'd forgotten to give her dangly earrings to Mags. "Put your earrings in the hat and any rings as well."

"I don't have any rings." Mrs. Bennick's voice shook, and Mags reached for the woman's hand in an attempt to calm her.

"No sudden movements!" His sharp tone caused Mags to shrink back and release the older woman's hand.

He moved on to Mr. Bennick, then Mr. Kellinghaus. The latter offered a sheepish expression before dumping a plentiful amount of cash and coins and an expensive timepiece into the hat.

Mags memorized the men's appearances for when they made it to Horizon safely. *If* they made it to Horizon safely.

The man's nose twitched. "How come you ain't got no jewelry, pretty lady?"

She straightened her posture as best she could, pretending not to be deterred by the evil around her. "I have nothing of value."

His mouth twisted to one side, causing the fake beard to lift and reveal a large scar on his chin. He regarded her, his gaze probing through her.

A knot of air caught in her chest. Did he not believe her? Would he suspect she was hiding valuables in the pocket beneath her dress? Would Mr. Kellinghaus divulge such information if prompted? Mags's heart pounded so loudly in her ears that she feared she'd not hear another spoken word.

The man stood directly in front of her, waiting not so patiently for her to deposit her cash, gold coins, and expensive jewelry into his dirty hat. As if she had any to deposit. Once again, she was grateful she hadn't changed into the lovely pink dress. Her bland and worn dress was anything but one a wealthy woman would intentionally choose. "Sir, I do not have any valuables." Of all the lies Mags had told—and she'd told plenty—that statement was true.

"You telling the truth?"

"Sir, all I own was in that carpetbag over yonder." She pointed at the bag that had been tossed to the side near her two wadded dresses and a sewing kit. The man had filched the latter, adding it to Mrs. Bennick's earrings and Mr. Kellinghaus's valuables.

Mags scrutinized the left side of the man's head, as a part of the beard hung a little lower than on the other side. Admittedly, the false facial hair better disguised the men than handkerchiefs.

"What are you looking at?"

Mags startled and tore her eyes away. Mrs. Bennick gasped and held a hand to her bosom. Mrs. Washut teetered, and Mr. Washut barely caught her before she collapsed into his arms.

"Hurry up over there," the tall, thin man admonished another outlaw who pilfered the money in the strongbox before moving on to the mailbag and the trunks stored on the top of the stage.

Yes, please do hurry. The sooner they left, the sooner they could continue on their way to Horizon.

Preferably without injuries or death.

An idea popped into her head. Dare she? "Sir?"

"What 'dya want?"

"You're not planning to rob any more stagecoaches, are you?"

He scowled. "What's it to you, lady?"

Mags shrugged. "I'm only asking because there's another stagecoach that will be coming along in the next hour."

"How do you know this?"

"I checked the schedule. I almost had to take that second one myself. You see, the bridge is washed out, and…"

"Yeah, yeah, yeah. We know the bridge is washed out. That's how we knew to watch for the stage."

Would the man whose hand she hit return as well? She cringed to think of the revenge he would exact. But when Mags glanced around, she saw no one approaching in the distance.

The man who'd pilfered the loot returned and leaned so close Mags could see the hairy mole on his upper cheek, just above the false beard. "Why would you tell us that?"

Why would she indeed? She silently begged herself to conjure up a plausible reason. "They have two strongboxes. I'll tell you the exact route if you don't harm us."

Warning bells rang through her mind. She had best hush lest she cause more trouble for herself and the other passengers.

All four outlaws regarded her, and Mags did her best to remain stolid—a look she'd perfected years ago while acting like she didn't care about the way she was being treated by her aunts.

The bandits talked amongst themselves for the next few minutes, almost as if they weren't in the middle of a holdup.

"Might be that we should see about that second stagecoach."

"Yeah, couldn't hurt to see if she's telling the truth."

"Anyone seen Kir..." but the outlaw held his tongue.

Who was "Kir"? Mags memorized the beginning of the name, hoping that might help to nab the highwaymen once she reported them to the sheriff in Horizon.

A sick feeling washed over her. These men were dangerous. Had likely killed people. Would they allow Mags and the other passengers to leave after they thought they had secured all of their valuables?

The man who'd emptied the strongbox and mailbag wandered over to Mags. He smelled of cigars and whiskey, and stubby brown chin hair showed beneath the false beard. "Maybe you'd like to come with us."

Bile rose in Mags's throat. She held her tongue until the man repeated himself, obviously desiring an answer. "I think not, but thank you all the same."

"Feisty little thing, ain't you?"

For a minute, she forgot to breathe. What would she do if they attempted to take her with them? Would the driver and shotgun messenger be able to thwart their plans?

The tall, thin man's abrupt voice interrupted her trepidation. "Let's get out of here."

Guns held on the driver and shotgun messenger, the outlaws backed away from the passengers and climbed on their horses before galloping in the opposite direction.

The driver hustled the passengers back inside the stagecoach. No one said anything for several minutes until Mr. Kellinghaus directed a narrowed gaze at Mags. "You're just lucky I didn't say anything about the hidden valuables."

"Yes, and I—we are grateful for that." Her voice wavered. So much could have gone wrong with the robbery. Yet, here they all were, riding to Horizon with no injuries or, worse, deaths.

Mr. Bennick pointed a finger at Mr. Kellinghaus. "You, sir, are an impudent fool. While you lost everything on your person, we lost nothing, save for my wife's earrings."

"But Miss Davenport hasn't returned your valuables yet, now has she?"

"As if she would steal them." Mrs. Bennick clucked her tongue. "You are an audacious nincompoop, Mr. Kellinghaus. Magnolia saved us from losing both money and precious heirlooms. And what have you done except wag your tongue and cause strife?"

"Indeed," added Mr. Washut. "Serves you right that you lost everything."

Mr. Kellinghaus crossed his arms across his puny chest. "I have nothing more to say. But mark my words, you best count every penny and account for every *precious* heirloom from Miss Davenport's safekeeping."

While everyone else had stood up for Mags, the fact that Mr. Kellinghaus deemed her a thief stabbed at her heart. Her aunts' words flashed through her memory, and a time when Aunt Mikelanna outright accused her of stealing a handkerchief caused a lump to form in her throat. The item had later been found in Aunt Mikelanna's top bureau drawer, where she had forgotten she'd placed it. No apology was forthcoming.

But you are a thief, Mags's inner voice chastised. Guilt washed over her. Yes, she'd stolen, but never from kind folks like the Bennicks and Washuts.

Did you not steal train services? Mags attempted to shove away the frustrating reminder that she *had* stolen the ride from Chicago to Horizon. She would atone for it by paying it back once she earned money. That was a promise.

Mrs. Bennick again held up her shawl, and Mags dug into her pocket and removed the money and valuables and handed them to their respective owners. She gave in to the temptation to toss a certain passenger a haughty look. "Your worry was for naught, Mr. Kellinghaus."

Something about his demeanor reminded her of Aunt Thirza's husband. Mags rested against the seat as a recollection clouded her mind.

Aunt Mikelanna, Aunt Thirza, and Aunt Darla had conversed amongst themselves at the parsonage that day, saying harsh things about Ma and Mags. Words that permeated deep into Mags's heart and stung worse than anything she'd ever known. They could say all they wanted about her. But the words about her mother stung the deepest. Mags wanted to remind them that she was standing right there. But she hadn't. Instead, she silently wrung her hands and shifted her feet back and forth while they determined her future.

Life with Aunt Mikelanna had been nonstop work caring for six children, all on her own. Her aunt tottered about doing whatever she pleased, her uncle worked at the saloon, and they both drank heavily, many times arriving home drunk. Mags was given a meager portion of food, no pay, and a cold, damp corner in which to sleep.

But she'd had a roof over her head.

On an uncharacteristically cold day, Aunt Mikelanna urged her to her feet before sunrise. *"It's time for you to live with your Aunt Thirza now."*

"Might I do so after breakfast?" As if breakfast provided any type of nourishment. Mags had lost weight living with Aunt Mikelanna. The one time she'd eaten extra, her cousin ratted on her, and the punishment had been nothing but a crust of bread and water for two days.

"Today it's been exactly two years, and that is the agreement. Get up, get dressed, and we'll deliver you to Thirza's within the hour."

When she resided with Aunt Thirza and her ne'er-do-well husband, Mags had been sent to work at the factory. Aunt Thirza made her turn over her entire earnings from the factory for rent. Mags, thankfully, was still able to attend school most days of the week before work. She loved learning. But by the time she arrived at Aunt Thirza's apartment each evening after school and hours at the soap factory, she was exhausted, and Aunt Thirza demanded she prepare supper as well.

At sixteen, Mags had moved out, not of her own volition, but because Aunt Thirza had placed her carpetbag with her meager items on the stoop of the apartment building. *"You are now sixteen, and it's been exactly two years to the day since I graciously took you in. The agreement is that you'll now move on."*

Mags countered Aunt Thirza's insistence. *"But I will continue to pay rent."* The thought of living alone terrified her. Where would she go?

"You've never really been very helpful, just a drain," said her uncle.

"Please, Aunt Thirza." The words sounded desperate in Mags's own ears, for they were.

Aunt Thirza crossed her arms over her ample bosom. *"It's time for you to go."*

Mags had stood outside the apartment building. A drunkard staggered down the street, a bottle of whiskey in his hand, and a mangy cat knocked over a trash bin. In an apartment across the street, a shouting match ensued, and a group of men sauntered down the street bragging about how they'd stolen from a local hardware store earlier that day. Mags had hidden behind one of the two unpruned bushes, hoping they wouldn't see her.

She'd fallen asleep sitting up, her back against the prickly vegetation. A thought had briefly occurred to her about asking the pastor for help. But he and his wife hadn't been willing to take her in last time.

God had deserted her again.

The following day, she secured a dingy apartment in a dilapidated part of town in a tenement where she'd stayed until they had raised the rent on her.

But none of that mattered now. All these years later, Magnolia Davenport was ready to start anew.

Mags leaned her head out the window. She was about to ask how much further when she saw a sign with the word *Horizon*. Where were all of the people? Where were the factories? Of course, she really couldn't see much from her position.

The stage pulled into the depot, and Mr. Bennick addressed her. "You, young lady, saved us from losing about $10,000." Mags's jaw went slack. She knew that the cash, jewelry, and timepieces were worth a fortune, but she hadn't realized that it was that big a fortune.

"Yes, thank you," chorused all but Mr. Kellinghaus.

Mrs. Bennick nodded her approval. "It was quick thinking on your part, and we are ever so grateful. To have lost my locket and other valuables...I couldn't fathom it. Now, what can we do to repay you?"

"Oh, that's not necessary."

"Oh, but it is." Mrs. Bennick scrutinized Mags's dress, and suddenly she felt like a ragamuffin. "Are you a teacher? Perhaps with the deaf school?"

"I am not."

"I know you mentioned you're here to visit family. Do you assist at the family farm?"

An idea came to Mags, one that had been on the periphery of her thoughts as of late. "I plan to open a bakery."

"A bakery?"

"Yes." Reality struck her that there might already be several bakeries in town. What then? But she had one thing those other bakeries lacked. Ma's recipes that she'd memorized.

Mrs. Bennick tapped her chin. "Well, you deserve some sort of reward for your bravery and for saving our valuables."

The stagecoach came to a halt, and Mrs. Bennick gently pressed on her arm. "Before we alight, perhaps we can discuss how to help you in return. Bertram?"

Mr. Bennick mustered a rare smile. "As witnesses, we'll all need to discuss this matter with the sheriff so he can apprehend the outlaws and recover the money, mail, and valuables that were stolen. But Gladys and I would like to offer you free rent of our vacant building here in Horizon."

"You would?" There was a vacant building in Horizon, and it would be hers? Rent-free? Mags's heart ticked up to twice its normal pulse.

"That is, if you don't already have a building for your bakery."

"No, I don't. Not yet."

Mr. Bennick removed his timepiece as if the discussion lingered on far longer than he had time for. "We'll provide it to you rent-free for five years. Does that sound appropriate?"

"Yes, sir. More than appropriate, and you don't have to do a thing to repay me. I'm just happy I could help." The thought of Ma's ring in the hands of bandits still caused her apprehension.

"We know we don't *have* to," said Mrs. Bennick. "As you know, the locket is important to me, as is my wedding ring. The ring on my right hand was given to me by my grandchildren and has each of their birthstones in it. I would not have wanted to lose it, as it is important to me. Bertram's timepiece has sentimental value as well, and not to mention the dollars and coins that were saved due to your shrewdness. Once we speak with the sheriff, we'll secure the key for you."

"And if you don't want to house your bakery in the vacant building, we are not offended."

Why would she not want to house her bakery in the vacant building? It was a dream come true. "Yes, sir. Thank you, Mr. and Mrs. Bennick."

The sheriff ambled toward them, interviewed them all about the robbery, then informed them he'd be calling a posse together to attempt to apprehend them, based on Mags telling the outlaws another stagecoach was forthcoming.

Awe transformed Sheriff Zembrodt's face. "That was smart thinking, young lady. You may have just aided the law in capturing some dangerous individuals."

Pride welled within her. "Thank you. I should also tell you about their false beards, a man whose name begins *Kir*, and another man's scar I observed from beneath his beard."

Sheriff Zembrodt listened intently before excusing himself to prepare the posse.

Would they catch the outlaws?

Mags stood on the boardwalk, peering around at the small town. No, it wasn't bustling with a million people. It didn't contain tall buildings, numerous businesses, countless factories, or abundant apartments. Yet, profound joy still immersed itself within her.

Not only would she be embarking on her new adventure, but now she also had a place to open a bakery—her very own business. If she worked hard, she would be able to call for Phoebe, Larry, and the baby within months.

Her dreams were coming to fruition.

Chapter Eleven

Her stomach growled something fierce. The last time she had eaten was before she'd hitched a ride in the railcar, and that had only been a meager snack. Her lips were parched. A hand pump beside a trough offered a refreshing antidote to her intense thirst. She lifted the handle, and with one hand, she caught the precious liquid and guzzled it greedily before splashing it onto her face, not caring how unladylike she may appear.

A few passersby glanced at her but said nothing, and a morsel of doubt clouded her mind. Hopefully, the people here would be nicer than the ones she dealt with in her own family. Perhaps they would embrace the new bakery, and she'd be able to support herself with her dream. A mirthless laugh escaped her lips. What bakery? While she was grateful that Mr. and Mrs. Bennick would allow her to rent her bakery free of charge, she had nothing to put in it. No stove, no dry sink, no dishes, and no ingredients to make delectable desserts.

Mags had twenty-five cents to her name. She stopped in front of the mercantile. Perhaps she could purchase a can of fruit or some apples. Surely it wouldn't be long before her bakery produced an income. And she was so, so hungry.

Inside, rows and rows of goods greeted her. A shelf with honey, nuts, and eggs caused her stomach to rumble again. She wandered to the adjoining shelf, which held a few cans of cherries and several cans of sardines. Then she saw it, one lonely can of peaches. Mags could almost taste the deliciousness of the decadent fruit on her tongue. At fifteen cents, she'd still have ten cents leftover.

For next time.

Unfortunately, ten cents would hardly feed her.

Nearly all the money she'd saved for her new adventure had been stolen from her that day in the alleyway near Phoebe's apartment.

Her fingers tapped the tin can at the same time as another, much larger hand. For the briefest of seconds, it was a tug-of-war of sorts. She'd nearly laid claim to it when she realized how unladylike her actions were. "Oh, I'm so sorry." Mags withdrew her hand while at the same time turning to see who might also be desiring the can of peaches.

"My apologies, ma'am."

A tall, muscular fellow of about her age or slightly older, with dark, wavy hair, blue eyes, and a black cowboy hat, peered down at her.

"I, well, I guess I didn't realize you wanted the can of peaches. By all means…"

The corners of his mouth lifted. "The can is all yours. I was actually reaching for some…" but the way he paused and redirected his attention to the shelfful of goods led her to believe he might not be telling the entire truth.

"Really, I'll just take a can of cherries." Mags resisted the urge to retch. She'd never cottoned to cherries. But as hungry as she was, she'd settle for them. Or maybe the can of tomatoes. They were only ten cents. Yes, that would be a better deal. "Rather, I will take a can of tomatoes."

"Please. Take the peaches."

Her face heated under the man's perusal of her as he awaited her decision. The can of peaches did sound appetizing, and if he was offering it, then she ought to take it, even if she felt bad that he wanted it too. "Will more peaches be available in the future?"

"I reckon so. Seems the factories produce more than one can at a time."

"Oh. Yes, most certainly." Mags knew all about factories.

The man reached for the can of peaches and deposited it into her hand. Then he touched the brim of his hat. "Ma'am."

"Thank you." She nearly fumbled the peaches before clasping them tightly in her hand. She dipped her head lest the man see the warmth that crept into her cheeks.

At the counter, a pleasant woman took her money, and Mags remembered something important. "Ma'am, do you, by chance, have a can opener I might borrow?"

The clerk eyed her with curiosity for a moment before retrieving a cast-iron cow head opener from the shelf and offering it to Mags. Embarrassed that she must secure a temporary can opener just to partake in her meager meal, Mags turned slightly while using the tool before returning it to the woman. "Thank you."

"You're welcome." This time, the woman smiled.

"I'm Tabitha."

"Mags."

"Nice to meet you." The woman paused and gazed out the window. "Oh, dear. It looks like they're calling a posse together."

"Yes, there was a stagecoach robbery."

Tabitha held a hand to her heart. "Well, we haven't had one of those in a few years. Best pray for everyone joining the posse that the Good Lord will bring them back safely." Tabitha could pray if she wanted, but those prayers would only be a waste of time.

Mags finished the can of peaches, then walked up and down the boardwalk. She located the vacant building and peered through the dirty window. The space, while small, would be perfect. But how would she succeed since she had no supplies?

Magnolia Davenport, when did you begin to entertain such gloomy thoughts? She'd come this far by her lonesome, and while it would take time and money to purchase the items for her business, Mags wasn't about to concede to failure just yet.

She passed a restaurant and her stomach thundered even louder. Should she enter the business and offer to wash dishes or serve the patrons in exchange for a bowl of soup or a sandwich?

The aroma of steak and potatoes lured her inside the restaurant, where a round-faced, jolly red-headed woman greeted her. "Welcome to Wilhelmina's. May I help you?"

"Hello, ma'am, I was wondering if I might do some work for you this evening in exchange for supper."

The woman extended a hand. "I'm Wilhelmina, and you are?"

"Magnolia, but everyone calls me Mags."

"Magnolia, what a beautiful name. I don't have any job openings at present, but if you would like to scrub a few pans for me, I can see to it that you get your belly filled tonight."

"Thank you so much."

Mags was deep in the throes of removing crusted sauce from an oversized pan when she heard a somewhat familiar voice. She peered around the corner of the kitchen and noticed the sheriff standing by the first table. "I don't know her name. She has blonde hair and is slender. She's not from Horizon but arrived on the stage this afternoon."

"I believe I may know of whom you speak," said Wilhelmina. "She's scrubbing some pans for me in the kitchen."

A momentary flitter of panic rippled through Mags. Why was the sheriff looking for her? But then she quickly shoved the worrisome thought aside. She'd done nothing wrong. This wasn't like the times she'd been unfairly and severely punished by her aunts. Or the time she deserved a night in jail because she'd stolen some food.

The fruit stand had begged her to sample the apples and oranges so neatly stacked in rows. While Mags hadn't stolen before, the temptation, combined with desperation, had been her downfall that day. She'd filled a basket she'd found full of the plump fruits without paying a cent.

"*Stop her!*" the shopkeeper yelled, and a constable in the vicinity chased her.

Jail hadn't been a pleasant place to reside, even for such a short time.

Or when one of Aunt Mikelanna's youngest sons had run off while Mags was tending to them at the park. It had scared Mags something fierce, and she and the others had urgently searched for the five-year-old. They'd found him hiding behind a terrace, beaming that it had taken them so long to find him.

Mags wrapped her arms around him. *"Please don't ever run off like that again. You gave me a fright."*

Her cousin had giggled, then snuggled into Mags's arms. *"Sorry, Mags. I wanted to play hide and seek."*

When they'd arrived back at the apartment, Mags figured the other children had forgotten the incident, until her oldest niece reiterated the entire story to Aunt Mikelanna, along with some embellishments. As punishment, her aunt whipped her, and her uncle delivered her far from the apartment that evening and told her to find her way back home.

She'd nearly been accosted by a scoundrel and had almost frozen to death in the chilly nighttime spring temperatures.

Mags had never lost track of any of the children after that.

But she'd been punished for other infractions. Too many to count, although never again whipped and never dropped in the middle of the city again by her lonesome. Mags still wondered how Ma, such a sweet and loving woman, could have such hateful sisters. She'd never find the answer to that any more than she would find the answer to why Phoebe's grandmother had rejected her. If she ever had the chance to help a child, she would not deny them based on who their family was or wasn't.

Her hands shook as she scrubbed at a particularly stubborn patch of food.

"Miss Davenport?"

"Sheriff," she squeaked, her voice sounding nervous and fearful in her own ears.

"Can I speak with you for a moment at the sheriff's office?"

"She hasn't yet had anything to eat, Sheriff. Could she meet you there, in, say, an hour?" asked Wilhelmina.

"That'll do. When you're finished, I'll meet you at the sheriff's office. It's on the next block on the left-hand side."

Mags nodded and returned to her task. Had they caught the bandits? Perhaps that could be what he wished to speak with her about.

"I think that's good enough for now." Wilhelmina entered the kitchen, exhaustion lining her round face. "Why don't you go sit down and peruse the menu? I've left it on the table near the counter. Have whatever you like."

"Are you sure? I really didn't do that much."

"You did plenty, and you saved me hours of backbreaking work. Please have whatever you like."

Mags long ago became adept at hiding her true feelings. She had done well wearing a mask, disguising anything she really felt. But this time, in the midst of all that happened, Wilhelmina's kindness caused her resolve to fail. "Thank you." Her legs wobbled as she meandered to the table and nearly collapsed into the chair. The restaurant was now almost void of customers, and the only sounds were the slight murmur of the last couple of people chatting quietly at their tables and the clinking of pans in the kitchen.

Mags perused the menu. She salivated just reading the offerings and settled on some corned beef hash, potatoes, and a glass of milk. Wilhelmina brought them to her straightaway, and not caring that she didn't look the least bit ladylike, Mags shoveled the supper into her mouth.

Food had never tasted so good.

When she couldn't eat another bite, she rose, took her plate into the kitchen, and thanked Wilhelmina again.

"I will keep you in mind if I ever require assistance. Normally, my husband is here, but he had to take an unexpected trip to Ingleville. Now don't forget to stop by the sheriff's office."

Mags hurried from the restaurant, her stomach full and content, but her nerves slightly on edge at what the sheriff could possibly want. Perhaps he wanted to ask more questions about the outlaws.

She opened the door to find Sheriff Zembrodt sitting at the desk and a deputy standing beside him. Five familiar faces glared at her through the jail bars. "We can talk right out front." The sheriff ushered her outside. "Thank you for coming."

He led her to a bench just kitty-corner from the building. "I see that you caught the highwaymen."

"We did. I've got some excellent deputies and other townsfolk who ride out with me when I need to form a posse. We found them just where you described, waiting for the next stage." He chuckled. "The next stage that wasn't going to arrive."

She offered a slight smile, and the sheriff continued. "That was quick thinking on your part, as was when you hit the man's hand and caused him to fall from the stagecoach."

"It's amazing all the things a good shoe can do," she said, her voice wavering as she did so.

"The reason I called you here is not only because of your help, especially the part about telling us where we could find the notorious Schultz Gang, but also because the description about the beards being fake and the other information you offered was essential in assisting us with the arrests. I'm not sure you realized that there was a reward for their capture."

"A reward?"

"Yes. In the amount of $500."

She gasped. Had she heard correctly?

"Now, I did get some information from the driver as well, so he'll get a portion of that, but all told, I have $425 here for you."

The tears settled just at the edges of her eyes before streaming down her cheeks. The sheriff may as well have offered her a million dollars.

"These men have been wanted for a while and have committed some vicious crimes in three different states. I also applaud you on convincing the other passengers to allow you to keep their valuables so they wouldn't get stolen."

"Yes, all but one agreed."

"Let me guess—Mr. Kellinghaus." Sheriff Zembrodt chuckled. "That doesn't surprise me one bit. That being said, where would you like the funds?"

She didn't yet have a bank account, but she supposed it would make good sense to open one with the new bakery.

A bank account. Had she ever even dreamed she'd have enough funds to deposit into an account? Not only that, but the $425 would enable her to purchase a new stove, a dry sink, and other supplies. "Can you please keep it for me until tomorrow, when I can open a bank account?"

"Certainly. Bank opens at nine."

It was only after she'd bid the sheriff farewell that Mags realized she could have used some of that money for a hotel room for the night.

But she did have the key to the building that the Bennicks had given her. While not the most comfortable, it *was* a place to lay her head. That was, if she could sleep after all of the excitement of today's events.

Chapter Twelve

An entourage of children zipped into the barn. "It's time to eat," announced Carrie. Hosea tapped Timothy on the arm and signed the words, "We'll race you back to the house." Timothy signed back that he was up for the challenge, and the race was on.

"Wait for me, everyone," whined Little Hans. Timothy loved racing his nieces and nephews and always let them win, although he figured they were wise to his ploy. As he neared the house, he saw two of the youngest ones, Gloria and L.J., stumbling around by the front door, their mothers close by. His sister, Ruby, held Evelyn in her arms, and when the baby saw him, she squealed and raised her arms. Timothy lifted the petite redhead, held her tightly in his arms, and spun her around before resting her on his shoulders and carrying her into the house, where he returned the giggling baby to her ma.

Fifteen minutes later, after Pa blessed the meal, Timothy scooped a generous portion of mashed potatoes onto his plate and reached for some meatloaf. A man could never have too much meatloaf.

"Did everyone hear about the woman who was instrumental in assisting the sheriff and the posse in capturing the gang who robbed the stagecoach?" asked Ruby.

"We were there, Rubes," said Albert.

"I know you were all riding with the posse, but what I want to know is if anyone realized how you were able to capture them so easily."

"I didn't realize there was a woman who assisted the sheriff." Pa passed the biscuits, and Ma poured milk for L.J.

"Yes, it was quite astounding." Leave it to Ruby to be theatrical in her presentation. "The woman apparently told the robbers that there was another stagecoach about to arrive and that they should rob that one as well."

"And they believed her?" asked Ma.

Ruby's husband, Jake, set down his fork. "That would explain why they were so easy to locate."

Landon, who was married to Timothy's sister, Mae, nodded. "My parents told me something about that. Apparently, she also saved the life of the driver."

Timothy had ridden as part of the posse with Pa, his brother, and his brothers-in-law many times. Only twice had they been unable to capture a wanted man. This time, they'd captured five.

Ruby buttered a biscuit and fed tiny bites to Evelyn. "This will be quite the story."

"Says the one who says that about everything," teased Timothy.

Jake leaned toward his wife and smirked. "Wasn't my story supposed to be quite the story?"

"Oh, it was. The very best story." She kissed Jake on the cheek, and Gus covered his eyes.

"Eww. Can you let me know when you're finished?"

A round of laughter commenced before Ruby continued. "Mr. Meldrum assigned me the piece. Of course, I haven't asked Miss Davenport if she'd be amenable yet, but I'm sure she'd love to share her story."

"Congratulations," said Ma. "I'm so thrilled there's a better editor now."

"Yes, it's a blessing that I no longer have to work for Mr. O'Kane." Ruby had cut back considerably on her writing while raising her children and helping her husband on their farm.

"Pa?" asked Gus, turning toward Jake. "If I promise to eat my supper, can I have cookies first?"

Jake chuckled. "I think you should eat your meatloaf and potatoes first. There will be plenty of cookies after you've finished."

"Not if I eat them all," said Simon.

"Now, Simon, do you remember our Bible lesson last night?"

"I know, I know. Put others ahead of yourself."

Timothy laughed. He appreciated Albert's ability to be able to turn just about any situation into a life lesson.

"So, Timothy," Rubes was saying, "why don't you come with me to interview this woman?"

"Why would I need to go with you?" His sister and her crazy reporting shenanigans. Although it was how she'd found the man she would eventually marry.

"I just thought you would be curious about how it all happened."

Timothy was curious—that was true. He wanted to know all about how the woman had convinced the robbers to await a second stage. He'd also heard something about false beards. And she'd saved the life of the driver? Interesting. Still... "I don't know, Rubes, I'm pretty busy. When are you planning on interviewing her?"

"Next Wednesday. Surely you can carve out some time for some investigative journalism? I promise to throw in some ginger cookies."

Curiosity mixed with the opportunity to eat one of his favorite types of cookies didn't bode well for his ability to decline Ruby's request.

Suddenly, the room grew quiet. Even the babies refrained from any noise as all eyes were on Timothy. He finally relented. "All right, what time on Wednesday?"

"How about eleven, just before the noonday meal?"

"And am I eating these cookies before we meet with her or after?"

Ruby tossed him a pointed look. "After, of course, dear brother."

The conversation turned to other happenings in Horizon. Landon informed them that the spur from Cornwall to Horizon was just about fixed, and soon, temporary stagecoach travel would again no longer be necessary for the immediate future.

Not that Timothy traveled much anyway. He was what folks called a homebody. He appreciated spending time on his farm and would rather be there than just about anywhere else.

Mags stood at the counter and penned a letter to her sister. The words flowed easily. Oh, how she wished Phoebe were already here!

Dearest Phoebe,

I miss you already. I just arrived in a town called Horizon, Idaho. It is a charming village, much different from Chicago. There is one mercantile, and as of yet, no bakeries. However, I plan to change that. I hope to open a bakery and make some of the delicious desserts Ma used to bake with us, especially her gooseberry fool and rolled jelly cake. I had quite an exciting moment when I rode on a stagecoach because the train from the last town to Horizon was unavailable due to a washed-out bridge. Needless to say, I had never ridden on such a contraption before, and it vastly differed from the comforts of the train.

Mags paused. She wouldn't tell Phoebe about how she'd traveled for free or how she'd ridden in the boxcar. If she did, Phoebe would have all sorts of questions, and more importantly, Mags didn't want Phoebe to be disappointed in her due to Mags's chicanery. No, some things were better left untold. However, she knew her sister would desire a smattering of details regarding the robbery, especially since that was the reason Mags had ultimately been able to afford to open her business.

When we were on the stagecoach, some unscrupulous men decided to attempt to rob us. Fortunately, I was able to secure everyone's valuables in a pocket in my dress. I also assisted the sheriff with locating the highwaymen. As such, I was given a reward that enabled me to purchase items for my bakery, and I've also set aside some funds to send to you, Larry, and the baby. Please let me know if you have been able to convince him to relocate.

Mags suspended her pencil mid-air. She hoped Larry would acquiesce and agree to relocate.

You would like Horizon. The people are nice, and you can see for miles. There are abundant farms and mountains in the distance.

Has the baby come yet? How are you doing? Please write and tell me how you fare.

I love and miss you something dreadful.

Love,

Your Sister Mags

She folded the letter and placed it into the envelope. Emotion clogged her throat as a memory flooded her mind unannounced.

The entire family had been sick, but Ma and Pa had succumbed to it. At first, Mags hadn't believed it was real. She knew her fever had broken, and when she glanced at Phoebe in her bed beside her, Phoebe had slowly opened one eye. "How are you feeling?" Mags had asked.

Phoebe groaned. "Like I've been run over by a horse and wagon."

Mags felt much the same. She clutched her middle, nausea churning her stomach. Every part of her body was weak, and her heart seemed to be beating faster than normal.

Yet she felt much better than she had yesterday.

"I'm going to check on Ma and Pa."

"All right," Phoebe mumbled, then closed her eyes. She lay so still that panic rippled through Mags.

"Lord, if you can hear me, can You please let my sister recover?"

Didn't the Bible say God heard all prayers? Her mind was so foggy. She'd have to ask Ma about that verse and where it was found.

Ma. How were she and Pa faring after contracting cholera? *"Ma?"* she called, her voice feeble and low.

No response.

"Pa?"

No reply.

Mags had attempted to prop herself up on her elbow to no avail. She fell back onto the soiled blanket. Several more attempts later, she'd finally achieved her goal. Slowly, carefully, painstakingly, she'd urged her legs over the side of the bed, and she steadied herself on the straw mattress before she took her first step.

Her legs failed to hold her up, so she instead crawled into her parents' room. Were Ma and Pa sleeping? If so, she didn't want to wake them. But as Mags drew closer, impending fear coursed through her veins.

She wasn't sure how long she'd collapsed against Ma, begging her to awaken. Begging her to be all right. Begging God, who was supposed to hear every prayer, to allow her parents to survive the horrific illness that befell the entire family.

But God hadn't listened.

Hadn't answered.

Hadn't cared.

Hadn't intervened.

Hadn't heard a word of her wailing, beseeching, or strangled cries.

She and Phoebe clung to each other at the graveside. They were all each other had now. No home, and no hope. And on that day, Mags realized that while there was a God, He wasn't interested in her.

A tear fell and smeared the words of Phoebe's address on the envelope, returning Mags to the present. Why did life have to be so hard?

Chapter Thirteen

The following day, Mags awoke from a sound sleep. For the briefest of seconds, she contemplated where she was. On the floor in a tiny room with plain walls and only a blanket to sleep on, and one to cover her. Oh, yes, that was right. She was in the building that would soon be her bakery. Had she ever thought she would stumble upon such a wonderful happening?

Long ago, when she was a little girl standing beside Ma rolling out dough for cinnamon rolls and putting plump mounds of dough into bread pans, she entertained the thought of someday being a baker. However, she had practically given up on that dream until Mrs. Bennick's inquiry. Now that dream was about to come true. The stove would be delivered in a few days. She had found some old dusty dishes in the attic, and she had enough funds to purchase other necessities, including a dry sink and a table. Perhaps even a bed would follow. But most importantly, she wanted to save enough funds for Phoebe, Larry, and the baby to travel to Horizon and perhaps have their own little house.

If she believed God heard her prayers, Mags would have thanked Him immediately for this good fortune. But alas, the reason for the most recent excellent turn of events was nothing short of her own decision to assist with capturing the highwaymen, even if it was miraculous that no one had been injured or worse.

She opened up a can of peaches and ate them for breakfast, thankful Tabitha had received a new shipment of her favorite fruit. Once Mags received her oven, she would be able to make something better for breakfast, but for now, she would be content partaking in canned goods, sandwiches, and an occasional trip to Wilhelmina's. She'd only been there twice, but she found that she liked the restaurant owner immediately.

The first item on her agenda was to walk to the train depot and pay Mr. and Mrs. Bennick for the ticket for her trip from Chicago to Horizon. That would do wonders for her guilty conscience.

Many passersby greeted her as she strode down several blocks to the edge of town. She hoped to catch the couple before they left Horizon.

"Excuse me, sir," she said to the conductor. "Have you seen Mr. and Mrs. Bennick?"

The conductor pointed her in the right direction. "Magnolia, so nice to see you." Mrs. Bennick reached for Mags's hands. "Did you come to see us off?"

"Yes, and also something else."

Mr. Bennick excused himself. "I need to talk with someone before we board."

Mags nearly lost her resolve. But, no, she had to do this. Had to set this to rights. "Mrs. Bennick, may I speak with you privately?"

"Certainly. You know, we wouldn't be leaving so soon were it not that Bertram was called to Denver for an issue with the railway there." She exhaled an exaggerated breath. "Such is the case of being a railway magnate's wife, I suppose." Mrs. Bennick led Mags to a quieter area on the west side of the depot.

"Mrs. Bennick, I have a confession to make."

"Go on."

"I owe Bennick Railways money for my train ticket from Chicago to Horizon."

"I don't understand."

"I—" Mags's breath hitched. Mrs. Bennick thought her a heroine for what she had done during the stagecoach robbery. Mags rather liked being thought of as someone important. After she confessed, however...

"Please go on."

"I, well, I didn't pay for my ticket. I lied about being a newspaper reporter and..." Did she have to share about hitching a ride on the boxcar as well? "I wasn't forthright and honest and instead found ways to secure a ride without paying."

Mrs. Bennick's brows knitted. "Why would you do such a thing?"

"I didn't have the funds. I know it was dishonest, and I am so very sorry." She fought the tears that threatened. "But I have the funds to pay for my ticket now, and I'd like to give that to you." Mags opened her reticule and removed the clump of dollar bills. When she'd discovered the cost of such a trip, she'd been aghast. Thankfully, with the reward money, she was able to pay what was owed. Mags handed the money to Mrs. Bennick.

"I'm not really the one you need to pay."

"Can you deliver it to the office where it needs to be accounted for?" Mags may lose her courage altogether if she needed to explain the situation a second time.

Mrs. Bennick pinned her with a gaze that Mags couldn't decipher. Was the woman happy about Mags's honesty? Disappointed she'd been deceptive? "Mrs. Bennick, I am sorry."

The woman peered down at the money in her hand. "Be that as it may, I do know something good came from your hoodwinking."

"Something good?"

Mrs. Bennick's shoulders rose and fell with a few deep breaths before she spoke. "Yes. If you hadn't been with us, perhaps the driver would have been killed. Our valuables would have been stolen. The outlaws would have potentially escaped and endangered more lives on stagecoaches or trains." She stared at something in the distance. "I'm only now beginning to learn how God works in our lives, but suffice it to say, the words I heard in Sunday's sermon were about the Lord working all things for good. Now, I'm not knowledgeable about the context of that verse as I've only recently begun to examine the things of our Lord, but I do know that nothing happens that is beyond His knowledge. That He can take something bad and turn it to good, should that be His will." Mrs. Bennick paused, and her eyes glistened. "Listen to me. I sound as though I've been a follower of Jesus for longer than mere months."

Mags wasn't sure how God would have intervened in this situation since He seemed so far from her. From her life. From her concerns. But Mrs. Bennick's genuine words gave Mags hope and comfort. Not only because she desired to make things right, but also because if God really did take bad and turn it to good, then maybe, just maybe, He would allow her to truly begin a new life in Horizon.

"You don't have to pay this, Magnolia."

"I want to. In part to assuage my guilt, yes, but also because it's the right thing to do. My parents would have wanted me to rectify things. I'm only sorry I had to steal in the first place."

"You're forgiven. And before you ask, no, I won't utter a peep to Bertram or to anyone else. I'll add this to the coffers and allow the accountants to deal with it." One side of Mrs. Bennick's mouth curved upward. "After all, that's what we pay them for."

"Thank you, Mrs. Bennick, for your grace and for your forgiveness."

Mr. Bennick strutted toward them. "It's time to board, Gladys. Bid Miss Davenport farewell. You'll see her again when we return next month."

Mrs. Bennick shook her head. "You're so impatient, Bertram. I'm coming." To Mags, she added, "Do not give this a second thought. All is atoned for."

A newfound vigor nudged Mags back to the bakery. The abundance of items on her list today no longer overwhelmed her.

First, she grabbed the new broom and prepared to give the place a good sweeping. Next Wednesday, she'd be meeting with a reporter from *The Horizon Herald* for an interview and telling the story about assisting the sheriff with capturing the criminals. Mags laughed. She hadn't exactly *helped* him capture them, but she had been able to give valuable information. Who would have thought she, Magnolia Davenport, would be able to succeed at such a feat?

Second on the list was a climb back into the attic to see what else she could find. The more items she was able to unearth, the fewer she would have to buy. Careful not to trip on the skirt of the dress with the formerly torn sleeve, she ascended the ladder into the attic. Wilhelmina had told her that people once believed there was hidden loot somewhere in the building. Due to an extensive search that disproved the rumor, most townsfolk now dismissed it as gossip. However, Wilhelmina mentioned there was an occasional visitor who inquired about it. Mags chuckled to herself. If they thought gold coins were stashed in the attic, they'd never find them. Not in the dirty, dusty, cramped loft. Perhaps someday she could turn it into living quarters. Were it not for the wall-to-wall crates, boxes, and who knew what else, the area would be a delightful spot in which to retire for the evening. Her aunt had such a loft, and two of her children had slept there. Mags hadn't been allowed to sleep in the cozy area, but she had visited it a time or two to check on her cousins.

She crawled to one of the corners, dug through one of the crates, and extracted a pair of men's trousers and a white button-up shirt. Underneath the clothes were some boots. Perhaps she could change so as not to waste her dresses on such a filthy chore.

Mags held the trousers up to her. They would fit in length, but they were a little wide in the waist. No problem. She would find a piece of rope and make herself a makeshift belt. She removed her dress and pulled on the white shirt, which also overwhelmed her slender frame. Next, the boots, which had seen better days, but were still in better condition than her own shoes.

Soon, she was dressed in the trousers, the shirt, and the boots, and ready for delving into the great unknown, otherwise known as the attic. She proceeded back downstairs to the back room, where she tucked her dress. Mags tightened a piece of rope around her waist, knotted it, and climbed back into the attic. She found an assortment of baking items in the southwest corner. Two cooking pans, a rolling pin, three mugs, and two plates. She located an old pot beneath a layer of yellowed newspapers. She would need to wash all of the items, but at least this enabled her to purchase fewer bakery necessities.

Speaking of purchases, she visited the mercantile yesterday and placed an order. The items were not in stock but should arrive today. Another jolt of joy rippled through her. It was all coming together. And to think her three aunts consistently told her she would amount to nothing.

"Just wait until you see the bakery when it's finished," she said aloud. Not that they would ever see the bakery, finished or not, but a sense of pride welled within her. She would not only be successful in her bakery endeavor, but she would also do whatever it took to make sure she found a way to belong in Horizon.

Mags unloaded the boxes and set several items around the edge of the opening into the loft for easier access. Much more practical to line them up at the opening, rather than climbing up and down each time and continually having to go fully into the attic to retrieve the boxes. These would be at the ready. A sense of contentment flooded her. While the building was small, she would create all kinds of nooks and crannies to store the dishes.

She stood for a moment at her place on the ladder and stared around the room. Wouldn't it be something if she were able to purchase two tables and set them neatly in the front area? Folks who would rather sit and stay a spell while feasting on cookies, cakes, pies, and bread could do so.

The place needed a good whitewashing, which was one of the items that Tabitha had ordered for her. Not just any color, but a can of lemon-yellow paint. She'd always loved the color yellow because it was Ma's favorite color.

She teetered slightly on the ladder due to the oversized boots and firmed a hand on the side to avoid falling as her heart leapt into her throat. It would do no good to tumble to the floor in a heap. Not when so much work beckoned her.

After catching her breath, Mags figured it best she venture back into the attic, taking methodical and deliberate steps so as not to lose her footing. Someday she'd purchase a new pair of women's boots, perhaps the latest leather Oxfords, but for now, the bakery and money for Phoebe came first.

A successful businesswoman must always have priorities. She stood tall in the center of the loft. Yes, she aimed to be a successful businesswoman. And she would succeed. She hoped.

How many times have your hopes been dashed before? a little voice in her mind taunted her. She attempted to ignore it.

"You've never succeeded at anything, Magnolia Davenport, except causing trouble." This time, words from Aunt Thirza flitted through her mind.

"Why can't you ever do anything right?" Aunt Mikelanna had snarled.

"I certainly wouldn't allow someone like her to stay with me." Aunt Darla's upper lip curled when she'd repeated the words more than once.

With effort, Mags pushed the dismal voices aside. She was no longer in Chicago. No longer residing where she was unwanted and unaccepted. This was a fresh start. A new start. And with a little luck, a fruitful start.

Chapter Fourteen

Timothy hadn't anticipated having to travel to town, but since his order had arrived at the mercantile, he figured it was just as good a time as any. He steered the wagon around the corner just as someone up ahead waved at him. Timothy squinted, attempting to see who it was on the horse. Likely a friend, so he waved back and never did find out who it was as they galloped into the distance.

Oh, he'd been wearing his spectacles at home and at the meal with his family on Saturday evening. Of course, that had caused his sisters to rib him unmercifully. Even Mae, who was characteristically quieter and soft-spoken, followed Lucy and Ruby's lead. *"Maybe someday you'll have to get your own spectacles,"* Timothy had told them.

"I would like some spectacles," his niece, Pansy, had offered. Timothy figured it would be different for a girl to wear eyeglasses than for a grown man. A farmer, who needed to be out plowing the field without having to worry about his eyeglasses slipping down his nose. Even Goose hadn't recognized him at first after he'd donned the ridiculous spectacles. She'd howled, barked, and ran around him in circles as though he were a stranger.

Perhaps a little more sleep was all he needed, and his eyes would clear up. As of late, he'd been so excited to do his chores that he hadn't been able to get some good shut-eye.

Timothy halted the wagon in front of the mercantile. The place was packed with people. Apparently, he wasn't the only one hoping to retrieve his ordered provisions. Ma had even given him a list. Not that he minded. He always considered himself a helpful sort.

Where was the mayor? Usually, he was here assisting his wife. But it was only Tabitha behind the counter.

"Hello, Timothy, I'll be with you in just a moment," she called out to him. He waved and nodded. But as she brushed by him to retrieve a few spools of yarn, she stopped. "If you're not terribly busy, might I ask a favor of you?"

"Absolutely."

"Thank you so much. The mayor is out delivering items, and we are unable to catch up. Not that I'm complaining, this is a blessing, but if you could deliver that crate and those cans of paint to that formerly vacant building next to the newspaper office, I would be much obliged. It's already paid for."

"Someone moved into that vacant building?" But Tabitha had already progressed to the next customer. Timothy figured, since he had to wait anyway, why not assist?

He would have to come back for a second load, but it was no use driving the wagon such a short distance, so he first grabbed the crate and said to Tabitha as he was walking out, "I'll be back for the paint cans." She nodded, and he walked out the door and down the boardwalk.

What could they be putting in that vacant building? No one had rented it in years. As a matter of fact, Timothy couldn't remember the last time there was a business renting it. Gossip of old indicated there was loot hidden in the walls or the loft or somewhere in the attic, but no one had ever found it, and the townsfolk had given up believing such ridiculous notions.

Still, it was a small area that needed a lot of work, and was filthy to boot. Nothing that a little good elbow grease couldn't fix. Still, he pitied the poor man who was tasked with rifling through the items in the loft. Once, when he was a young'un, he and his friends found the door unlocked. On a dare, Timothy climbed the ladder and perused the attic. A catastrophe was the best way to describe it. As if a tornado had rushed right on through it and left a disaster in its wake.

Poor new owner if they hoped to weed through all that junk. The man ought to hire someone to assist with removing the clutter. And what new business would open in the building? A small general goods store? Hardware store? Another bank or barber?

Timothy first tapped on the door with his foot, but when there was no answer, he set the crate down, turned the doorknob, lifted the crate once again, and walked backwards into the building. He noticed a man halfway into the loft, tottering slightly while wearing dirty tan trousers and a bulky white shirt with oversized boots. Timothy didn't recognize the man from behind, and he couldn't see his face or anything above his waist.

"Hello, sir? Excuse me, sir?"

He heard a thump as though maybe the man had bumped his head on something, before he started back down the ladder. Timothy was unprepared for what happened next.

"I am most certainly not a sir!" A woman glared at him. A woman wearing britches, an old white shirt, and clunky men's boots. A woman with wisps of blonde hair framing her pretty face.

"Oh, no, you're not a sir."

No, she was definitely not a man. Timothy couldn't remove his gaze from her face, a face he couldn't see as clearly as he'd like due to his poor eyesight. However, he *could* see that the woman of about his age was beautiful even in tattered clothing with smudges on her face, and her hair in disarray. He vaguely recognized her as the one who'd fought him for the peaches at the mercantile a few days ago.

Timothy gulped. "I'm sorry, sir, I mean, ma'am."

She wobbled precariously on the third rung, her enormous boots failing to grip the step. Timothy rushed toward her, and she gripped his arm as he gently assisted her to the floor. But she immediately yanked her hand away. "I do not need the help from someone so blind as to think I am a man."

"My deepest, most sincere apologies," he said, bemoaning the fact that he had just used his sisters' favorite term. "I figured—you know, what with the attire you're wearing—that you were a man. But I see now that you're not a man, you're a woman." Good thing he didn't utter that she was a beautiful woman. "And I'm not blind, I'm just..." *supposed to be wearing my spectacles,* but he didn't utter that spoonful of information aloud either.

"What is it you want?" Irritation infused her tone.

"I just came to deliver that crate." He pointed at it and continued. "There are a couple of paint cans I still need to retrieve for you. Your order came in at the mercantile."

"I see." Her gaze held his.

"Well, I guess I'll just—" he hiked a thumb toward the door. "I'll just go back down to the mercantile and get those paint cans."

"Yes, if you would please. And I will be having a word with your boss."

"My boss?" Should he tell her he was his own boss? That he'd have it no other way, were it up to him?

"Yes, Tabitha at the mercantile. While I do realize that Horizon is not a large city and folks here probably haven't been coached in proper etiquette, that was a rather serious faux pas."

"Faux pas?" He shook his head. "I'll be back with your paint." While the woman was pretty, she could use some manners. Who didn't thank someone for taking time out of their day to make a delivery?

A few minutes later, he deposited the final paint cans inside the building. "Is there anything else I can do for you before I go on my way?"

"I'm fine." Her mouth opened, closed, then opened again. "Thank you for delivering the items," she said, rather begrudgingly.

He tipped the brim of his hat and left. He took one last glance back where she stood in the window, a hand on her slender hip, watching him. Curiosity bested him. Who was the woman? Why was she in Horizon, and what type of business was she opening in the vacant building? A sewing shop? Perhaps. But if so, she would do well to perhaps sew herself some clothes first before serving the general public.

Perhaps she had been a little harsh toward the mercantile's deliveryman. After all, he had brought the items to her so she wouldn't have to retrieve them herself. But goodness. She was not a sir. The poor man needed spectacles.

Mags caught a blurry glimpse of herself in the bakery window. She would admit she did appear a bit tattered, but still a woman all the same.

Who was the deliveryman? Had he been working the day he surrendered the peaches to her? Mags chewed on her bottom lip. She best return to the work at hand lest she never be ready to open her bakery.

Mayor Trabert, a skinny older fellow, approached Mags just as she finished hauling things down from the attic.

"Miss Davenport?"

"Yes?"

"On behalf of the town, I'd like to invite you to our town hall meeting tomorrow evening at six."

A town hall meeting? She'd never been to such a gathering. Before she could ask further questions, the mayor bid her goodbye and left as quickly as he'd arrived.

The following evening, curious and thinking it was a good idea to meet other Horizon folks, Mags approached the town hall, a clapboard structure with an unrailed porch. Either side of the door boasted two large windows. She took a step up one of two stairs and peered hesitantly in the right-hand window.

Would this be an opportunity to form a connection with others who called Horizon home? Would she finally belong?

Slowly, gingerly, somewhat cautiously, Mags took another step and reached for the doorknob.

"Hello, Magnolia."

Mags startled and turned to see Wilhelmina standing behind her.

"Are you going to go in?"

"I am. I just—it's my first meeting."

"Yes, I remember how nerve-racking that can be. I hardly knew anyone when Hubs and I moved to Horizon all those years ago. But you'll fit right in, I promise you that. Besides, I hear we will be honoring you at this meeting."

"Honoring me?" Before she could say anything more, Wilhelmina opened the door and ushered her inside. Mags took a seat in the far back. Folks visited with each other, and for a moment, Mags wished she had lived here her entire life rather than just days.

Would she ever feel so comfortable with others that she would prattle on with them at a town hall meeting? Mayor Trabert stood behind the lectern and led the *Pledge of Allegiance* before a man named Pastor Albert gave a prayer. Then the mayor discussed the items on his agenda, including the annual visit from the orphan train from New York. Pastor Albert stood at the lectern and spoke about a barn raising to help a family who'd lost their barn in a rainstorm. He also mentioned a family in Horizon in need of food, clothing, and a job for the father. "A crate has been placed just inside the church door for donations," Pastor Albert concluded.

A man named Landon spoke of how the bridge washed out by the rainstorm had been repaired, and rail service was again available from Horizon all the way to Cornwall. Wilhelmina conveyed information about the county fair coming up in a couple of months, and another woman named Miss Greta informed everyone that the Gingham Ball was right around the corner.

Sheriff Zembrodt told onlookers that all five of the Schultz Gang, including the notorious Mr. Kirchner, had been captured and wouldn't be robbing any more stagecoaches. "Thanks to our dedicated deputies and posse, along with

Miss Magnolia Davenport's wisdom in telling the gang another stagecoach was forthcoming, the outlaws were waiting not far from the location where the previous burglary took place. We were able to nab them without incident." The crowd cheered, and when they quieted, the sheriff continued. "Miss Davenport also informed us that the men were in disguises, which aided our ability to locate them. Needless to say, the Schultz Gang was wanted in three different states. But while that was important, even more important was that Miss Davenport saved the life of the stagecoach driver when she thwarted one of the highwaymen's attempts to shoot him."

Applause roared throughout the room. "Miss Davenport, would you please come to the front so we can recognize you?"

Mags rose on shaky legs and walked to the front of the room. On her way, several people congratulated her. She stood between the mayor and the sheriff. "And would Mr. Vipond also come to the front of the room? Many of you know Mr. Vipond as the driver of the stage. He resides in Cornwall, but also wanted to offer his gratitude to Miss Davenport."

The man stood on the other side of the sheriff and nodded at Mags. "If you hadn't been there that day, I probably wouldn't be here today. I thank the Good Lord for your quick thinking every day." Everyone clapped, and someone whistled.

Mayor Trabert again spoke. "As mayor of Horizon, it is my honor to present Miss Davenport with this carved plaque." He handed the beautiful oval wooden plaque to Mags. Tears smarted her eyes, and the people in the audience blurred.

But it was then that she noticed a familiar face. She spied the man who'd thought she was a sir. *And the man who let you have the peaches,* her inner voice reminded her.

Mags again focused her attention on the mayor and the sheriff. All three shook her hand.

And before Mags left the town hall meeting that day, almost everyone in the room had offered their thankfulness and congratulations to her.

Chapter Fifteen

Timothy parked the wagon in front of the makeshift home where the Agnew family was staying. "Here we are."

A shadow crossed Albert's face. He said nothing for a few seconds; likely, the sight bothered him as much as it had bothered Timothy when he'd first come upon it. Or perhaps even more, it reminded Albert of the life he'd lived before becoming a Shepherdson.

Finally, Albert spoke, "The family definitely needs our help."

"That they do. As I warned you, Mr. Agnew is not an easy person to talk to."

"I've been praying that God will give me the words to speak. If the man doesn't want help for himself, I hope he won't deny assistance for his family."

Albert had always been an optimistic sort. Timothy appreciated that trait in his brother, and he added his own prayer that Agnew would be amenable to the fact that they and the entire town only sought to come alongside a family in their time of need. "I think it's best we speak with Mr. Agnew before we unload everything."

"Yes, I agree with you."

Mrs. Agnew hung laundry over tree branches, the girls at her side. When Ozias, who had presumably been fishing, spied Timothy and Albert, he dropped his fishing pole and bounded toward them. "Mr. Timothy! Mr. Timothy!"

Timothy was only thankful that Ozias was not in town attempting to sell discarded newspapers. He hoped the words he had to say to the boy's parents about an honest profession for Ozias would be met with acceptance.

"Whatcha doing here?" Ozias's eyes darted around as if looking for something. Or someone.

"We're here to speak with your pa. Ozias, this is my brother, Pastor Albert. Pastor Albert, this is Ozias Agnew."

Ozias extended a grimy hand toward Albert. "Pleased to meet you, Pastor Albert. He's over there." The lad pointed to the same spot where Mr. Agnew sat last time Timothy visited. "Whatcha gonna talk about with my pa?"

Timothy adjusted his spectacles. It hadn't been an easy decision to wear the annoying eye pieces, but it was easier than listening to Albert pester him about Timothy's need for the magnifiers, which, if Timothy were honest, truly did clear his vision. Agnew sat up in his chair and gazed in their direction, a grimace on his face.

"What are you doing here?" Agnew asked when they approached him.

"Mr. Agnew, this is my big littler brother, Pastor Albert." Timothy hoped his attempt at humor would soften the man's harsh demeanor.

Such was not the case.

"Like I told you, I ain't interested in religion."

"It's a pleasure to meet you, Mr. Agnew." Albert extended a hand. Agnew didn't accept the greeting. "I'm not here to talk to you about the Lord. However, Timothy mentioned your family had fallen on hard times, and we wanted to help.

We have some crates of food, clothing, and blankets in the wagon."

"Appears to me your brother not only needs spectacles, but a hearing horn. I told him last time that we don't accept charity."

Timothy marveled at how Albert remained calm, collected, and gracious. He'd always admired and respected his older brother, and perhaps even more so today.

"Mr. Agnew, if you don't mind my asking, how is your foot?"

"Not that it's any of your business, but it's doing better." Challenge hardened his voice, but Albert remained unflappable.

"We're glad to hear that," he said.

Agnew's youngest daughter, a happy little girl of about three, bounded up to him, barefoot and in a faded calico she'd long outgrown. "Close your eyes and open your hands."

Agnew did as she asked, and the little girl set a rock in his hand. "I found it just for you, Papa. It's a pretty rock, all smooth and shiny."

"Thank you, I'll add it to my collection." Agnew's voice cracked, and he cleared his throat.

"I love you, Papa." The girl wrapped her arms around him and planted a kiss on his cheek. "I'm gonna help Mama now."

Agnew watched his daughter half-run, half-skip away. She stopped, turned, and waved at him, then headed toward her mother. Emotion stirred in the man's dark eyes. He redirected his attention to Timothy and Albert and rubbed his jaw. "Any chance you have any dresses for little girls?"

"Yes, sir, we do." Albert punctuated his answer with a smile.

"All right. Seeing as how they both need dresses, and Ozias needs some trousers that aren't up to his knees, I'll accept your charity."

"We'll unload the items straightaway."

Agnew gave a clipped nod, and Timothy prayed that now was the right time to address the other two matters. "Mr. Agnew, I do have a job opening for Ozias on my farm. He'd be working with my other nephews—two of whom are Albert's sons—picking rock. It wouldn't be every day, but maybe a couple of days a week for the next several weeks. I have some land I need to clear for crops. Would you be amenable to Ozias earning a fair wage picking rock?"

"Guess I could allow that."

A half hour later, after unloading the crates and visiting briefly with a grateful Mrs. Agnew, Timothy and Albert returned to town. Something stirred deep within Timothy. While it hadn't been easy to convince Agnew to accept the donations, it had been worth it to do all they could to aid the struggling family.

Mags sat down to pen another letter to Phoebe. Had her sister received her previous one yet? Mail delivery was painfully slow, but hopefully her missive had reached Chicago.

Dearest Phoebe,
I hope this finds you doing well. I miss you terribly. I couldn't wait to write and tell you that I was honored with an award for the capture of the outlaws. The mayor awarded it to me at a town

hall meeting. Can you believe your sister attended a town hall meeting?

Has the baby come yet? How is Larry?

Mags paused her writing. She certainly hoped that scoundrel Larry was treating her sister with respect. What Phoebe ever saw in him was beyond Mags. She put pencil to paper and continued.

You'll never believe what happened. I was climbing into the attic at the bakery, and an employee from the mercantile arrived to deliver the paint I'd ordered. He thought I was a sir! Never in my life have I been mistaken for a man. Although, to his credit, I was wearing trousers and a man's shirt and boots.

Mags halted, contemplating her next words. She wouldn't tell Phoebe that the man had relinquished a can of peaches for her. Phoebe would only fret that Mags wasn't getting enough to eat.

Oddly enough, the man is somewhat dapper. He has thick dark hair, blue eyes, and a muscular stature. However, his eyesight is rather poor.

She'd be sure to seal the envelope well. No sense in anyone else discovering that she found the man to be handsome.

This afternoon is my interview with The Horizon Herald. I hope I don't sound like a buffoon when I answer the reporter's questions. Please let me know if you have convinced Larry to move here. There is a charming little house at the end of the street that would make a fine home for you three. If you are planning to move here, as I hope you are, I will inquire as to the cost to rent it or perhaps purchase it. It would be the most wonderful thing to see you again and to live close by.

I love and miss you something dreadful.

Love,

Your Sister Mags

After mailing the letter to Phoebe, Mags did her best to tidy up the building before wandering outside and locating a couple of unwanted chairs in the alleyway behind the bank. She asked permission first, and when Mr. Sanders, a crusty man with a sour disposition, told her they were not needed and that she might have them, Mags had nearly jumped up and down with glee. She lugged the chairs back to the building, and if Ruby Lynton sat on one chair and Mags sat on the other, it would work well for the interview.

Mrs. Lynton, who told Mags to call her Ruby, arrived on time with an adorable baby in her arms and a man at her side. A man who looked oddly familiar.

Mags opened the door. "Please come in, Mrs. Lynton—Ruby."

Ruby walked in, and the familiar man followed her.

Mags looked askance at him. "What might you want today, sir?"

"Oh, this is Timothy, my assistant, and my daughter, Evelyn."

She figured Ruby to be quite prestigious if she had an assistant. Even if that assistant was the one who thought Mags to be a sir and who was also a mercantile employee. The baby girl, with her curl of red hair, reached for Timothy, and he took her into his arms while Ruby secured a notebook and pencil.

"Thank you so much for agreeing to be interviewed. As I mentioned previously, the article will be in *The Horizon Herald*."

Mags thought of how she'd pretended to be a reporter and of the famous editor who also boarded the train. "Do you often write for *The Horizon Herald*?"

"I formerly wrote for it each week; however, when I married and became a mother, I decided to write on a less frequent basis." Ruby had a way of putting her at ease, and Mags found she liked the woman immediately.

"I was quite impressed by your story of courage. I'm contemplating calling the article 'One Woman's Bravery Puts Evil Villains Behind Bars.'"

While Mags appreciated the sound of the article title, she didn't really consider herself brave or courageous.

"Can you tell me a little bit about yourself? I know you're not from Horizon."

"No, I hail from Chicago."

"What brings you to our fine town?"

Mags contemplated her answer. Yes, she'd moved here for a fresh start. A new beginning. A chance to find somewhere where she and Phoebe could begin anew. But she wouldn't elaborate to a stranger, and especially not to one who would pen the words she spoke for an article countless people would read. "I have always wanted to open a bakery."

"A bakery?" Timothy glanced about.

"Yes, I have much to do before its grand opening."

"Timothy will be your most frequent customer."

A streak of red crossed Timothy's face. "Reckon I'll stop by to peruse the offerings."

"Magnolia, if you don't mind me mentioning so, Horizon is a lengthy distance from Chicago."

"Please, call me Mags. Yes, it is. I knew I wanted to move to a special place, and Horizon came highly recommended. It is indeed a welcoming little town." Would an area so small provide her with enough customers?

"I've lived here my entire life, as has Timothy." She pointed at the man, whose sheepish grin reminded Mags that she found him slightly annoying.

Ruby asked her numerous questions, including how she knew about the beards, how she'd thwarted the man from shooting the driver, where she came up with the idea to store the other people's valuables, and the idea to tell the robbers that another stage was on its way. Then, after the interview concluded, Ruby rose. "Thank you again for taking the time to speak with us. When the article is published, I will bring you a copy."

"Thank you."

"And thank you for your bravery. It not only saved a life and potentially the lives of several others, but it also saved folks a great deal of money by hiding their valuables."

"Your directions aided us when we captured the outlaws as well," added Timothy.

"When you captured the outlaws? But don't you work at the mercantile?"

A smirk rose on the man's face. Oh, he was a handsome one. But handsome or not, he had an irksome way about him. "The mercantile?"

Ruby laughed. "I'll have to remember that."

"You won't remember that," countered Timothy.

"Oh, but I just might. Not only are you a farmer, but you also work for the Traberts." Ruby took a squirming Evelyn from Timothy's arms. "Timothy rode with the posse when they apprehended the highwaymen."

"Oh, I see."

Poor unfortunate fellow. If his eyesight was anything like Mags determined it to be due to his faux pas, he ought not to be riding with the posse, but she didn't say as much.

Ruby, Timothy, and Evelyn left after the interview concluded, and Mags set about her work, determined to put the half-blind man out of her mind.

Suffice it to say, she failed.

Chapter Sixteen

Mags set about the task of washing the bakery's front window. She'd made impressive strides over the past few days and was clearing out the main area in anticipation of the stove that would be arriving soon. She pinched herself just to be sure this was all happening.

Not long ago, she'd boarded the train in Chicago for Horizon, not knowing what lay ahead. Still, the bakery venture could prove to be a failure, and if so, she would figure out another way. She always did.

"What an improvement!" Mags turned around to see a woman walking along the boardwalk holding a little girl's hand.

"Thank you."

"What type of business will this be?"

Mags was genuinely surprised that word hadn't gotten around in the small town that she was planning to open a bakery, especially since she'd informed Ruby and thought the woman might perchance include that tidbit of information in her article about Mags.

Once the day drew closer for the bakery's opening, Mags would have to be sure to tell anyone and everyone she came into contact with. If she expected to be successful, people had to know about the decadent desserts she planned to sell.

"A bakery? Oh, that sounds delicious." The woman smiled at her. "My name is Velma Shepherdson, and this is my daughter, Gloria. My husband is the pastor at the church."

Gloria waved a chubby hand at Mags "Hewo," she said. Gloria reminded Mags of one of her cousins that she cared for, only happier and likely with a much better mother, especially if she was a pastor's wife.

Speaking of which, before Velma could invite her to church, Mags spoke. " It's nice to meet you. I'm Magnolia Davenport, but everyone calls me Mags. I'm really not one to attend church." The words emerged from her mouth even as worry at being invited tinged her heart.

"Oh," said Velma, although there was no judgment in her eyes, only surprise. "Well, it is very nice to meet you as well."

Relieved, but feeling guilty that she'd incorrectly speculated the woman's reason for approaching her, Mags attempted to redirect the conversation. "Your daughter is adorable."

"Thank you."

"Tank you," mimicked Gloria.

"When do you plan to open?"

Mags set the rag on the bench outside the bakery. "I'm hoping in the next week so I can establish a clientele before winter." Winter. That was something Mags dreaded. Memories of wind whipping through her threadbare coat and the drafty air of the apartment never warmed due to the lack of enough wood for the fire. "What kind of winters do you have in Horizon?"

"Cold and snowy. I take it you're not from Idaho?"

"No, I hail from Chicago."

"Chicago, goodness, but you're a long way from home."

Mags would never again consider Chicago her home.

"Aren't you the one who received a plaque at the town hall for saving a man's life and assisting in the capture of an outlaw gang?"

"Yes."

"That was quite something. Have you met many of the townspeople?"

"Several. They've been quite welcoming."

"We are glad you're here." The warmth in Velma's voice comforted Mags. Perhaps she really *did* belong here.

Gloria patted Mags on the leg. "There's a hee," she said, pointing to a horse.

"A hee?"

"It's what she calls horses," said Velma.

Mags lowered herself to Gloria's height. "Do you like horses?"

"Yes, Gworia like hees." She nodded, her sparse brown curls bobbing.

"How old are you, Gloria?"

"Gworia dis many." She held up two fingers.

Mags straightened into her full height. "She's so adorable and smart."

"Thank you. After having sons, a daughter has been a special delight. Not that I don't love my boys." Melancholy shadowed Velma's eyes before she recovered and smiled again. "Would you like to join my family for Saturday night supper?"

"Oh, I couldn't impose."

"It's not imposing, and we'd love to have you. There are quite a lot of us. We meet at my in-laws' home. Tyler and Paisley Shepherdson. Have you met them yet?"

"I don't believe so."

"Albert and I live in the parsonage, so we could retrieve you on the way to supper at six on Saturday."

"I'm not sure." Hesitation crept into Mags's thoughts. She didn't belong at a large family gathering any more than she'd belonged at Aunt Mikelanna's home.

"No pressure at all. Why don't you think about it, and you can let me know. Gloria and I have a few errands to run, but we will be back at the parsonage this afternoon."

"All right, thank you." She bid Velma and Gloria goodbye and returned to her window washing duties.

Two hours later, Mags had made up her mind that she would attend the supper with Velma and her family. It might be an excellent way to share about the bakery, and maybe make some new friends in the process. As quickly as she contemplated it, something niggled deep in her gut. *Why would you want to try to make friends? People always disappoint you. Haven't you learned that yet? And if they don't disappoint you, they leave. Like Ma and Cassius.*

But Phoebe hasn't left, she argued with herself. As a matter of fact, Mags was the one who had decided to leave Chicago.

So she walked to the parsonage and found Velma and Gloria in the front yard planting some flowers. "I've decided to accept your invitation."

"Delightful. We'll retrieve you at six." They chatted for a few minutes more before Mags returned to the bakery. If she were a praying woman, she would have prayed that Velma's family would be as accepting of her as Velma seemed to be.

Saturday came quickly. Mags unfolded the dresses from her carpetbag, where she stored them. It wasn't like she had many choices. She could wear the trousers and white shirt, then laughed to herself at that suggestion. She could wear the dress with the torn sleeve that she recently repaired, but it did look tattered and worn. She could wear her day dress, or she could wear the lovely one that she'd fished from the trash bin. Yes, that one would do. She wanted to make a good impression, after all. Besides, the only other time she'd worn it while in Horizon was when Ruby interviewed her.

She'd don it only for special occasions, and this could be deemed as such. Mags brushed her long blonde hair and twisted it into a chignon. She had no mirror, so she had to do the best that she could, but she could look in the front window. She exited the bakery and glimpsed herself in the window. Would they approve of her? Velma was a pastor's wife, so she wasn't wealthy, but maybe the other family members were. If so, they would undoubtedly find her properly attired for the event.

At six, a wagon pulled in front of the bakery. A man whom she recognized from the town hall meeting, climbed down and assisted her into a backseat that had been built into the wagon and which held two boys.

"We're Simon and Sherman," one of them offered.

"Nice to meet you, Simon and Sherman. I'm Mags Davenport."

Pastor Albert, Velma, and the two boys spoke almost non-stop about their day. Gloria offered some words every now and again as well. Mags marveled at their easy camaraderie. Her aunts and their families were almost always angry, complaining, and arguing with each other, their voices clipped, harsh, and acidic.

Albert and Velma reminded her of Ma and Pa with the way they looked at each other so fondly. Her heart surged in her chest. Oh, how she missed her parents. How she missed Phoebe.

"Here we are," announced Sherman.

"Just wait 'til you meet everyone else," said Simon. "There are a bunch of us."

Sherman stood and grabbed a basket of fruit. "And there will be a test on our names."

His brother's mischievous smile gave Mags pause. "And if you pass it, Miss Mags, you get an extra slice of apple pie."

Her stomach growled at the thought. It would be wonderful to be able to have a real meal again.

The Shepherdson farm was surrounded by green fields, a tidy red barn, several other wagons, and a buggy. Several children ran to the wagon, forming a greeting committee of various ages.

A boy of about seven turned to face the others. "Simon and Sherman are here!"

The boys waved. "Hi, everyone. Do you want to play some baseball?"

A girl with long braids tossed a ball in the air. "Can I be on your team?"

"Sure. We'll divide into teams. Becky, you can be on Sherm's team, and I'll take Carrie."

"As long as I get Hosea," said Sherman.

"That's fine. I'll take Gus."

"I'll take Polly."

"I'll take Little Hans."

"What about me?" A petite girl wearing a blue-and-white checkered pinafore peered up at the older children.

"You can be on my team, Pansy."

The children ran to a clearing sandwiched between the house and a field with Pastor Albert's admonishment that they remember to be Christlike in their actions and to be ready for supper when they're called.

Pastor Albert then assisted Mags from the wagon, and she followed the couple and their daughter to the front door. A case of the nerves bundled in her stomach. Perhaps attending the supper with people she didn't know hadn't been such a good idea. Even if it was better than spending the evening alone once again in the cramped bakery.

Velma introduced her to four women, who were standing in the kitchen when they entered. This is my mother-in-law, Paisley Shepherdson."

"It's so nice to meet you. We're thrilled you're here." Mrs. Shepherdson's soft and gentle tone reminded Mags of Ma's voice.

"And these are my sisters-in-law, Mae, Lucy, and I believe you already know Ruby."

"Oh, yes, we met the other day during the interview. It's delightful to see you again," said Ruby. The women warmly welcomed her, and Mags's jitters calmed somewhat.

Mags assisted the women with food preparation, and when the menfolk and children entered the house, she noticed a familiar man. *He* was part of the Shepherdson family?

"I just finished the article and submitted it to my editor," Ruby was saying. But Mags's attention was on Timothy. Obviously, he was Mr. and Mrs. Shepherdson's son and a brother to Ruby, Lucy, Mae, and Pastor Albert. Tonight he wore spectacles, something he hadn't worn during the interview. Perhaps he'd be able to see better. He noticed her staring, and Mags tore her eyes away as the heat warmed her cheeks.

"That was quite brave of you," said Mae, a delicate and soft-spoken woman wearing a lovely dress with leg-o-mutton sleeves, pearl buttons on the high-necked bodice, and a bell-shaped skirt extending from her slim waistline.

"Thank you. I'm just thankful it was successful."

"And here they thought their beards were brilliant disguises," said the man to Ruby's right, who, if Mags remembered correctly, was named Jake.

"Yes, I thought it was rather suspicious how all of their beards matched. One blew off one of the men, and another was twisted to the side."

"When we rode out with the posse, the sheriff shared that with us. It helped us to know who we were looking for," said Mr. Shepherdson.

Mags attempted to keep her attention on the comments, but something about the man named Timothy kept her attention fixated on him. He was more distinguished looking today than he had been the day he'd wandered into the bakery or the day he attended the interview with Ruby. She recalled the words she'd penned to Phoebe about his dapper appearance. Not that she was truly noticing, for she most certainly was not.

"It's my understanding that the first time Timothy met Mags, it was not under the best of circumstances." A glint shimmered in Ruby's eye.

"Ooh, do tell," said Lucy.

"Would you care to tell the story, Timothy?"

"No, thank you, Rubes. I'm not even sure it's a story to tell."

"You wouldn't want to keep anything of interest from your family, would you?" A challenge mixed with a cheeky smirk crossed Lucy's face.

Timothy shifted in his seat, removed his spectacles, and rubbed his eyes. "As I mentioned, Lucy, there isn't much of a story to tell." He veered his gaze Mags's way.

Mags's face and ears felt impossibly hot, and she fiddled with the napkin in her lap.

"With your permission, dear brother, may I tell the story?" Ruby fed Evelyn a bite of mashed potatoes.

"Whether he grants his permission or not, you'll probably tell us, Rubes."

"Truer words were never spoken, Albert." Timothy had replaced his spectacles once again and ran a hand through his dark hair. "Go ahead and tell your version, Rubes."

"It just so happens that when Timothy entered the bakery, he saw Mags and thought she was a sir."

Timothy shook his head. "That's not the entire story..."

"You thought Mags was a sir?"

"Ma, I can explain."

"Let me guess," said Mr. Shepherdson. "You weren't wearing your spectacles."

"I wasn't, but in this case, they wouldn't have helped. Miss Davenport was wearing men's clothing."

The entire family laughed, and while Mags was horrified at first that they knew the story, at the same time, she was intrigued by their camaraderie. Their closeness. Their friendly wit.

"There was no clear way to tell she was a woman, what with her clothing and the fact I could only see half of her, with the other half of her stuck in the attic. Come on, Lucy. Aren't you going to defend me?"

"Sorry, but no."

"But I allowed you to push me in the pram when I was far too big to be riding around in it."

A smile tugged at Mae's lips. "Lucy was always so motherly when we were children. She was thrilled when Ma and Pa added Ruby and Timothy to our family, and she could care for them and push them in the pram that Miss Greta gave to Ma as a gift. All was going well until... "

"We can skip this part," muttered Timothy.

"Oh, no, we're not skipping this part."

"How would you remember Rubes? You were too little at the time."

"I don't remember, but Albert, Lucy, and Mae remember."

Pastor Albert began to chuckle. "We're just thankful Timothy didn't get hurt when Lucy hit that rock and the pram tipped over."

Mrs. Shepherdson sipped from her cup before adding, "That was part of the problem. You see, Timothy was too big for the pram by this time. I was in the yard hanging clothes, and Tyler was in the field. Lucy, our loving little mother hen, decided to put Timothy, who was a well-fed and chunky two-year-old, into the pram."

Mags attempted to imagine a plump little boy riding in a frilly pram and tipping over.

"Because I allowed you to do that, you should at least defend me." Timothy scowled at Lucy, but he, too, was soon laughing about the pram incident.

Mags sat befuddled, not sure what to think. Not since the days with Ma, Pa, and Phoebe had she ever seen such a joyful family. Even Timothy, who bore the brunt of the story, failed to hide his amusement.

For a good part of the time, the family discussed the incident with the pram. Timothy found it hard not to notice Magnolia Davenport. Sure, she'd glowered at him at first when the "sir" incident was mentioned, but then—and he could see clearly with his fancy spectacles—a pleasing blush covered her face, followed by a pretty smile.

But even with his eyeglasses, he wasn't really noticing her beauty.

He wasn't really paying attention. Nope. Not at all. What he was thinking about was the spongy angel food cake Ma made for dessert. He'd almost interjected that the first time he'd met the woman was when they'd both wanted the same can of peaches at the mercantile, not the "sir" incident.

Timothy was surprised to see her here, but then, Velma possessed the gift of hospitality, perfect for being married to a pastor.

The ribbing from his siblings continued, although he didn't mind. He'd done his own share of ribbing over the years.

"Perhaps this will be a lesson for you," said Lucy in her typical bossy voice.

"How do you mean?"

"A lesson to wear your spectacles at all times," added Albert. "Not just on the farm."

Velma attempted to wipe off a squirming Gloria's chubby cheeks. "It could save you from further embarrassment," she said.

Timothy gritted his teeth. He would no more wear those spectacles around town or at church than admit that he found Magnolia, or Mags, as she preferred to be called, a comely woman. Although he did secretly hope she'd someday forgive him for his grievous error.

Chapter Seventeen

The sunset cast an orangey glow, and Mags stood near the wagon as Pastor Albert and Velma prepared to leave. The children chatted with their aunts, and Ruby put an arm around Carrie, as she told her, Becky, Polly, and Pansy a brief story, which caused gales of laughter.

One of the boys was telling Mae about his adventure catching a frog yesterday. Lucy was holding Evelyn, and she and Velma discussed an event at the church while Gloria did her best to escape her mother's hold.

Clearly, the children were close to their aunts, and the ache was so profound that it caused a noticeable pain in her chest. The burn of unshed tears caused a choked sob to settle in her throat. Why couldn't her aunts have loved her the way these aunts loved their nieces and nephews?

Why couldn't she have been good enough to earn their love? Important enough? Worthy enough?

As she often did when the sting of sorrow was nearly too much to bear, Mags tucked the anguish deeper within herself. There was no sense in wanting things that would never be.

After several minutes, Pastor Albert assisted Mags into the wagon, and he and Velma drove toward town.

"We're so glad you joined us tonight," said Velma when they'd stopped at the bakery.

"Thank you for inviting me. I do have one question. Why does everyone move their hands around in a wild frenzy when they speak? I've never seen anything like it."

"It's called sign language, and it's the language taught to deaf people."

"You mean each one of those movements means something?"

"Exactly. Mae formerly taught at the deaf school and had to learn sign language. When she and Landon adopted Polly and Hosea, everyone wanted to be sure they felt included. So, we all set about learning sign language."

Pastor Albert flicked the reins. "It does take some time and some fine-tuning. There have been many times when one of us has signed something that actually meant something else. But Polly and Hosea have been so patient with us."

"You all learned a new language for Polly and Hosea?"

"We did," said Pastor Albert. "Mae says it's much easier to learn when you're a child, so we've taught the younger ones sign language from the time they started speaking. For us adults, it's been a learning experience to say the least."

Mags was mesmerized by how a family could care so much for each other that they would be willing to learn an entirely new language. Of course, thinking back, Ma and Pa would have done something like that, too.

Velma shifted a sleeping Gloria onto her other arm. "If you'd ever like to learn it, I'm sure we can find several people who would be happy to teach you."

Mags tossed and turned that night after supper at the Shepherdsons' house. Being their guest reminded her of the good times in Chicago—the times with Ma, Pa, and Phoebe. She wrapped the thin blanket around her and stared at the ceiling. A memory came rushing back, flooding her mind as if it had happened yesterday.

It was a bright and sunny Saturday, and Ma didn't have to work at the factory. Pa had a few milk bottles to deliver and, after breakfast, asked if either Mags or Phoebe would care to accompany him on some deliveries.

Phoebe, who had planted herself on the worn sofa with her latest sewing project, shook her head. *"Now that I'm twelve, I won't be delivering milk any longer,"* she said. *"Take Mags, she's only eleven, so she'll go with you."*

Phoebe could certainly be stuffy sometimes, and bossy, and Mags wanted to argue about going, but changed her mind. She always loved delivering milk with Pa.

"Besides," said Phoebe, *"I have some sewing to do. Ma and I are working on a new project."*

"We can work on it when you get home," Ma offered.

Phoebe shook her head so forcefully her dark curls bounced. *"No, that's all right, I'll stay."*

At first, Phoebe's constant clinging to Ma lately irked Mags. But Pa had mentioned to Mags that Phoebe needed Ma, especially during this time in her life. And since Phoebe shared Cassius with Mags, Mags would share Ma with Phoebe. As best as she could, anyway, because Mags loved Ma more than anyone in the entire world.

Pa planted a kiss on Ma's cheek. Mags loved to witness the fondness between them, and less than ten minutes later, Mags and Pa had traveled down the busy streets of Chicago delivering milk.

Unfortunately, they'd had to stop at mean Amanda's house. The words of the girl earlier that week in school remained firmly rooted in Mags's mind. Perhaps she could ask Pa the question burning through her mind before they returned home. She had to know if Amanda was correct or just being malicious.

"Pa?"

"Yes?"

"Could I ask you something?"

"You know you can ask me anything, Mags."

"And will you give me an answer?"

Pa had halted the wagon and pulled it over to the side of the road beneath several large oak trees. "Sounds serious, but I'll aim to do my best, provided I know the answer."

Mags had worked her lip between her teeth. She'd pondered whether she really could ask Pa the question on her mind. He waited patiently as he always had. She'd never met a more patient man than Cassius Davenport. "My pa, I mean not you, but my other pa, he wasn't a nice man, was he?"

"Reckon he wasn't."

"He hurt Ma, didn't he?"

"Yes. Why all the questions, Mags?" Pa hadn't said it to be condemning, but rather in his kind, gentle voice he always used unless riled, which occurred only rarely and for good reason.

Mags had shrugged before divulging the reason for her inquiry.

"Amanda at school said that she heard that I had a bad pa. I told her my pa was the best pa there ever was, and she said, 'not Cassius, your real pa.'"

Pa had put his arm around Mags and expressed his gratitude for her kind words about him. He then released her and reached for the reins. But Mags hadn't been finished with her questions. She still needed clarification.

"How come my other pa isn't still here?" Mags had asked.

"Mags, this is something you need to ask your ma. She's better equipped to answer this than I am."

But Mags couldn't work up the courage to ask Ma about such a delicate matter. Not if what she suspected was true. She'd told Pa she couldn't ask Ma, then stared out over the front of the wagon at all the passersby. All the people who weren't distressed over what kind of man their real pa might be.

"My ma and pa—they weren't married, were they?"

"Magnolia..." Pa only called her by her full name when the matter was serious.

"I need to know the answer."

"You will need to ask your ma."

Mags rarely argued with Cassius. She'd just been so grateful he'd agreed to become her pa all those years ago that she didn't want him to figure she was too headstrong and renege on his offer. But that day, she contended she needed answers and wouldn't surrender until receiving those answers.

"I can't ask Ma. I have to ask you. Please tell me."

"It's not my story to tell. It's your mother's story."

Mags had known she couldn't ask Ma. What if what she suspected conjured up horrible memories for Ma? She never, ever wanted to do anything that would hurt her mother.

"I'm eleven years old. Old enough to know the truth."

Pa had run a hand through his thick, wavy black hair. Worry had shown in his hazel eyes. *"Some men are..."* Cassius Davenport rarely said anything spiteful about anyone. She'd pressed him for answers.

"Are not men of good character," he finally said. Sadness had clouded his features.

"Like my pa?"

"Yes."

They'd sat in silence as the seconds ticked by. Finally, Pa said the words that Mags would always hold close to her heart. She'd never forget the single tear that slid down Pa's cheek, and how he'd hastily wiped it away with the sleeve of his work shirt. Probably hoping she wouldn't hold it against him that she'd seen a grown man cry.

"Magnolia, God formed you in your ma's womb, and you are fearfully and wonderfully made." It hadn't surprised her that Pa would discuss the Lord, for he did often.

"I know that, Pa."

"And you know that you have no choice as to who your real father is."

"I know."

He rubbed the back of his neck. "After I tell her I told you..."

"I won't tell her. I promise."

Pa had been content that Mags wouldn't tell Ma, but he said that he, as Ma's husband, wouldn't keep what he'd told Mags from Ma. "Honesty is best, especially in a marriage."

Mags understood that, but at eleven, she wasn't planning to marry anytime soon, so she figured she didn't need that advice. But she *did* need to know the truth. Why was Pa so hesitant?

"Mags, you do realize that you are not responsible for who your father is or what he did. Promise me you will always remember that."

"I promise." A lump had settled firmly in her stomach. What was Pa about to say? Mags chewed on a thumbnail and debated asking the next question, but she needed to know. *Had* to know.

"He hurt Ma, and they weren't married, were they?"

Pa said nothing. Just stared straight ahead, his eyes glistening with moisture.

"Did she know him?" Mags's voice had squeaked with the question. Whenever Mags had asked Ma about her real pa, Ma typically changed the topic of discussion or feigned not hearing her. One time, she said she figured Mags's real pa was no longer alive.

Mags had asked for further clarification about how the man had died and why she hadn't ever met him. Ma had hugged her and said, *"We'll discuss it later."* But they never had.

Pa cleared his throat. *"Your ma was working late at the factory one night and was walking home and..."* his voice caught, and while his attention was directly in front of him, it was as if he wasn't seeing. *"I'll say no more."*

Mags figured she knew exactly what her pa was trying to say. *"So, a mean man hurt my ma when she was walking home one night, and then there was me."* Her lips trembled, and she'd squeezed her eyes shut and clenched her fists. *"How dare some mean man hurt my ma!"* Grief, anger, loyalty, and a need for revenge for what the man had done to her mother meshed altogether in a tight wad of angst. Her shoulders shook, and the knowledge of what had happened paralyzed her. Her breathing had come in gasps, and the world seemed to spiral out of control.

Pa had put his arm around her, and together, they'd cried. Pa, a man so brave, so strong, so manly, had been overcome with emotion. Finally, after some time, he held Mags's hand in his own. *"Magnolia, it was not your ma's choice how you came to be any more than it was your choice. But it was your mother's choice to love the precious baby that grew within her. To raise her,* to cherish her, and to see her as the gift from God that she was. Despite the circumstances, she chose life. She chose you."

Her tears amplified, and a peculiar numbness magnified the unrelenting tightness in her chest. It all made sense now. Why she'd never met her real pa. Why Ma hadn't wanted to talk about it. Why she'd never met Ma's family. They likely blamed her.

"I want you to hear me clearly when I say this." Pa had framed her face in his hands.

She couldn't find her voice, so she just nodded instead.

"God created you, and you are very special to Him, to your ma, and to me."

The tears had slipped from her eyes and rolled down her cheeks. "I—I know that. And anyway, you're my pa, not that other man." Her voice quivered.

"Yes, I am, and I'm proud to be your father."

When they returned home after the deliveries, Mags headed straight to Ma and wrapped her arms around her waist. "I love you, Ma."

"I love you, too."

Then Mags had taken a step back and peered into Ma's face. The face of a woman who'd been horribly hurt, then rejected by her family. The face of a woman who'd chosen to love and raise Mags no matter the circumstances surrounding how Mags had been formed in her womb. Her respect for her mother grew to a magnitude Mags couldn't even explain.

Mags had never told her mother what she knew, but she figured Pa had because he never kept secrets from the woman he loved.

She sat up on the thin blanket and exhaled several deep breaths. She so desperately sought peace within her heavy-laden soul. Ma and Pa had believed so strongly that

God was the author of that peace. Why couldn't Mags believe it too?

Chapter Eighteen

Pride was not an easy thing to overcome, especially when it came to spectacles. Timothy figured if he put the eyeglasses on his face intermittently, perhaps in time, he'd become accustomed to them.

So far, he'd worn them at home while tending to chores and doing his farm work. On occasion. Much to his embarrassment, he'd worn them to the supper at Ma and Pa's. A supper that included a somewhat mysterious woman named Magnolia Davenport.

Why she was still on his mind, he had no idea. There were at least three Horizon women who'd set their caps for him. Yet, he had no desire to ever marry. Not with being content farming. Besides, he had his family, his nieces and nephews, and he had Goose. The latter of which still waited patiently for her breakfast.

Timothy fed the dog, then prepared to go to town for his appointment. He peered at the eyeglasses in his hand and debated about wearing them for just a few minutes during the trip to Horizon. It was nice to be able to see an eagle soaring on the wind more clearly, or to be able to ascertain who it was who passed and waved to him.

At first, the spectacles rubbed on his right ear, but Timothy had bent them slightly and fixed that issue. They did become smudgy and dirty far too quickly, what with all the dust, which was cumbersome. He didn't have time for the nonsense of cleaning them each night.

He parked in an empty space beside the barbershop. He needed a haircut, but he didn't need the ribbing that would follow if he wore his spectacles in this particular place of business. So instead, he tucked them into his chest pocket. A chest pocket that Ma had sewn on for him after he'd shown her a picture of a shirt with such a pocket in an advertisement in *The Horizon Herald*. He'd sworn Ma to secrecy not to tell anyone that his reason for the pocket was for his eyeglasses. She'd smiled at him and patted him on the shoulder. *"Your secret is safe with me, son,"* she said.

Timothy folded the spectacles, then opened the door of the barbershop. He squinted, noticing that, as usual, three older men frequented the business. The Lieutenant, who was married to Miss Greta and ran the boardinghouse; Leonel, a man with sparse black-and-white peppered hair and a leathery face full of wrinkles; and Leonel's best friend, Pablo, a toothless man married to a kind woman named Maria.

"Well, hello, Timothy. You're right on time," said Bjorn. He rose from the barber chair, dusted it off, then gestured for Timothy to take a seat.

Timothy nodded at the three men sitting against the wall, all of whom he could see in the mirror. The trio were more like busybodies with the way they constantly prattled on and gossiped about the ongoings in Horizon.

"Is that there a chest pocket?" asked the Lieutenant.

"Yes, it is."

"Whatcha got in there?" asked Leonel.

Timothy should have left his magnifiers in the wagon, but he couldn't chance them getting accidentally crushed. Or he should have left them at home, although not if he'd wanted to slowly ease his way into wearing them in public places. "It's nothing, really."

"Nothing, you say?" This from Pablo, who looked for a minute as if he might catapult himself out of his comfortable chair to see if what Timothy said was true.

Timothy ignored the men and sat down in the barber chair. Bjorn positioned the cape over Timothy's shoulders. "It almost looks like you have a pair of spectacles in your pocket." Timothy caught his alarmed gaze in the mirror at Bjorn's comment. How could the barber have ascertained that?

"Did you say spectacles?" asked the Lieutenant. "You mean, like mine?"

Leonel scratched his head. "Why would Timothy wear them things? He's not old enough to be wearing spectacles."

"Yeah," agreed Pablo. "Only old guys like us wear spectacles."

"That's true." The Lieutenant removed his eyeglasses, buffed the lenses on his shirt, then placed them back on his face.

"Say, maybe Timothy is a young man with elderly eyes." At Leonel's statement, the other men chuckled.

Timothy could feel the heat rising up his neck. Good thing Bjorn hadn't yet shaved off his whiskers. It wouldn't be so bad if eyeglasses weren't only for the elderly. Then Timothy may not mind wearing them, especially because they did make things a lot clearer.

He scrutinized his image in the mirror as the barber lathered soap on his face, hoping the men would change the topic of discussion.

They didn't disappoint him. While they changed the topic, their discussion remained, unfortunately, on Timothy.

The Lieutenant stretched his legs out in front of him and crossed them at the ankles. "Heard ol' Timothy over there is the most eligible bachelor in Horizon."

"You don't say?" Pablo stroked his chin. "You lookin' to court anytime soon, boy?"

Leonel slapped a hand to his knee. "Yeah, if you don't hurry along, you'll be as old as the Lieutenant before you ever settle down."

"Says the man who don't even got hisself a wife." Pablo shook his head. "Besides, won't be a problem anyhow for the young Timothy. He'll already look as old as the Lieutenant, what with those spectacles. I hear Widow Arscott is lookin' for another husband."

That caused another round of chortles. "Aww, she ain't but seventy-five if she's a day. Near as old as the Lieutenant." Leonel covered his mouth and pointed at the Lieutenant. "You are about seventy-five, ain't ya?"

"I'm not that old, and at least I'm not as old as you two. One foot in the grave and such."

The men started joshing each other, and Timothy exhaled a breath of relief. At least that would keep them from joshing him for the time being.

Until three minutes later. "Maybe he needs to wear those spectacles so he can see the lovely ladies who are pining away after him, wanting him to ask them to court him."

"Yep, that's true, seeing as how he's blind as a bat and can't see them."

Timothy jerked forward, nearly causing Bjorn to take a chunk of his chin with the razor. "I'm not as blind as a bat.

I just need a little extra clarification for when things are far away."

"Extra clarification, he says," said Pablo.

"Miss Greta says Mary Lou has set her cap for you." Timothy couldn't discern it from this distance, but he imagined the Lieutenant's eyes brightening when he spoke of his beloved wife.

"And you know Miss Greta knows everything that's going on in this town and then some. Did you know Mary Lou has set her cap for you, Timothy?"

"I didn't know men spoke of such things," he said, trying to deepen his voice as though he were an authority on the matter.

"Oh, we do on occasion," said Leonel. "'Specially when we're concerned you'll go grow old and gray before you decide to court, let alone marry."

"Maria says Alma has a crush on him, too. And what's that other young woman's name? The one whose pa works at the livery?" Pablo scratched his head.

"Artemisia, or something and such," said the Lieutenant.

"Maria says that Alma has set her cap for him because she's always making him desserts and such."

"Your wife might be right, Pablo, but she doesn't know as much as Miss Greta. She says Mary Lou has, in her words, been right fond of the young Timothy since they were still in school. My bet, if I were a gambling man, is that Timothy will choose Mary Lou."

"Naw, he'll choose Alma. Man needs to eat, and we all know Timothy has a reputation for eating more than his share."

"You're wrong about that, Pablo. You too, Lieutenant. He'll choose that Artemisia woman. She's got some eye condition with the way she's always fluttering her lashes at the young Timothy. Maybe she can buy herself a pair of spectacles too, and they'll match."

The roaring of the men's laughter echoed through the barber shop and likely out onto the boardwalk and beyond. Timothy lowered his voice. "How long do you reckon the haircut and shave will take?"

Bjorn chuckled. "Not long. You're not one for gossip?"

"Those three over there are worse than chattering hens."

Leonel broached another subject. "Hey, did you all hear about that woman who helped the sheriff and his posse capture all them stagecoach robbers?"

The Lieutenant cracked his knuckles. "Yes, I know all about her. I was riding with the posse, and I attended the town hall meeting."

"That's right, you did ride with the posse."

The Lieutenant grunted. "Just more proof I'm still a somewhat young and sturdy man who knows how to assist the law when necessary, unlike some folks."

"He ain't somewhat young, but he sure is sturdy. Check out that belly." Leonel pointed at the Lieutenant's abundant girth. That started another whole round of insults between the three.

"You're just jealous because you ain't handsome enough to get a wife, and, Pablo, you're jealous because Maria doesn't cook as good as Miss Greta does."

And on it went. Timothy thanked the Good Lord above that the conversation had permanently turned from him. After he paid Bjorn, he bid the men goodbye and commenced to what he came to town for besides a haircut and shave. He needed to purchase a new rake and a few other necessities at the mercantile and check his balance at the bank.

Once out of the men's line of sight, Timothy removed his spectacles from his pocket and reluctantly put them on. He would wear them for one block before removing them when he entered the mercantile. Three townsfolk passed him and waved without even so much as a word about his extra set of eyes.

He walked past the bakery just in case Miss Davenport had opened it for business. He patted his stomach at the thought. Either the food would be delectable like Ma's and Wilhelmina's, or it would be atrocious like Alma's.

Fortunately for him, while his siblings had to endure Ma's cooking before she became proficient, Timothy hadn't suffered that hardship. By the time he was ready to eat more than his fair share, Ma had already perfected her skills in the kitchen.

When he glanced through the front window of the bakery, it looked much the same as it had during the interview. However, he did notice a concerning issue. Miss Davenport was standing on a chair on the other side of the window in those hideous trousers and oversized men's boots. But that wasn't the concerning issue. The unsettling matter was that the dilapidated chair she stood on leaned to one side, and she was attempting to balance herself on one leg while reaching to the top of the window. What was that woman doing? If she wasn't careful, she'd meet her demise when she flipped off the chair.

He best be the gentleman Ma raised him to be and inform the woman of her precarious predicament.

Timothy opened the bakery door and stepped inside. The noise must have jolted Miss Davenport because she teetered and tottered before losing her balance. Timothy bolted in her direction, held out his arms, and caught her just as she slipped from the chair.

"Oh!"

She peered up at him with pretty blue eyes, not that he was noticing whether or not she had blue eyes, but with his spectacles on and being this close, her eyes did seem to sparkle more than he recalled. He cleared his throat. "You ought not to be climbing on chairs like that."

"I—well, I was attempting to clean the top of the window."

"Still, that chair doesn't look the most stable." Seeing it up close, he noticed one leg was shorter than the other three, and the slats on the top were curved and bent as if once upon a time someone had set far too much on top of it.

"I'll have you know that that chair is of quality. I found it in the alley. Mr. Sanders from the bank said I could have it."

"That explains a lot of things." Mr. Sanders was not known for his generosity or benevolence.

"While I do appreciate your quick actions and your concern, I am just fine."

"You're just fine? You were about to fall and break yourself."

"I would have caught myself," she said, but her voice wavered as though even she was skeptical about her statement. "I

f you'll kindly put me back on my feet, I do have things to do."

"Oh, yes. Sure. Put you back on your own feet." Why was he stumbling all over himself? Timothy set her down, and she wobbled slightly. "How about I reach those tall places for you?"

She regarded him. "All right." Miss Davenport handed him the rag, and he swiped at the places she couldn't reach.

"How's that?" he asked.

"Thank you." She chewed on her lip. "I suppose I should thank you for catching me as well."

A rosy blush covered her otherwise pale face. "You're welcome. Can't see us allowing the new bakery owner to injure herself, not when cakes, pies, and cookies are in jeopardy."

"Oh, well, yes, that's true. It's challenging to prepare decadent desserts when you're injured."

"When do you plan on opening for business?"

"I'm just waiting on the stove and a few other items."

"That's good to know."

"Do you think...oh, never mind."

What had she been about to say? "Please go ahead," urged Timothy.

"Do you think the bakery will be well patronized?"

"Well, that depends on the quality of the food you're offering." He thought of Alma's pies and cakes, and nausea churned in his stomach. A woman's ability or inability to cook wasn't the most important thing, but Timothy would have to eat lest he waste away to nothing. If Miss Davenport baked items like Alma's, she'd be out of business before she even started.

※

Mags could deny it all she wanted, but if Timothy Shepherdson hadn't caught her when she toppled off the chair, she could have been injured, and such a matter was not in her plans, not if she wanted to be successful in Horizon. She did owe him plentiful gratitude for rescuing her the way he had. It was pure luck he'd happened upon her at just the right moment.

Since she was staring, she quickly averted her attention to a speck on the window. Timothy didn't even look like himself today, what with his clean-shaven face, haircut, and spectacles like the ones he'd worn at the supper at his parents' home. He was a dashing and dapper man with those broad shoulders and blue eyes, but she'd not let him know she thought as much.

Besides, what was she doing contemplating Timothy Shepherdson's appearance? She couldn't allow any distractions to stand in the way of opening her bakery and making a new life in Horizon. And with the exception of Cassius Davenport, she hadn't known any man to be kind and upstanding. Not her uncles, not some of the flirtatious men at the factory who were already married, and not the man who had harmed her ma all those years ago. Not even Phoebe's husband, Larry.

"If you need help with the stove, let me know."

"Oh, yes, thank you." His offer drew her from her musings. "Hopefully, it will arrive soon."

If she didn't receive the stove posthaste, she'd have to make alternative arrangements.

"Mind if I take this chair home with me?"

"You don't trust that I won't climb on it again?"

"Not only do I not trust that you won't climb on it again, but I'd also like to see if I can repair it for you."

"Might I ask why you're being so kind to a stranger?"

Timothy jerked his head back as if shocked by her question.

"Why wouldn't I be? I consider myself a helpful sort. Besides, my ma always taught me to treat women with respect, and my pa would have my hide if I treated them any other way."

"I see." She could understand that after having met Mr. and Mrs. Shepherdson. "Then, yes, I would be much obliged if you could look at it and see if it could be repaired. I found it and several others in the alleyway. I have three more in the living quarters, and I plan to have a few tables for customers to sit at while partaking of desserts."

All of a sudden, she forgot who she was speaking to as the excitement of what she'd planned for the future came rushing back. "Of course, people can shop and take the food with them, but as is the case at Wilhelmina's, wouldn't it be a pleasant thing to have them also be able to sit down and enjoy a cookie on an otherwise busy day?" She thought of such places in Chicago. She visited a bakery with her parents twice, once for her birthday and once for Phoebe's.

The side of Timothy's mouth quirked upward, and her face grew warm.

"I mean—oh goodness, listen to me prattling on. I'm not usually one to share such information with a stranger."

"Sounds to me like you have some fine ideas for this place, Miss Davenport."

"Oh, please do call me Mags. And thank you for that compliment."

"Mags, it is then. Well, I must be on my way. I can take any of the chairs that need fixing and return them in a few days or deliver them to you on Sunday at church."

"I won't be at church, so it would be better if you could just bring the chairs by on Monday if that is suitable." Would he judge her for declining to attend church? She just hadn't been able to reconcile in her mind how a good and loving God, the one her parents adored, could have taken so much from her. And how One who supposedly heard all prayers never heard hers.

"All right, well, that's what we'll do then. I will bring any repaired chairs back to you on Monday."

She pulled the other chairs into the main area of the bakery, and Timothy inspected them. Mags was grateful he didn't argue with her about her lack of religion.

Timothy left the bakery before either of them could say another word. She watched as he sauntered down the boardwalk, taking two steps before setting down the chairs, removing his spectacles, and stuffing them into his shirt pocket.

Chapter Nineteen

When Mags awoke the following morning, she'd just changed into her day dress when she heard a knock at the bakery door. Who could be visiting this early?

But as she peered out, she noticed several familiar faces. Timothy, Mr. Shepherdson, Pastor Albert, Jake, Landon, and Hans stood at the door.

"May I help you?"

"Hello," said Mr. Shepherdson. "Your stove and dry sink, along with some other supplies, just arrived at the mercantile on today's train. Thought we'd deliver them and assist with the setup."

The breath whooshed from her lungs. They were here to help her with the stove and dry sink? She rubbed her eyes. Surely, she was dreaming a fanciful dream. For how many times had she wondered how she'd be able to complete such a task on her own?

"Thank you. I—yes, that would be most appreciated."

"If you'll just show us where you'd like us to put the stove, we'll go retrieve it," said Jake.

"Yes, of course." She led them inside the bakery, and when Timothy, who was carrying the repaired chairs, accidentally brushed her arm with his, her stomach did a peculiar flip-flop. Obviously, it was because of the news that her order had arrived. Who knew receiving the stove and dry sink could be so thrilling?

Mags paid Tabitha the money for the items, then the men hauled them to the bakery. Oh, but to begin making Ma's gooseberry fool and rolled jelly cake!

Although there would be no making gooseberry fool until she'd located some gooseberries, but the rolled jelly cake was another matter. While she now owned pans, bowls, towels, spoons, dish towels, and the like, she couldn't very well bake anything without ingredients.

While the men tended to the large items, Mags loaded a crate with flour, sugar, eggs, baking powder, strawberry preserves, oats, butter, milk, lemons, raisins, and a can of peaches. In her excitement, she'd nearly forgotten frugality. Purchasing the entire mercantile would never afford her the ability to send for Phoebe.

After the men placed everything in its proper place, Mags stood back and eyed the transformation of her bakery. She shut her eyes, opened them, shut them, and then opened them again just to be sure this wasn't a dream.

"Thank you so much." The words of gratitude wobbled from her lips.

"You're more than welcome," said Pastor Albert.

"Let us know if you need any more help," added Mr. Shepherdson.

Tears clogged her throat, jumbling her next words. "I will. Thank you again."

Timothy offered a broad smile, and her pulse quickened all the more. "I fixed the chairs. You shouldn't have to worry about falling."

"No, I won't. Fall, that is. Thank you. For the chairs. For the help."

"You're welcome." He waved, then followed the other men out the door.

A thought entered her mind unannounced. Perhaps there were other nice menfolk in this world besides Pa. Timothy and his family had proven that.

Mags set about preparing her first dessert, a delectable rolled jelly cake. She cut a slice of the spongy deliciousness and popped it into her mouth. The savory taste of lightly browned cake and the strawberry preserves melted in her mouth. It tasted exactly like the ones Ma used to make.

Timothy finished tending to a few errands in town when he decided to walk through the alley as a shortcut to the bank. He caught the aroma of something delicious, and he sniffed, trying to determine the semi-familiar smell. His nose led him behind Mags's new bakery. A makeshift table was perched with three pies on it. As he drew closer, he recognized a young boy reaching for one of the pies and attempting to slither around the corner.

"Ozias Agnew!" He hurried his pace, but when Ozias saw him, he started backing away from the table.

"Did you pay for that pie?"

"Maybe?" Ozias's statement was more like a question, causing doubt to firm itself in Timothy's mind.

"Hand me that pie, please."

"I can't."

"You know stealing is wrong."

Ozias held the rim of it to his thin chest, causing a dollop of peaches to spill onto his shirt. "If it's out here all by its lonesome, it don't belong to nobody. Until now."

"No, it's out here because it's cooling. Now hand it over, please."

Ozias's eyes darted around him as if weighing his options. Finally, he relinquished the pie.

Timothy was about to set it back on the table when a familiar voice caused him to startle.

"Timothy Shepherdson! Are you attempting to steal a pie?" Mags rushed toward him, dish towel in hand.

"No, it's not what it looks like."

But it was too late. Mags was already whacking him on the arm with the dish towel.

He juggled the pie, holding tightly as it nearly fell out of his arms. It wouldn't do for all of her hard work to be for naught.

"You need to return the pie posthaste, Mr. Shepherdson."

"Timothy. It's Timothy. Mr. Shepherdson is my father."

It was clear from the way her eyes narrowed into slits that his proclamation hadn't amused her. He edged back slowly. "If I could explain..."

"I figured you to be a man of good character. You allowed me to have the last can of peaches at the mercantile the day I arrived. You saved me from a disaster on the chair. You fixed two broken chairs, and you, along with your family, delivered the heavy items from the mercantile. But I must have been sorely incorrect."

"Not sorely incorrect, ma'am. It's just that..."

"You are a grown man who has one of the kindest and most charitable families I've ever met. They will be so disappointed to hear about your shenanigans."

"Shenanigans? What shenanigans? I was rescuing the pie."

Mags shrugged and peered around at the vacant alley. "From what?"

"From the real thief." But his excuse sounded feeble in his own ears.

"A thief. Hmm. If you hadn't been so gracious in helping me, I might be of the mind to fetch Sheriff Zembrodt."

Timothy wasn't worried that the sheriff would think he was a thief, but he was worried about the ribbing he would receive if she did follow through with her threat.

"You see, what was happening was that I came upon Ozias attempting to steal the pie."

"Ozias? Who is Ozias? And where is he?"

"With all respect, ma'am, he's not going to stick around after being caught."

She clearly had no time for his voiced protests. "I expect to see hooligans such as yourself in Chicago, but not somewhere like Horizon."

"A hooligan?"

"Is there an echo in the alleyway?"

"No, ma'am, no echo, but I can assure you I am not a hooligan." Timothy placed the pie on the table and raised his hands. "Please, allow me to explain."

"Proceed."

"Ozias Agnew, a boy who lives with his family outside of town, was attempting to steal the pie when I came upon him. He ran off, of course, and I was left holding it." Timothy peered down at it, and his stomach rumbled.

"You weren't attempting to steal it?"

"Not at all."

Mags worked her lip between her teeth. "My apologies, then."

"Accepted. Albert and I have been attempting to help Ozias's family. His pa was injured in a farming accident and is in a bad way. They live in a makeshift shelter outside of town, squatting on another man's property. While his pa did accept some crates of food and clothing, the man refuses much charity. Ozias has been to my farm once with my nephews to pick rock and will be working again next week." Timothy shook his head. "He knows better than to steal." But even as Timothy said the words, he knew it would take some time and patient teaching on the part of his parents and himself to remind the boy that taking what didn't belong to him was wrong.

"How sad. I'm glad you're helping him."

"That's how Horizon is. When we see a need, we attempt to fill that need."

Something indistinguishable crossed Mags's face before she spoke. "I've seen that firsthand, and I appreciate it."

"Do you need help carrying the pies back to your bakery so no real hooligans attempt any shenanigans?"

"I would appreciate that. Yes."

Timothy carried two of the pies while Mags carried the other one. When he entered the bakery, his jaw dropped. "This is impressive."

Her face lit, and something inside him stirred. He wished he could repeat the same words a dozen more times just to see the joy in her countenance.

"Thank you. I've even had a few customers today."

"And you'll no doubt have more when the word spreads."

"I hope so."

His stomach rumbled again, reminding him it had been a few hours since his last meal. He stuck a hand in his trouser pocket and jingled the coins. "I'd like to buy that peach pie if it isn't reserved for another customer."

Five minutes and fifteen cents later, Timothy walked out with the very pie he'd saved from Ozias's clutches. It didn't make it home, and it instead proved to be a delicious snack for his short journey back to the farm.

Chapter Twenty

MAGS WAS SLEEPING SOUNDLY when she heard a thump. At first, she thought she might be dreaming, and she rolled over and closed her eyes. A rattling sound, followed by footsteps, echoed in the quiet night. Was someone in the bakery? She jolted upright, her heart's erratic rhythm pounding in her ears.

She slithered from bed and slid against the wall out into the front bakery area. Sure enough, in the moonlight shining through the front window, she noticed a man slowly crouching through the building. Her breath caught in her throat, and her heart pounded so loudly she feared he could hear it. Who was he, and why was he there? Had he seen her? She couldn't see his face or determine any of his other features. She stooped low, wishing she could somehow make it to the front door and escape before he saw her.

Mags tiptoed behind the counter and peered through one of the wooden slats. In the glow of the moonlight, she watched as he walked near the front window, running a hand along the wall. What was he looking for? Fear raced up her spine. Would he hurt her if he saw her? Could she wriggle past him and out the door?

The man slithered to the counter.

He rustled through the items, clanging one of the baking trays before removing the dish towel from a plate and helping himself to a cookie. He chomped and smacked his gums as he devoured a gingersnap, then reached for a second. His noisy chewing continued before he began mumbling to himself.

"It's got to be here somewhere; it has to be."

What was he looking for? Three cookies later, Mags wondered if he'd leave behind any for tomorrow's customers. Would he harm her if he saw her? Was he just some drunkard lost and trespassing? Or was he dangerous? Pins and needles developed in her right leg from remaining in one position. She extended her foot, shook it, and that's when it happened. She accidentally hit the side of the counter with her arm.

"Who's there?"

If she stayed really still, would he think he was just hearing things? It was moments like these that she truly missed being able to pray.

"You there!"

She glanced up to see the man bending over the counter, peering right at her.

Beads of sweat formed on her forehead.

She popped up, hoping to seem braver and more confident than she felt. Better to be facing him eye to eye than in a vulnerable position on the floor. "Who are you and why are you here?"

"Where's the loot at?"

"Loot?"

"Yeah, the stolen gold and silver from the stagecoach robbery."

The words she'd read in Ruby's story in *The Horizon Herald* trilled through Mags's mind. Hadn't Ruby mentioned the fallacy of the scuttlebutt? That people had explored and examined every nook and cranny thoroughly and had found nothing? "There isn't any."

"Poppycock!" He angled toward her, and she inhaled the rank smell of body odor and urine. The man drew closer, invading her sense of space. "Now, where is it?"

"It's not here. That was years ago, and they've already searched many times over for it."

"It's got to be here." He gripped her arm, his sharp fingernails digging into her tender flesh. "You. Will. Tell. Me. Where. It's. At." He punctuated every word through clenched teeth.

"Unhand me this instant!"

"I won't until you tell me where the loot is." He squeezed her arm tighter, and Mags winced. "Is it in the attic? Down here somewhere? Tucked in a tea caddy? Or maybe hidden in a sugar bowl?"

"As I said, there isn't any, and it's not here." Her voice shook, much to her regret. She attempted to pull from his grasp, and he reached for her other arm and shook her.

"Tell me where it is.

Is it in the attic?" he repeated.

There was no way this man was going to believe her, so she might as well tell a bold untruth. Perhaps when he started up the ladder, she could bolt from the bakery. "Yes, you are correct. It's in the attic on the far-left side toward the back."

He stood there a moment longer, glowering at her, a cookie crumb stuck in a corner of his unkempt beard. "You'd better be telling me the truth, woman."

"It's over there," she said, nodding to an area just beyond one of the chairs.

"Over where?" He released her right arm and followed her nod.

Mags felt around on the counter, her fingertips brushing the end of the rolling pin. Just a little farther...

She grasped it, swung it around, and clobbered the burglar in the head, all in one fluid motion.

He crumbled to the ground. Stunned, Mags towered over him and released a ragged breath before sprinting out the door and to the sheriff's office.

By the time she reached the lawman, her unbridled heartbeat pounded in her chest. She threw open the door and stepped inside.

"Mags?" Sheriff Zembrodt looked up from something at his desk, and one of the prisoners in one of the cells woke up and peered at her through the bars.

"There's someone in the bakery."

"A burglar?"

"Yes, I think he's looking for the loot."

"All right, I will go check it out. Go to Miss Greta's, and tell her I sent you."

Mags was about to object when Sheriff Zembrodt continued. "Don't worry, we'll take care of the fee later, you just get to safety. If you see the Lieutenant, send him over."

She scurried out of the sheriff's office, thankful for a sky full of stars and a bright moon that assisted her to Miss Greta's Boardinghouse.

Mags rapped on the door, regretting that she would be awakening the already somewhat cantankerous woman in the middle of the night. The Lieutenant answered. "What are you doing out here so late, Mags?"

She had to repeat her breathless words twice due to the Lieutenant's struggle to hear her. He leaned his right ear toward her, and she raised her voice. "I was hoping I could stay here."

"You can come back in the morning and speak with Miss Greta about a reservation."

"No, I don't need a reservation. Sheriff Zembrodt sent me because of a burglar in the bakery. He needs your assistance."

Miss Greta appeared at the front door in her nightdress. "What is all this commotion about? Goodness, child, don't you know what time it is?"

"Yes, ma'am, I do apologize for that. I can explain everything. But for now, the sheriff would like the Lieutenant to report to the bakery in case he needs help with a burglar."

"Let me just grab my trusty pistol. The sheriff called on the right person. Having served in the war and having been in the military, I'm well equipped to handle such matters."

"Do be careful." Miss Greta planted a kiss on the Lieutenant's weathered cheek.

"Don't worry, my love, I will always come back to you."

"Yes, please do. I didn't wait half of a lifetime to lose you now."

"With all respect, I don't think he's in any danger," Mags interrupted. "It's probably just in case the sheriff needs the Lieutenant to help him carry the man to the jail cell."

"Oh, is that all?" The Lieutenant's broad shoulders deflated.

"I'm just surmising."

"All right, well, reckon it's a worthwhile idea to be prepared anyhow." The Lieutenant put the gun in its holster and slapped a cowboy hat on his head. "I'll be back soon. Try to get some sleep, Miss Greta."

"You know I won't be sleeping until you return safely."

He answered with a clipped nod and strutted down the street.

"Now, why is it you are here?"

Mags rubbed her arm, attempting to assuage the pain caused when the burglar clawed her. She explained the situation to Miss Greta, her voice trembling due to the chilly evening and the lingering fear. "Well, I don't know why the sheriff didn't send you to the hotel, but I suppose you can stay in the hummingbird room. It's the only one I have available at present. Breakfast is at seven. If you miss it, I won't serve it twice."

"Thank you, ma'am."

Mags stood beside the bed with its beautiful quilt. She hasn't slept in such an actual room in a bed since Ma and Pa were alive. She plopped down, allowing the softness of it to engulf her. Hopefully, they would catch the burglar, but she didn't have any more time to think about it because she had fallen fast asleep.

She slept so soundly that Mags hadn't awakened even once. When the scrumptious aroma of what smelled like pancakes drifted beneath the door, she sat up in bed and stretched. Reluctantly emerging from the magnificent bed with its plump bedding, she dressed, fixed her hair, and walked downstairs.

No one was at the table when she arrived, and only Miss Greta was in the kitchen. "I thought you were going to sleep all day."

"No, ma'am, I just don't recall the last time I slept in the bed." She regretted the words the instant she said them because Miss Greta eyed her suspiciously.

"You don't have a bed in the back room at the bakery?"

"No, ma'am, not yet.

Miss Greta furiously scrubbed a spot of hardened grease on a frying pan. "Well, I suppose it was rather exhausting for you to have a burglar trying to find loot that's no longer there and probably never was."

"Yes, it was quite frightening. I do wonder how he's doing after I hit him over the head with a rolling pin."

"You did that?"

"I did."

A look of admiration crossed Miss Greta's face. "
Good for you. You can't be too careful these days with those intent on breaking in and stealing. Years ago, before I married my dear husband, we had someone try to break into the boardinghouse. They nearly met their end when they came face-to-face with a frying pan. Now, I understand I may not look as spry as I once was, but I've always been able to wield a mean hit with that frying pan."

Mags giggled at Miss Greta's exaggerated tone. She wouldn't have wanted to be the one who broke into the boardinghouse that day.

Miss Greta regarded her. "I suppose since you had such an eventful night and you were probably exhausted, I do have some eggs left in the pan if you would like to help yourself."

"Thank you, Miss Greta."

"You are most welcome, but do not let word get out that I let anyone eat after breakfast has already been served. I can't have folks thinking I've gone soft."

Mags pretended to button her lip. "I won't tell a soul." Miss Greta spooned a generous clump of eggs onto a plate along with a pancake. "Thank you so much. Please let me know the charge for last night's stay, and if there's anything I can do to help you in return, I'd be happy to do so."

"Don't really need you to do much around the place, but I wouldn't decline some of those sour cream cookies you sell at the bakery."

"I will be sure you get some." Mags could barely contain herself from shoveling the food into her mouth at a rapid pace. She hadn't tasted a breakfast this delicious since Ma used to make pancakes and eggs. When she and Phoebe assisted in the kitchen, Ma would allow them a dabble of batter to taste to ensure the food tasted just right before it was served. *"You'll be my taste testers,"* Ma said.

Of course, the food always tasted delectable. Ma had a gift for making delicious meals. Tears burned her eyes as she remembered standing beside Ma in their kitchen, both of them wearing matching aprons. Pain stabbed Mags squarely in the heart.

"Do you have children, Miss Greta?" she asked, attempting to push away the thoughts of Ma.

"Yes, the Lieutenant and I have one son. He's almost a full-grown man, and he works on a ranch just outside town. We're right proud of him."

Mags finished eating and offered to assist Miss Greta with the remaining dishes. The woman waved away her offer, and Mags turned the corner on her way up to her temporary room when she nearly ran into the Lieutenant.

"Watch where you're going, young lady."

"I'm so sorry, Lieutenant."

The older man was very suspicious with his hands behind his back. His eyes darted about before settling on Miss Greta. "Would you look at that beautiful woman?"

Mags swiveled around and focused her attention in the direction the Lieutenant pointed. Miss Greta's back was to them, and she was busy wiping a plate with a cloth. "Ain't she just the most beautiful thing ever?" Mags stifled a grin. She admired how the Lieutenant viewed his wife. While Cassius was not as vocal, she knew her pa loved Ma something fierce. Another stab of pain reminded her of how she wished she'd had her father for longer than six years. She often thought of how, should she ever marry, she would want someone kind, gentle, and thoughtful, and willing to be a father to a child who wasn't his. Just like Cassius Davenport.

"From the first second I laid eyes on her, I knew she was the one for me," continued the Lieutenant. "I don't want her knowing I picked these flowers for her. I'm fixing to put them in a vase and set them on the table all surprise-like."

"I could help you with that if you tell me where the vases are."

The Lieutenant adjusted his thick spectacles on his nose. "All right. There is one in the parlor. You'll have to fill it with water from the pitcher. Don't let her see you."

Mags scuttled away to the parlor and found the vase the Lieutenant spoke of on a shelf with several other knickknacks, and poured water into it from the pitcher, all without Miss Greta even so much as noticing her. It helped that the woman was humming a tune and absorbed with cleaning the kitchen.

"Here you are." She handed it to the Lieutenant.

"Thank you. You're much more discreet than I am."

Mags didn't doubt that with the man's booming voice, large presence, and even larger feet. He put the flowers in the vase and positioned it on the table before gesturing at Mags to follow him as he tiptoed away and onto the porch. "No sense in letting her see us," he said. "Sometimes a man's got to do some covert activities around this place. Miss Greta's an observant woman."

Miss Greta didn't seem particularly astute to Mags, but she didn't say as much. "Do you leave her vases of flowers often?"

A brilliant red flushed the Lieutenant's weathered face. "Not only vases of flowers but also other little gifts now and again." He puffed out his chest. "When you wait as long for your true love as I did, you've got to make up for lost time."

"Were you able to catch the man who broke into the bakery?"

"Yes, but not sure why you'd doubt our ability. Sheriff Zembrodt is one of the best in the state, and of course, when he has an assistant like me, we can't help but be successful. Helped a mite bit that the burglar was thumped on the head with that rolling pin. Seems he'll have a bruise the size of Idaho on his head after that.

Can't believe folks still think there's loot hidden in that building. We would have found it long ago if there was."

For a second, Mags wished there truly was hidden loot in the attic or in the walls or even tucked in some old sugar dish. If so, she could buy Phoebe and Larry a house here in Horizon for them to raise the baby. But as quickly as she entertained the thought, Mags remembered that if there was such a find, she would have to return it to its rightful owner.

She bid the Lieutenant farewell and was about to tell Miss Greta goodbye when the woman spoke in a hushed tone. "Have you seen the Lieutenant?"

"Yes. He's outside."

Miss Greta was holding the vase of flowers and inhaling the intoxicating fragrance of the blooms. "Have you ever seen anything so lovely? That Lieutenant is such a sweet man. Do you think you could do me a favor?"

"Certainly."

"I baked his favorite cookies. Would you mind taking them out and setting them on the bench inside the barn? That's where he fixes things. I want to surprise him."

Mags did as instructed. The woman was correct. The Lieutenant wandered into the barn, and when he did, he was overjoyed by what he found.

"Have you seen Miss Greta?" he asked after devouring two of the cookies.

"Yes. She's in the house."

"That woman is such a thoughtful sort. Do you think you could do me a favor?"

"I'd be happy to." Mags figured that at this point, she might never return to the bakery.

"She loves apples, and I found some rosy ones from the tree just a bit ago. Would you mind setting them on the dry sink?"

And on it went for several more rounds before Sheriff Zembrodt arrived at the boardinghouse with the good news that she could return to the bakery. "I just asked Mr. Meldrum if Ruby could write another article about how there is absolutely no loot in the bakery. Maybe if we keep reiterating it, folks will get the message."

"Especially since many have looked for it with no success," said Mags.

"Exactly. At one point, nearly the entire town was stuffed inside that little building, searching. They left no part of that place uncovered. Yes, the former owners before the Bennicks purchased it and left a lot of clutter up in the attic, but hidden treasure isn't among it."

Mags returned to the bakery, cleaned up some items, then set about baking, grateful to be back and that nothing aside from a few cookies had been stolen. She was hard at work when several children bustled through the door, followed by Timothy Shepherdson.

Timothy stopped at the church to fix something for Albert. His sisters and several other women were engaged in a women's Bible study on the lawn, and the children played baseball nearby. When his nieces and nephews saw him, they dropped their game and rushed toward him.

"Uncle Timothy!"

They all started talking at once, their hands making sign language gestures as they did.

"Can you speak one at a time, please?"

Becky and Carrie told him about how they'd been working on their projects for the upcoming fair. Simon then asked, "Can you go with us to pick something out for Pa's birthday?"

"Reckon that sounds like a good idea." Timothy had in mind what he planned to purchase for Albert.

"Hey, can we come too?" asked Gus.

Polly's hands flew with the request that she'd really like to stop by the bakery. He signed back that that would be amenable. Especially since Timothy had plans to stop there as well to check on Mags after he'd heard about the news from Ruby, who'd heard about it from Mr. Meldrum, who'd heard about it from Sheriff Zembrodt, about a burglar breaking in last night looking for hidden loot. Spending time with his nieces and nephews and stopping by the bakery and the mercantile shouldn't preclude Timothy from accomplishing a list of tasks on his farm this afternoon.

The group descended upon Mags's bakery several minutes later. Timothy counted the coins in his pocket. "Everyone can have one cookie of their choice," he said.

His nieces and nephews cheered, and Timothy followed them inside. A lemony aroma wafted on the air.

"Hello, Mags."

"Timothy. Hello."

He held her gaze, and for a few brief seconds, it was as though he and Mags were the only two in the bakery. A wisp of blonde hair framed her pretty face.

But, no, Timothy wasn't really thinking about Mags's beauty or how he *might* be growing fond of her. Two important considerations filled his mind. First, Mags hadn't expressed interest in church. Did she know the Lord? That was of utmost importance to him. Second, he honestly didn't have time to be thinking any sort of sappy thoughts. Not when he owned a newer farm with countless chores beckoning him at any given time. And third, he had no ambition to court or subsequently marry.

He cleared his throat and instead focused on the lemon pie with raisins on the counter, and his mouth watered. After peaches, lemons were his favorite fruit.

"What brings you to the bakery?" she asked, a sweet lilt to her voice.

In their enthusiasm, the children spoke at once.

"Uncle Timothy is buying us cookies."

"Do you have molasses cookies? Those are my favorite."

"It's Pa's birthday tomorrow, so we're shopping for a gift."

"I've had the sour cream cookies before, and they're delectable."

"What are you mixing up in that bowl, Miss Mags?"

"How about we speak one at a time?" Timothy suggested. He tucked an arm around Little Hans and Polly. "Remember, ladies first."

The boys nodded, and Sherman deferred to Becky.

"Hello, Miss Mags. Do you have any gingersnaps?"

"I certainly do, and you all arrived at just the right time." Mags wiped her hands on her apron.

"The right time?" Hosea signed.

Timothy translated.

"I am in need of some taste testers."

"What are taste testers?" asked Gus.

"When I was a little girl, my ma asked my sister and me to test the batter to make sure it tasted good before it was baked."

"Ooh, I'd like to do that," said Pansy, followed by a "me, too!" from the rest of the children.

"Perfect! I'm trying a new recipe called lemon loaf cake." She spooned a small sample for each child.

"This is decadent," said Carrie.

"Uncle Timothy, can we have lemon loaf cake *and* cookies?" asked Little Hans.

Mags passed out cookies, and Timothy slid the twelve cents across the counter. "Thank you. And for you?"

"A gingersnap, please." He'd return later for the lemon pie with raisins.

The children sat at the two tables, and Timothy leaned an elbow on the counter. "I heard about the burglar. Are you all right?"

"Yes, thankfully. He was in search of the hidden loot."

"That's what I heard. I also heard that you whacked him with a rolling pin."

She smiled, causing his heart to pound a little harder in his chest. "Word travels fast here."

"That it does."

"I stayed at Miss Greta's last night after fetching Sheriff Zembrodt."

"Reckon that was an experience."

She nodded. "It was. Those two are certainly unique."

"Indeed. My ma tells a story of when she first arrived in Horizon and stayed there. My pa built an outhouse to pay for her accommodations. Miss Greta was a mite more persnickety back then."

She laughed, a laugh so contagious and so full of joy, he couldn't help but join her.

"I'm glad all is well after the robbery. I suppose I should usher these children to the mercantile so we can purchase a gift for Albert's birthday." He lowered his voice. "I'll be back for the lemon and raisin pie if you could set that aside for me."

"Certainly."

"Will I see you Sunday at church?"

A shadow crossed her face, and a catch in her voice halted her words. "I don't think so."

"Just know if you'd like to attend, you could sit in my family's pew, or should I say, pews. There are a lot of us these days."

"Thank you. I will keep that in mind." A weary sadness had replaced the joy, and Timothy reminded himself to pray for her.

Chapter Twenty-One

TRUE TO HIS WORD, Timothy returned for the lemon and raisin pie. Mags appreciated seeing him twice in one day. Any man who would take his nieces and nephews for cookies couldn't be all that bad. Maybe even a little like Pa.

His question about church had startled her. She'd seen folks meander down the street on Sunday to attend the whitewashed church with its tall steeple and cross. It might do her well to attend a service, but would God even notice she was there?

The postmaster entered the bakery for some spice cake and deposited a letter that had arrived from Phoebe. She could barely wait until he left before opening the missive. Was she an aunt yet? How did Phoebe fare? Mags perched on the bench just outside the bakery and unfolded the letter. Phoebe's perfectly slanted letters leaped from the page.

My Dearest Magnolia,

I'm glad to hear that you are enjoying living in Horizon. It sounds like a lovely place. Have you made lots of friends? Have you decided to return to church? I know that is something we ought not discuss, but truth be told, I have been concerned about you. When I went to live with Grandmother, we began attending a church near Grandmother's apartment where the Word of God is preached. If we found ourselves in the situation we had after our parents' passing, I am confident this pastor and his wife would have been more willing to perhaps take us in, or at least you. As you know, I have guilt over the fact that Grandmother did not offer you a home with us.

We spent so, so many years apart. I searched for you, but had no idea where you resided. If only we'd found each other sooner. But alas, I am grateful for the time the Lord gave us. While you did not tell me all of the details of residing with your aunts, I can only imagine the heartache and difficulties you faced. I will forever be saddened that I didn't do more to help you. I hope you can forgive me.

When Pa married your ma, I wasn't sure about a sister, but I soon realized that you were one of the best gifts God had ever given me.

The baby has not yet arrived, and I have been quite ill. The doctor was concerned for both my health and the baby's, and as such, determined I needed someone to help care for me. Logically, that would have been Larry; however, I am sad to say he left two weeks ago, and I was given divorce papers. Never in my wildest dreams would I have imagined causing such a scandal. I am not sure now why I married Larry, but suffice it to say, I am overwhelmed with excitement to meet this baby.

Lest you worry—as I know you are prone to fretting—I have moved in with Grandmother once again. She has been taking care of me. I'm not sure what I would have done without her. The baby is due any day now, and I am relegated to my bed. The apartment is much the same, although Grandmother has fewer belongings. Times have been difficult for her with her health. She is now hunched over and suffers from rheumatism. I do regret that I am causing her some distress, but she assures me she is happy to have me here.

After the baby is born and is old enough to travel, I would love to accept your offer to move to Horizon. There is nothing I would like more than reuniting with my favorite sister. I love you and hope to see you soon.

All my love,
Phoebe

Tears had already begun to burn Mags's eyes. Why had she ever thought to leave her sister behind? If she were still in Chicago, she could be helping take care of her, preparing with her for the baby in Larry's absence. Speaking of Larry...Mags swallowed a few unkind words that came to mind about the man who charmed her sister. Phoebe had deserved so much better than that ne'er-do-well.

Tears trickled down her cheek and landed on Phoebe's letter, smearing the words.

"Oh, Phoebe, there is nothing to forgive," she said aloud. "And, oh, how I wished we had found each other sooner as well. Please forgive me for leaving."

"Mags?"

She looked up to see Mrs. Shepherdson standing beside the bench.

"Hello, Mrs. Shepherdson." Had the woman heard her lament?

"Mind if I have a seat?"

Mags nodded and patted the bench beside her.

"Is everything all right?" While Mrs. Shepherdson reminded Mags in many ways of Ma, she wasn't about to share the concerns of her heart. Not with someone she'd only met so recently, and for certain not with someone who might reconsider her friendship if she knew things that Mags kept tucked deep in her heart.

"Yes, just reading a letter from my sister."

"Does she still reside in Chicago?"

"She does."

Passersby waved, and some offered greetings. Mags was thankful no one stopped to chat. It was hard enough to hold all of those emotions inside with Mrs. Shepherdson, let alone if there was a crowd.

"It's such a lovely day today."

"Yes, it is." Mags folded the letter and tucked it back into the envelope.

"Is your sister your only family in Chicago?"

"She is. Our parents have passed."

"I'm sorry to hear that."

"Thank you." Phoebe's face flashed through Mags's mind. Was she in pain? Was the baby all right? In the time it took for the letter to be delivered, had Phoebe already had the baby? Why, oh why, hadn't Mags stayed in Chicago? Why has she so selfishly decided she wanted to start a new life while leaving the only person left who cared about her all alone with a scoundrel of a husband and a difficult pregnancy?

A choked sob escaped her throat, and Mrs. Shepherdson wrapped in arm around her shoulder. "Are you sure you're all right?"

"I suppose I'm not," Mags muttered.

"Would you care to discuss it?"

"I'm just worried about my sister."

"Is she ill?"

"She's about to have a baby, and there might be complications. She has moved back in with her grandmother."

"I'm so sorry. Would you like to pray for her?"

"No, but thank you all the same. I don't believe God answers prayers, or at least my prayers." She waited for a chastisement, and when there was none, she sneaked a peek at Mrs. Shepherdson's profile.

The older woman's brow knitted. "I understand. Sometimes it's hard to believe that God even hears us."

"I know He doesn't hear me. I begged Him to allow my parents to live, and He didn't. Then I begged him when I had to go live with..." She stopped herself before revealing any more.

"I remember praying for my pa. He had something wrong with his mind and couldn't remember us. He wasn't himself, and Ma and I were so terribly worried. God did not answer that prayer the way I wanted him to. I hoped that Pa would recover and return to the man we knew him to be, but that wasn't God's will."

"I'm so sorry about your pa. Is your ma still alive?"

"No, unfortunately, when the floods came, the waters swallowed both of my parents. To this day, I'm not sure how I survived, barring a miracle from the Lord. But I did pray we would all survive it, and that again, wasn't the Lord's will.

Mags suddenly wanted to comfort Mrs. Shepherdson. "I'm so sorry about your parents. That must have been awful." She couldn't imagine the pain of seeing your parents succumb to floodwaters.

"It *was* awful. There were times I thought I wouldn't overcome it. Times I wasn't sure I could go on."

Mrs. Shepherdson had felt that way? "But you seem like a woman of strong faith."

"I'd like to think of myself as a woman of strong faith, but even those of us who profess Christ struggle at times. When we surrender our lives to Him, it doesn't mean our lives will be easy. Or that we won't struggle. Or that we don't grieve."

"What I don't understand is why everyone thinks God is so loving and good and gracious and kind. Or at least that's what we were taught at the church we attended when Phoebe and I were young. Our parents believed that, too, but I don't believe it anymore. If He is so loving and good and gracious and kind, then Phoebe's husband wouldn't have left her, she wouldn't be having a difficult pregnancy, she wouldn't have to live with her grandmother again, our parents wouldn't have passed, and other things that happened, and your father wouldn't have had a sickness that affected his mind, nor would your parents have passed." She stopped and took a deep breath. Would Mrs. Shepherdson judge her for her long tirade? At least there was nobody on the boardwalk at the moment to hear her. For that, Mags was grateful.

Mrs. Shepherdson said nothing, but took Mags's hand in her own. Finally, after a few heartbeats had passed, she spoke. "I cannot pretend to understand why things happen the way they do. I know God does have a plan, and we don't know what that plan means, but we have to trust He knows and that He loves us."

"He loves us so much that He would allow painful events to happen?" The instant she said the sarcastic words, Mags regretted them. Mrs. Shepherdson had been so kind to her, and she'd even started to grow slightly fond of Timothy. Being so precocious would likely change their minds about her. Her heart hurt at the thought. And once they found out about the real her, the woman who'd stolen to travel to Horizon, the woman who deserted her sister because she selfishly wanted her own adventure, the woman who'd once spent a night in jail...they would no doubt distance themselves from her, and rightfully so. Her bakery would never have a chance to succeed, and all of her plans would be for naught. She would have to find somewhere else to move or return to Chicago.

"I surely don't have the answers for why bad things happen. There is so much pain and so much anguish in this life. But I do know one thing. We never walk through those painful times alone. In His Word, God tells us He never leaves us. He walks through those times with us, that He is close to the brokenhearted."

"If He is close to the brokenhearted, then He wouldn't allow them to be brokenhearted in the first place."

Mrs. Shepherdson gently squeezed her hand. "But if only good things happened in our lives, we wouldn't need a Savior."

Mags had heard the message about what Jesus had done for her many times in the church where she and Phoebe grew up. It never really resonated with her. She thought it was nice that He would do such a thing for people, but she'd never truly understood its magnitude.

"If we had a perfect life here with no sin that we commit and no sin that anyone else commits, we wouldn't realize our need for Him. We would depend fully on ourselves."

"Would it be so awful to depend on ourselves?"

The last thing Mags desired was a sermon or a lecture, but something about the way Mrs. Shepherdson spoke—softly, warmly, calmly, and kindly—didn't really sound like a sermon or a lecture, or at least not like the ones that she'd heard in Chicago. Maybe it would be okay to express more of her fears, concerns, and doubts.

"I know when I depend on myself, it never goes well," said Mrs. Shepherdson. "I have done that many times in my life. Tyler and I were married for convenience's sake. We grew to love each other after we made our vows. Needless to say, I made numerous errors in those days. I still do. I had no idea where I would go when I ended up in Horizon, but I did know God would take care of me. Left to make my own way would have been disastrous for sure, not to mention I would not have succeeded without His help. Without His guidance. Without keeping my eyes fixed on Him, even when it wasn't easy."

"I'm just overcome with guilt for leaving Chicago when I should be there taking care of my sister." Should she return? Board the next train back to Chicago? Shouldn't Phoebe have come before the bakery?

"Whether you should return to Chicago is something you will have to lift up in prayer and allow God to guide your steps. I will say that you have already impacted people's lives here."

"I have?"

"Yes. Who knows the outcome of the stagecoach robbery had you not been there. You saved a man's life. Not to mention, you are a wonderful addition to our town. If, after prayer, you decide to return to Chicago, that is ultimately your decision. But I can tell you that you would be missed."

Would people miss her if they knew the real her? If she turned to the Lord again, would He forgive her for stealing, for leaving Phoebe, for abandoning her faith? "Do you think God forgives everything? Even turning my back on Him?"

"There is nothing you can do, Magnolia Davenport, that He cannot forgive. That is why Jesus endured all of that pain on the cross for us. The flogging, the beating, people turning their backs on him, the betrayal, He endured all of that for us so that we can be forgiven and spend eternity with Him."

The words seeped deep into her soul as if she'd heard them for the first time.

"Without Him, I would not have made it through those agonizing times in my life, and there were many. The loss of my parents was horrific. But through it all, He never left my side. My favorite verse is found in Habakkuk. It talks of the fig tree failing to blossom with no fruit, that the olive fails, fields shall yield no fruit, and there'll be no herd in the stalls, yet, '*I will rejoice in the Lord, I will joy in the God of my salvation.*' But my favorite part is verse nineteen. '*The Lord God is my strength, and he will make my feet like hinds' feet, and he will make me to walk upon mine high places.*'"

Mags took in the words, so reassuring and so comforting. Could it be that she could find joy in Him even though she'd lost so much? Could it be that the Lord would be her strength, too?

She picked at a button on the dress. "There's so much to think about."

"Indeed, there is. There is so much richness in God's Word. So many promises and not one of them will He fail to keep."

"I do appreciate how everyone in Horizon has been so kind." Here, she didn't have to worry about malicious aunts or loathsome men at the factory. Wilhelmina had given her a temporary job to earn her supper that first night, and Miss Greta had allowed her to stay in her home when the bakery was burglarized. Folks patronized the bakery and warmly welcomed her. "It's almost perfect."

"Horizon is a delightful place, and I wouldn't want to live anywhere else. But it's not perfect, and its residents are not perfect. We are all fallible, and we do have some who are unkind. My daughter, Ruby, would be able to tell you that firsthand. If Horizon were perfect, we wouldn't long for heaven."

"Thank you for taking the time to listen," Mags said. "You've given me much to ponder."

"You are more than welcome. If you ever need to talk again, please let me know. And while I'll not pressure you to attend, I'd love to invite you to church. Please feel free to sit in our pews with our family."

Timothy had said much the same. "Thank you. I'll consider it."

"I'll be praying for Phoebe, the baby, and your decision about whether or not to return to Chicago."

That night, Mags rested her head on the new pillow she'd purchased at the mercantile. She fell asleep with thoughts of the Lord on her mind.

Chapter Twenty-Two

THAT SUNDAY, TIMOTHY BARELY made it through the blockade of four women who'd eagerly greeted him the second he dismounted from his horse. The church door beckoned him. Close, but so far out of reach.

"Hello, Timothy."

"How are you, Timothy?"

"Isn't it such a pleasant day, Timothy?"

"Have you been thinking about the Gingham Ball, Timothy?"

"I made you some of my famous green tomato pie." This from Alma, who thrust the dessert toward him. He'd never been overly fond of tomatoes, especially unripe ones, but he wouldn't hurt Alma's feelings.

"Thank you."

"Oh!" she tittered. "Did you hear the way he thanked me?"

The other three women swooned. Timothy peered around in the hopes of seeing Mags. Ma mentioned she'd spoken to Mags the other day, but hadn't elaborated on the topic.

"Uncle Timothy!" He turned to see Ozias running toward him. It didn't surprise him that the boy had begun to call him "uncle" after working with Timothy's nephews.

"Excuse me, ladies. Hello, Ozias. It's good to see you here."

"Ma and us kids are coming to church today."

Mrs. Agnew and her two daughters approached Timothy. "It's good to see you here today, ma'am."

"Ma, them are my cousins over there. Can I go see 'em?" Ozias pointed to where Timothy's nieces and nephews stood talking amongst themselves.

"Yes, you may."

"Us, too, Ma?" the older daughter asked.

"Yes, but please keep an eye on your sister." The two girls held hands and ran behind their brother.

"I was unable to talk Harvey into attending, but he wasn't opposed to us visiting the Lord's house today."

Timothy marveled at how God was already answering prayers in regards to the Agnew family. "We'll keep praying."

"This town has done so much for us." Tears rimmed the woman's eyes. "Ozias loves working with your nephews. I hope you don't mind that he thinks he's related."

Timothy chuckled. "I don't mind at all. We'd be happy to call you family."

Mrs. Agnew held a hand to her mouth. "Thank you."

"I've been meaning to stop by and let your husband know I may have found him a temporary job. It would only be for a few months while the permanent employee is visiting his family in Pennsylvania, but it would bring in an income, and perhaps by the time it ended, Harvey's foot would be healed."

"A job?"

"Yes. I'll stop by tomorrow and speak with him about it. It's with the railroad as a ticket clerk. He'd be able to sit during the course of working."

"Thank you. For everything. I'll not breathe a word, but I do want you to know that you and your family have been an answer to prayer."

Mags removed a pan lined with chocolate cookies from the oven when two young women about her age entered.

"It smells scrumptious in here," said the taller one, a black-haired woman with a pale face and widely spaced hazel eyes.

"Yes, it does." The shorter, slimmer one with blonde hair and oversized and intense brown eyes took a deep breath.

"Do you know Timothy Shepherdson?"

"I do," Mags answered.

"He is so utterly dapper." Both women swooned and giggled, making them seem much younger than they were.

The taller one extended a hand. "I'm Mary Lou, and this is my best friend, Alma."

"I'm Mags Davenport. Nice to meet you. What brings you into the bakery today?"

"Well," said Alma, "I'm hoping to win the heart of a very handsome young man."

"If I don't win his heart first." Mary Lou nudged her friend. "If you'll recall, I've known him longer than you have."

Alma scrunched her shoulders against her neck. "No matter. We will see who he chooses at the Gingham Ball."

"The Gingham Ball?" Mags had heard it mentioned, but wasn't sure exactly what it was.

"It's where all of us eligible ladies wear gingham dresses."

"Married folks attend too," countered Alma.

"Indeed," said Mary Lou, "but for those of eligible ladies, as we are sewing our dresses, we cut a strip of material and sew a man's necktie. We place it in an envelope, and then the eligible young men who attend the ball each randomly choose an envelope. They match their tie to the woman's dress, and that gentleman dances with her throughout the evening." She held a hand to her neck. "Isn't it just romantic? To think of being in the arms of a handsome gent while you dance the night away."

"Only if he is indeed a handsome gent. What if it's someone despicable like Mr. Troxell?"

"Or Mr. Sanders, who is quite old."

"Not as old as Leonel."

Mary Lou puckered her lips and scrunched her nose. "Mr. Sanders and Leonel might be eligible bachelors, but I can't think of any woman in her right mind who would like to dance the night away with either of them. Leonel is nearly a hundred years old, and Mr. Sanders and Mr. Troxell are just plain contemptible."

"Hence the reason neither is married." Alma held a hand to the side of her mouth. "But you didn't hear that from us."

"I'll not breathe a word," promised Mags.

Alma surveyed the bakery, then lowered her voice. "If there is a way I could cheat, I sure would."

"You know cheating is wrong, Alma. It will be whatever it's to be. Besides, I'd rather win fair and square."

"Well, be that as it may, I plan to win Timothy Shepherdson's heart, even if it's not by his choosing the envelope with the tie that matches my dress."

"Surely, not with your, ahem, baking skills."

"Very funny, Mary Lou. I happen to have an idea. Besides, I heard a rumor that Mrs. Shepherdson could barely boil water when she and Mr. Shepherdson married all those years ago. That hardly kept Mr. Shepherdson from marrying her. The way I see it, the same could be for Timothy and me."

"I don't see how. As you mentioned, Mrs. Shepherdson could at least boil water."

The friends' banter amused Mags. They were as opposite as opposite could be, but from all indications, both had set their cap for Timothy.

Alma scowled at her friend. "Well, that won't matter after I execute my plan."

"Which is?"

"To purchase a delectable dessert, deliver it to Timothy at church on Sunday, and..."

"Pretend as though it is your own?"

"Exactly."

"He won't be fooled by your tomfoolery, Alma. He knows your baking skills or lack thereof. Besides, I thought we were having an outing today just to visit the bakery and sample some of the food for ourselves. I've heard it's quite good."

"Thank you, I appreciate that." Mags was barely able to get a word in before the women continued to gush about Timothy.

"He is only the most eligible man in Horizon."

"Not just Horizon," clarified Mary Lou, "but probably the entire county."

"Those blue eyes and those muscular shoulders..." Alma closed her eyes. "Can you imagine being asked to court him?"

"Lest you forget, he's not only handsome but a fine man of character, too. He loves the Lord, is honest, forthright, and true-hearted. Of course, I know these things because I've known him since we were children."

"Be that as it may," said Alma, "since he hasn't yet asked for your hand in courtship, I'll not concede to you winning Timothy's heart. Now, which dessert do you think he would like the best?" Alma tapped a finger on the counter as she and Mary Lou perused the offerings.

Something told Mags that Timothy wasn't particular about desserts or any kind of food, for that matter. He'd bought a peach pie and a lemon and raisin pie, so she wouldn't suggest those since Timothy would probably recognize them as ones Mags had baked.

"What about rolled jelly cake?" suggested Mary Lou.

Mags regarded her. On the one hand, she should be honest. Ma would say that was the best policy. But on the other hand...a perplexing niggle wormed its way into her heart and settled in her belly. Could it be that she was growing fond of Timothy as well? No, that couldn't be. She had no time for such foolish notions. Not when she was trying to make a home for herself in Horizon.

"Ooh, yes. We ate rolled jelly cake once in Cornwall. One of the best desserts, if I do say so myself. Brilliant idea, Mary Lou."

Mary Lou bowed. "Thank you. Glad I could be of service."

Alma giggled and clapped her hands together. "This is one of my most splendid ideas."

"You truly are a flibbertigibbet, Alma."

"Oh, yes, I know." To Mags, she said, "When can we retrieve the rolled jelly cake?"

"I can have it finished for you tomorrow afternoon."

"Perfect! That will enable me to deliver it nice and fresh to Timothy on Sunday at church." She angled her head. "Are those fruit jumbles?"

"They are. Freshly made just before you arrived."

Alma licked her lips. "I haven't had a fruit jumble since Wilhelmina made them for one of the church potlucks last summer."

"How have you ever survived?" Mary Lou quipped.

Alma nudged her friend. "It's been challenging to say the least. I'll treat you to a fruit jumble."

"I happily acquiesce."

"Two fruit jumbles, please. Pray tell, do they include currants, cinnamon, and cloves?"

Mags served two of the baked pastries onto a plate. "Yes, they do. It was my mother's recipe."

"I can almost taste them now. I'm so glad you opened the bakery, Mags."

Alma's words warmed Mags's heart. The woman plunked the coins on the counter. "This is so thrilling. Finally, Timothy will have no choice but to consider me for courtship after he tastes the scrumptious dessert."

"What if he asks you to make it again?"

"Pshaw, Mary Lou. I will just come right back into the bakery and order another one."

"You don't think he'll ever grow wise to your shenanigans?"

"It's hardly a shenanigan, my dear friend. Desperate times call for desperate measures, or so they say."

"You don't think it's the slightest bit dishonest?"

Alma blanched. "I know that you have set your cap for him too, and that we are best friends. I desire nothing to come between our friendship. Not even Timothy Shepherdson. So if you would prefer I not partake in such a plan, then please say so."

"Far be it from me to tell you what sort of plans and schemes to partake in. You've always been a strong-minded girl. And I'm just like you—I want nothing to come between our friendship. You have my blessing to deliver the cake to him on Sunday. I do have to admit it is a rather good idea." Mary Lou and Alma both giggled.

"Yes, I think so too, if I do say so myself. I was sleeping last night and awoke suddenly with it fresh on my mind. I thought to myself, '*Alma, if you can't bake something, find someone who can help you.*'"

"I could give you lessons," offered Mags.

"Oh, I don't want lessons. I know Mrs. Shepherdson had to have lessons after she and Mr. Shepherdson were married, and Wilhelmina kindly obliged, or so that's what Ma says. But lessons are not for me. As a matter of fact, cooking and baking aren't for me. But don't say I said so."

"True," agreed Mary Lou. "You'll never catch a husband that way."

Thoughts of Timothy swirled through Mags's mind. Would he grow wise and discover that Alma had not baked the rolled jelly cake? And what would happen if he and Alma were to marry and he determined she couldn't bake at all?

The women took their seats at one of the tables. Their camaraderie and chatter reminded Mags of all those times with Phoebe. Would she ever be so accepted in Horizon that she also had friends she could prattle with?

After they'd finished eating, the women returned their plates. "We'll see you tomorrow, Mags," said Alma. "And, ladies, do take note of my ring finger." She splayed her hand to Mags and Mary Lou. "Because the days are dwindling where it is void of a wedding ring."

"Aren't you getting a little ahead of yourself?" asked Mary Lou.

"You always were a naysayer."

Mags watched as the two left the bakery.

A wistfulness took up residence deep within her heart. How she longed for friendship.

Mags exited the mercantile when she spied Sheriff Zembrodt. In front of him was a man who was obviously being arrested. A man who looked familiar. "Mr. Yates?"

The man dropped his chin to his chest.

"Mr. Yates?" she asked again.

He slowly peered up at her. "Hello, Mags."

"You know this man?" Sheriff Zembrodt caught her eye.

"I do. Why are you arresting him?"

"He's a stowaway. Thought he would secure a ride on the train without paying. According to the law, that's theft. Now, if you'll excuse us, I need to get him into a cell."

"But you can't arrest him."

"He was breaking the law, Mags."

She followed them to the sheriff's office. There had to be a way to help the man who had saved her life. Mags stood to the side until the sheriff locked Mr. Yates into a jail cell, then requested to speak with Sheriff Zembrodt in private.

He met her in front of the boardwalk. "Mags, I know you mentioned that you know this man, but I have to follow the law and arrest him. I hope you understand."

"I do understand, and I do agree that what he did is thievery, but Mr. Yates, he…" Her voice cracked. "He saved my life." She thought again of attempting to climb aboard the railcar. Her hands slipping, her feet dragging. The wind rushing past her as the train sped down the track. Her fingers losing their grip. "Can I at least speak with him?"

Sheriff Zembrodt gestured toward his office. Mags stumbled through the door. Mr. Yates sat on the cot with his head in his hands. Thankfully, all of the other cells were empty.

"Mr. Yates, is it true you were hitching a ride on the train?"

"I was. Mags, I hope you don't find this to be rude, but this isn't any of your business."

"But I want to help you if I can. Do you remember when you pulled me onto the train? If you hadn't done that, I would have fallen beneath the train and been run over. And then you refused to turn me in when you and Mr. Haswell were arrested."

"I was glad I could help you, but just because I did those things doesn't mean you owe me."

Mags brushed his comment aside. She *did* owe him. For her life. For her second chance. "Did you see your family in Cornwall?"

"I did. One of the best days of my life."

"Was your wife willing to give you another chance?"

"At first."

Tears clouded Mag's vision. "At first?"

Mr. Yates's jaw twitched. "I had me a job in Cornwall. I spoke to my wife and told her I was now sober. It was only God's grace that she was willing to give me a chance. Also, only by His grace has she not remarried. Two days later, I reported to work, and several of us men were laid off. Not the employer's fault, but because times were hard for that business. He wasn't even able to pay us the full amount owed to us, but my wife didn't care to hear the reason. She just told me she wasn't surprised that I failed to retain another job. Since she was no longer willing to give me a second chance, I prayed about it, not really sure what God would have for me. I figured I would go to California and see if there are any jobs to be had there. I didn't quite have enough money to purchase the train ticket, so I figured I would hitch a ride. It's what we hobos do." He scraped a hand through his hair. "I know I shouldn't have done it, especially since I had promised to be honest and change my ways. But my wife was right. I'm incapable of changing."

"I think you just need another chance."

"After I do my time and pay the fine, I'm going to California. See what I can find there."

"But what about your family? What about reconciliation?"

He hiked a shoulder. "I appreciate you caring about me."

Something she once heard in church surged to the forefront of her mind. "Isn't it true that our God is a God of second chances and third chances and fourth chances?

"True, but I didn't think you cared much for the things of God."

"He doesn't hear my prayers, but that doesn't mean that what He has to say isn't true. And if He is a God of all those chances, we just need to give you another one."

"Don't waste your time, Mags. What burdens me the most is how I could have had my family back, but I threw that opportunity away."

"Through no fault of your own. You can't be blamed for the business closing."

While the Lord hadn't heard her prayers, perhaps He would hear the prayers she prayed for someone else. As she rushed down the boardwalk to the train depot, Mags lifted her gaze heavenward.

Lord, I know I haven't spoken to You since Ma and Pa passed. But maybe, perhaps, could you help Mr. Yates? He's in a bad way. He's a good man, Lord. He just needs one of Your many chances. Please?

Mags next arrived at the train depot and requested to speak with Landon. Surely, Mae's husband would have a job opening for Mr. Yates.

"Mags, hello, what can I do for you?"

"Hello, Landon, I was wondering if there are any jobs available with the railroad?"

"For you?"

"No, for a friend of mine. He's a hard worker." She fidgeted with the hem of her sleeve. "He just needs a second chance."

"I have a labor position in Ingleville. Send him here, and we'll see what we can do."

"Thank you, I appreciate it very much."

As Mags stepped back into the sunshine once more, her heart felt lighter than it had in a long time.

Chapter Twenty-Three

Timothy saddled his horse and rode to town for church. As he rounded the corner and onto Main Street, he saw a familiar sight. Mary Lou and Alma stood beside the tree in the churchyard. He cringed. They were likely waiting for him, especially since Alma held something in her arms. Something that appeared to be a plate. He would never have been able to see the detail had he not worn his spectacles, but today would be his first day wearing them to church. Today would be the first day he would be able to see his brother clearly as he preached. The first day he would be able to tell who was who from a distance.

He dreaded the comments. But he might as well partake in an act of courage. It was tough to swallow pride sometimes.

"Timothy, oh, Timothy!" Alma waved, and Timothy dismounted his horse and tethered it to the tree.

"Good morning, ladies."

"Oh!" tittered Alma.

"Hello, Timothy," said Mary Lou. She pasted on a broad smile. She was a nice woman, but he'd always considered her much like one of his sisters. Alma, on the other hand, drove him crazy. She belonged more in the theater than in Horizon.

"I made you a rolled jelly cake." She thrust the dessert, wrapped in brown paper, into his hands.

Timothy had grown accustomed to Alma's constant desserts she would bring to church. He felt bad that he never wanted to eat any of them because of the awful taste. It was probable that the poor woman had left out a key ingredient. Most likely, sugar.

"That was right kind of you, Alma."

She beamed, affection glowing in her eyes. Affection, he could not return.

"Will you be attending the Gingham Ball?"

Mary Lou elbowed her friend. "That's far too forward of you, Alma."

But Alma ignored Mary Lou and implored Timothy to answer.

"Reckon I might." But it wasn't to dance. Timothy had heard there would be all kinds of cakes, pies, cookies, pastries, and cinnamon rolls.

Alma trilled. "I'm so glad to hear that."

Behind Alma and Mary Lou, Timothy spied an unusual sight. Mags was walking toward the church. Did she plan to attend for the first time today? He hoped so. His family had been praying for her. She wore that lovely pink dress she'd worn to supper at Ma and Pa's house. He couldn't take his eyes from her.

"I know you're just going to love the rolled jelly cake." Alma folded her hands behind her back and lifted her chin.

If it tasted anything like the other desserts she'd made, he highly doubted it. But he'd never mention such. Ma would have his hide and then some if he ever showed unkindness to someone attempting to be generous. He reluctantly tore his gaze from Mags. "Thank you, Alma."

She giggled, twirled a wisp of hair around her finger, and whispered to Mary Lou. "Did you hear how he said my name? Gracious me! You're so welcome, Timothy. By the way, there's something different about you." She squinted, and Timothy braced himself for her next words. "It's the spectacles, isn't it?"

Mary Lou rolled her eyes. "Did you just now notice those?"

"Yes, I wasn't expecting them on a younger gentleman."

"Yes, well, apparently I have old-person eyes."

Both women laughed again at Timothy's pronouncement before they both pootled away. The savory aroma led him to unwrap the brown paper. Golden crust with a swirl of jelly greeted him. He hoped it was strawberry jelly. That was his favorite. He surveyed the area, and noticing that no one paid him much mind, he snuck a meager bite.

The savory dessert melted on his tongue, and he chewed slowly before taking another bite.

"Timothy?" He startled and turned around to see Mags standing behind him.

"Hello. Good morning. Happy Sunday. Nice day, isn't it?" He sounded like a dolt and folded the brown paper around the rolled jelly cake. "How you are?"

"I beg your pardon?"

"I meant to say, how are you?" He was such a nincompoop.

She laughed, a sweet, joyous laugh that drew him to her all the more. If only she was a woman of faith.

"I was wondering if I might ask you something."

"Sure."

Two other women who'd set their caps for Timothy walked by and waved. Apparently, he hadn't made it well known enough through his sisters that he was not planning to ever marry.

"Do you have any gooseberries on your land?

"Gooseberries? Yes, I believe I do in a sunny spot down on the eastern side of the property. Why do you ask?"

"When I was a girl, one of my ma's favorite treats to prepare was gooseberry fool."

"I've never heard of it, but I'd probably like it."

"It's a custard of sorts. Gooseberries aren't always easy to find, so I'm thrilled to know that you have some on your property. Might you allow me to pick a few?"

"Sure, help yourself."

"Thank you, I appreciate it."

"You're welcome. Tomorrow I will be arriving in town to retrieve my nephews and Ozias. I could give you a ride to the property if you were ready around seven or so."

"I can be ready then. I don't open the bakery until ten. That should give me plenty of time to pick the gooseberries." She tilted her head to one side. "Might you also be able to return me to the bakery?"

"Sure. The boys will be picking rock, so once I get them situated, I will be able to deliver you back to town. This gooseberry fool, will you be selling it?"

"Yes, but I might be persuaded to offer a bowl of it to someone who allows me to retrieve gooseberries on his property."

"And I might be persuaded not to eat the entire bowl of it in one fell swoop."

"How do you know you will cotton to it?"

"I have never met a cake, cookie, pastry, pie, or custard I didn't like." He patted his stomach. "I'm not picky when it comes to food." He watched as several churchgoers passed them. "It's good to see you at church today."

"Yes, well, I just—well—"

Was she having second thoughts? "You can sit in my family's pews."

"Thank you. I just—I haven't been to church in years."

He waited for her to continue.

Mags pinned her arms across her chest. "Do you think God always hears our prayers?"

"I do. He just doesn't always answer them the way we'd like."

"That I do know."

"One thing I marvel about the Lord is that He answers unspoken prayers as well."

She chewed on her lip. "How do you mean?"

"Well, for instance, we recently suffered a rainstorm. Of course, we prayed that our crops wouldn't be damaged. We prayed anyone caught in it would be safe. When I returned home the next day, I noticed God answered an unspoken and unthought-of prayer."

"Oh?"

"The water in the river was already high. It could have easily flooded from the torrential rains. But God held those rains at bay. There were no floods. My roof could have leaked. It didn't. So many times He takes care of us, and we don't even realize it."

"I suppose so."

Timothy hadn't meant to sound like Albert, but here he was, his excitement about the Lord flowing from his thoughts to his mouth. "For instance, did He deliver you safely to Horizon? Did He keep you safe when the stagecoach was robbed? Did He bless you with the bakery? Did He keep you safe when the burglar broke into the bakery?"

Mags's eyebrows drew together. "Yes." Her voice was hesitant, soft, and fragile. "You're right—He did do all of those things and more."

"It's never too late to come back. Of course, the thing that always strikes me over and over again is how He sent Jesus for us. We never asked for that. We couldn't have known we were wretched sinners in need of a Savior. But He knew."

Timothy's words probed a part of Mags's heart she'd closed off for the past several years. He gestured for Mags to go ahead of him, and he followed her into the church. She squeezed in between Mrs. Shepherdson and Lucy. Miss Greta began playing the brand-new piano in the corner of the church, and Albert led them in their first hymn, "Bringing in the Sheaves".

"This is one of Timothy's favorite songs," whispered Lucy.

Mags dared a glance in Timothy's direction at his handsome profile. He'd donned his spectacles today and stood sandwiched between Gus and Hosea as he lifted his voice to the Lord.

It had been so, so long since she'd sung a hymn, let alone acknowledged her Heavenly Father. Would He hear her words as she sang in worship? Could she cultivate a faith like that of her parents?

Bringing in the sheaves,
bringing in the sheaves,
We shall come rejoicing, bringing in the sheaves.

A single tear slid down her cheek. She remembered this song from when she and her family attended church in Chicago.

After three more hymns, the offering plate was passed before Pastor Albert made announcements. "The Gingham Ball is in two weeks. Please see Tabitha at the mercantile for more information. Our elder fund, which assists those in our community with needs, has recently benefited two Horizon families. Thank you for your generosity. And finally, I'd like to introduce Miss Jenkins with the orphan train."

Miss Jenkins stood. "Thank you for the warm welcome. I am pleased to announce that we were able to find homes for all of the orphans on this trip. We will be back next spring, and I hope that at that time, the fine residents of Horizon will once again open their hearts and homes to a child."

The congregation clapped, and Pastor Albert began his sermon about the peace that can only be found in Jesus Christ.

A peace Mags desperately needed.

Chapter Twenty-Four

When Timothy awoke that morning, he had his day all planned out. Chores, a trip to town to retrieve the boys, including Ozias, who would help clear rocks, and Mags, who planned to pick gooseberries. It was a plan no different from many days if he didn't count the bonus of getting to spend time with Magnolia Davenport.

But one thing Timothy hadn't planned was an encounter with a trapped skunk.

He first stopped to retrieve Little Hans, Hosea, Gus, and Ozias, who lived on the edge of town, before Simon and Sherman at the parsonage. Timothy then parked his wagon in front of the bakery.

Why was his heart racing faster than it ought? Probably because he'd been rushing around today in anticipation of preparing the field for rock-picking. Couldn't have anything to do with the fact that he looked forward to seeing a certain blonde woman. Could it?

The boys were talking some nonsense about whose pa had caught the biggest fish. As the conversation progressed, so did the size of the fish.

"You ain't seen nothing like the one my pa caught," bragged Gus.

"Pfft. Our pa is an expert fisherman, isn't he, Sherm?" Simon nudged his brother.

"Yeah, the best."

By Timothy's way of figuring, if Simon and Sherman were anything like Albert, it was pure exaggeration on their parts. Albert always thought he'd caught the largest fish God had ever made when he and Timothy were young'uns. In truth, Albert was only a fisher of men and had no hope of ever being considered a decent fisherman.

Hosea's hands took to flying with his signed words. "My pa caught a forty-inch trout."

The boys all laughed, and Simon shook his head and signed, "Are you sure about that, Hosea?"

"Sure as I can be."

"Hosea likes to brag a trifle about his pa," said Little Hans. "No one can catch fish like mine can. Nice, big old salmon, bigger than that forty-inch trout."

"You all are full of bananas," countered Ozias. "We live by the river, and all we do is fish. My pa caught the biggest burbot you ever did see. A whole twenty-two pounds and then some. That old cod fed us for days."

Sherman chuckled. "For days? I doubt it, Ozias. The way we've seen you eat when you've helped us on Uncle Timothy's farm tells me you probably ate that whole cod in one bite."

"Not so. I ain't that hungry."

But Timothy knew better. Ozias's family had finally accepted regular donations from the churchfolk, albeit reluctantly. Agnew would start his temporary job in a few days, and Timothy was grateful the man had softened to the help. His foot was healing, and Albert had been to the place the family squatted twice. Agnew still hadn't come to church, but he was less irritated that his wife and young'uns did.

God was moving in the lives of Ozias's family.

Timothy climbed from the wagon just as Mags exited the bakery. If he were honest, he would admit that the woman stole his breath. But he'd keep that tidbit of information to himself. No sense anyone thinking he was a romantic sort because he wasn't. As much as he was growing fond of her, he had his hands full with the farm. Not that she would ever entertain the prospect of courtship, as he doubted her feelings toward him were mutual, and he didn't know where she stood faithwise.

"Hello, Mags." He extended his elbow and escorted her to the wagon.

"Good morning, Timothy," she said with a smile. A smile that did something strange to his insides. But alas, lest he stand there looking like a fool, he averted his attention to the boys in the back of the wagon.

"Hope you don't mind some rambunctious young'uns."

"Oh, I don't mind at all. I helped raise my young cousins for two years."

Timothy assisted her into the wagon. "I'm sure your aunt appreciated that."

A melancholy expression crossed her face, but Mags said nothing. The more he came to know about her, the more Timothy surmised her childhood hadn't been a happy one.

"Hello, Miss Mags," the boys greeted.

"Hello, boys. It's good to see you all." She waved at them before settling onto the buckboard.

"And Goose came with us," Gus said, wrapping his arm around the dog. Of all the boys, Gus took to her the most. "She's a good old dog, aren't you, Goose?"

Mags turned around in her seat to face the boys. "I am curious. How did she get her name?"

Little Hans planted his round face between Timothy and Mags and pointed a thumb at his chest. "I would be the one responsible for that. When I was just a little boy, I thought she was a goose at first because she's white."

"And because your eyesight is poor," Sherman claimed.

"It is not," argued Little Hans.

"Yeah, before you know it, you'll be wearing old man spectacles like Uncle Timothy."

At Sherman's words, Timothy cringed. "Now, now, boys, that's enough about my spectacles."

"Yes, sir, but how come you don't wear them much?" asked Gus.

"I wear them plenty." By Timothy's way of figuring, by wearing them at home, whenever he went to his parents' house, and now at church, that was a copious enough amount of time.

Simon chose that moment to speak again. "My pa says now that you're wearing them at church, you oughta be seeing a whole lot better."

Sounded like Albert. Always the bossy sort.

"Ma says you wore them for exactly five minutes," countered Gus.

Sounded like Rubes. Always being nosy about other folks' business. "It was more than five minutes."

This time, Hosea leaned forward and signed, "My ma says it's because you're embarrassed."

Timothy shook his head.

"Why would you be embarrassed?" asked Mags.

Not her, too. "It's not that I'm embarrassed, I just figure they're unnecessary, and, well, I'm a little young for them."

Dare he look to see Mags's expression? He cast a furtive glance her way. She had angled her head to one side and was chewing on her lip. Did she believe his flimsy excuse? He didn't need those spectacles. Not really. Even now, he drove along the road just fine without requiring an extra set of eyes.

"There's nothing wrong with spectacles," she finally said. "Benjamin Franklin and Abraham Lincoln both wore them."

"Yes, but they're slightly older than I am."

"I think it makes one appear intelligent."

Timothy arched an eyebrow. "You do?"

"Yes, I do. As though one is book-learned."

"Hmm." Her words gave him pause. Did she appreciate menfolk who looked book-learned? Mags was an intelligent woman. Perhaps he ought to give heed to her words.

She shrugged. "If the eyeglasses assist you in clearing your vision, why not wear them?"

Thankfully, the boys were carrying on their own conversation and had discarded the topic of his spectacles. But Mags was still regarding him. "I just find them cumbersome, is all."

"Anything new can be cumbersome. It takes time to become accustomed to them."

The words slipped from his mouth before he could stop them. "Don't you think only elderly fellows wear eyeglasses?"

"Not always. In Chicago, even some children have to wear them. It's not something just for old folks."

"Even young boys?"

"Sure. Young girls as well, although I've seen boys wear them more often. Men your age, too."

He'd have to ponder her words in detail later. If she didn't mind how he looked wearing them, maybe the spectacles wouldn't be so bad after all.

They continued to the farm, and every now and again, Timothy stole glances at Mags. She seemed to be enjoying herself, riding on the buckboard and chatting with the boys.

"I really must learn sign language," she said.

"Oh, I can show you some of the sign language." Sherman leaned forward on his knees and propped his arms on the back of the buckboard. "This is how you say Simon's name in sign language." He took his index finger and pointed it at the side of his head near his ear, and turned it around in several circles. Then he placed his fully splayed hand in front of his head and added two forward bounces, fingers extended. All of the boys started laughing.

"That's Simon's name in sign language?" Mags asked.

"Don't listen to a thing they tell you," Timothy told her.

Ozias leaned forward as well and mimicked Sherman's signs. "Wow, now I know sign language."

"That's not Simon in sign language," grunted Little Hans.

"Then what is it?"

"It's how you say crazy great-grandfather."

The boys all started laughing, joined by Mags's sweet laugh. He turned to her. "I'd be happy to teach you some signs, or maybe Becky or Carrie. They're a little more accurate than the boys."

They reached the farm minutes later. Fortunately, the place where Mags would be picking gooseberries was near where the boys would be assisting him as he picked rock in preparation for adding fertile planting ground for more crops. He had never seen as many rocks as those that littered the Idaho terrain.

The boys unloaded, investigated the area as they always did, looking for snail shells or arrowheads before they began working. Goose started running around in circles and barking.

"What is it, Goose?" Simon asked.

"Look, Uncle Timothy! It has a jar on its head!"

"Is he going to be all right?"

Hosea's hands flew with the next question, asking if they should help it so it didn't suffocate.

Timothy wandered over to where the boys were to see what all the commotion was about. Then he saw it. A skunk with a jar on its head.

"Do you think it would spray us?"

"How do you think that happened?"

"Aren't skunks nocturnal?"

Gus edged closer. "He's so cute. Do you think my parents will let me have a pet skunk?"

Timothy may not have answered any of the other questions, but he did have an answer for Gus. "I doubt your parents will allow you to have a skunk for a pet."

The animal wiggled its head from side to side. "How are we going to free it?" asked Mags.

Timothy was already concocting plans to help the animal, but her concern urged him all the more to be a hero in her eyes. Even if doing so could prove smelly. "I'm not sure as I've never dealt with skunks before. Maybe I could get some oil, slick its fur, and it could slide its head from the jar that way."

Hosea tapped him on the arm and signed that he could fetch some oil. Timothy signed thank you and sent Hosea on his way to the house while Timothy continued to devise a plan. "One thing I do want is for everyone to stand back."

"Yes, children, let's stay right over here." Mags pointed to a safe distance away. "Simon, can you please keep a hold on Goose?"

Little Hans peered up at Mags. "Why does he have that on his head?"

"He was probably looking for food, and it was an accident," she explained.

Timothy noticed her kind and calm explanation. His nieces and nephews already adored Mags.

Hosea bounded toward them with the oil in his hand, and the questions started all over again.

"How are you going to catch it, Uncle Timothy?"

"Do you think it will hold still for you?"

Timothy hadn't really thought about that.

"We could block it so it doesn't escape," suggested Ozias.

"I'm not blocking it," said Sherman. "Have you smelled what happens when a skunk gets mad?"

Little Hans's forehead knitted. "He shouldn't get mad since you're helping him. Right, Uncle Timothy? He should be grateful. That's what my pa says. To be grateful when someone helps you."

"Yes, and your pa is right, but this is a wild animal. He may not know we're trying to help him."

Timothy dodged after the skunk, caught it, and gently held it in one arm. "It's okay," he said, hoping his voice sounded soothing to the animal. He smoothed the oil on the skunk's neck. The skunk watched him through the glass jar with beady eyes. So far, so good.

"All right now, I'm going to try to tug off the jar." Timothy attempted to do just that to no avail. It was still very much stuck on the skunk's head.

Goose barked again and stood on her hind legs. "Make sure you keep Goose over there. I don't need the skunk feeling threatened."

"And then he'll let out a big pewy," said Little Hans.

Think, Timothy, think. How else could he rectify the situation? Finally, a thought came to him. "Will one of you boys grab the hoe over by the barn?"

Sherman sped to the barn and returned a few seconds later. He handed the hoe to Timothy.

"I still want everybody to stand back, but I'm going to attempt to hold the glass jar down with the hoe and hopefully the skunk will pluck his own head from it in an attempt to get away."

"He's so cute and fuzzy," said Gus.

A glint shone in Simon's eyes. "We could play a trick on Carrie, Becky, Polly, and Pansy."

The boys chuckled.

"You'll do no such thing," reprimanded Mags.

"Aw shucks, Miss Mags. It was just a joke," said Sherman.

Timothy tamped the hoe onto the end of the jar and held it still. The skunk writhed and wiggled about.

"Come on, free yourself." Timothy hoped his plan would work. Prayed his plan would work. He tossed a quick glance at Mags and puffed out his chest. If anyone could save the day, it would be Timothy Tyler Shepherdson. "Please don't spray me," he muttered. He'd heard the horror stories of people getting sprayed by skunks and didn't want to be added to their ranks.

After what seemed like an eternity, the skunk broke free. The children clapped, and for a second, Timothy thought I would be well. Until...

Goose broke free from Simon's grasp and lunged toward the skunk. "No, Goose!"

The skunk hissed and stomped. Goose remained undeterred.

Timothy backed up just as the skunk lifted its tail, and a stream of something wet collided with Timothy's leg. It released a foul mist before running off.

"Aww, pew," said one of the boys.

"Did it just spray you, Uncle Timothy?" asked Ozias. Timothy didn't need the wind to change course to know the answer to that question. The pungent odor filled his nostrils.

No, today had not turned out one bit like he anticipated.

Timothy could definitively say he'd never been sprayed before today. While Goose got the brunt of it, Timothy's legs and feet had been sprayed by the fine mist—an unrelenting and fetid mist. He gagged and his eyes watered, and nausea briefly overcame him. His pant legs had been saturated, as had his boots. The skunk ran off, and Goose started to whine. Timothy groaned when he saw his precious dog with her singed whiskers as she batted at her snout.

The boys began to speak all at once.

"Did you just get sprayed, Uncle Timothy?"

"Pew! How long will you smell like that?"

"Is Goose okay?"

"Do you think the skunk will come back and spray us?"

"The Lieutenant had a pet skunk, leastways that's what he said."

"You're fibbing, Gus. The Lieutenant never had a pet skunk."

"Oh, yes, he did. It was his favorite pet until Miss Greta made him get rid of it."

One started laughing, and they all followed suit. Mags tiptoed toward him. "Are you all right?"

"Not really."

She covered her mouth with her hand, and Timothy wondered how long he could hold his own breath.

Mags watched as Timothy brushed off his lower legs as if that would rid the material of the obnoxious odor. "You might not want to do that because once it gets on your hands…"

"Uncle Timothy, let's have Goose get in the river, and we can wash her off." The boys kept their distance despite Goose attempting to garner their attention.

"Think I'll join them in the river." Timothy removed his socks and shoes. "I'll just kill two birds with one stone, as the saying goes, and wash my clothes and myself at the same time." He sat on the riverbank and called to Goose.

"We'll jump in and help wash her."

Soon, all of the boys, Timothy, and Goose were in the river water, although there was clearly more splashing than washing, and the boys maintained a safe distance from Timothy and Goose.

"We once had a skunk spray one of the other tenants in the apartment where I lived with one of my aunts," mentioned Mags. "I have an idea of how we could eliminate some of the smell.

"Washing off will do the trick just fine. I don't need any fancy schmancy remedies."

She was about to protest when he continued. "Besides. No sense in wasting daylight. I need to get washed off and de-skunked by the noonday meal."

They had just eaten breakfast, and Timothy was already thinking about the noonday meal?

Timothy signed while simultaneously speaking, asking if Hosea would go to the house for a bar of soap. The boy nodded and bolted to the house. The rest of the boys remained in the river, scrubbing a rambunctious Goose with their hands.

When Hosea returned with the bar of soap, he handed it to Timothy and jumped back into the river. Before long, any attempts to bathe Goose soon turned into a game of playing fetch with the boys, splashing around, laughing, and enjoying themselves on the hot summer day.

Mags was not a proficient swimmer, so she hoped the boys wouldn't require rescuing. She kept a watchful eye on them, however. "Gus, please don't get too daring." The boy managed some sort of acrobatic maneuver beneath the water.

He stood up. "Don't worry about me none, Miss Mags. I'm an expert swimmer."

Boys were such odd creatures. No rock picking would get done today, but at least she would achieve her goal of securing gooseberries. While keeping one eye on the boys and one eye on her bucket, she plucked the berries from the bushes. Timothy continued to furiously scrub his pant legs and feet with the soap.

"If that doesn't work..."

"I know, I know," replied Timothy, slight agitation in his voice, "tomato juice, right?"

"Yes, you could try tomato juice, especially for Goose. But what I was going to say is apple cider vinegar works wonders."

"Unfortunately, I don't have tomato juice or apple cider vinegar in the house."

Sherman stopped scrubbing Goose. "One of us could ride over to Grandma's house. She always has apple cider vinegar."

Mags took a step closer to the river. "You might consider it, as it effectively aided that poor man who was sprayed by the skunk in the tenements."

Timothy seemed to consider her proposition.

With a hat shielding his eyes, she couldn't entirely read his expression.

Poor man. She could smell the rank stench a mile away. "I recommend that when the boys finish with Goose, one of them ride over to their grandma's house and fetch some apple cider vinegar and tomato juice."

Simon raised his hand. "I can. Once that sun and the breeze hit my clothes, I'll be dry faster than you can say *Uncle Timothy was sprayed*. Besides, you have only a few days to rid yourself of the smell before church."

"That's true," said Sherman. "Likely you'll have that whole pew to yourself come Sunday."

Mags snickered.

Timothy stood up and straightened his back. "I don't think this is going to be a problem one bit. By the time I'm done with the soap, this odor should be gone by tomorrow."

Should Mags tell him the truth? "You should probably know that the smell can last three to four days."

Timothy scowled. "That's for folks who don't set out to remove the odor right away. There are other options to consider. Besides, while I appreciate your suggestion, it sounds like a heap of flummadiddle to me. I'm not interested in smelling like vinegar or tomato juice. But I do think tomato juice is a good idea for Goose in case we can't get the smell out of her fur."

Little Hans waded through the water but kept a safe distance from Timothy. He cocked his head to one side. "Uncle Timothy, what if we can't get the smell out of you?"

Unfortunately, the smell had not dissipated after he used the soap. Simon rode over to Ma's house for some tomato juice and apple cider vinegar. When he returned, Timothy had filled a bucket with water and tomato juice, and the boys helped him scrub Goose once more. Unfortunately, by the time they were finished, Goose's beautiful white fur was tinged pink. He'd never anticipated owning a pink dog.

Few rocks were picked that day, but Mags seemed satisfied with the number of gooseberries she procured from the bushes. He returned everyone to their homes, and Mags sat as far away as possible on the edge of the buckboard. Good thing the skunk only sprayed his lower legs and feet.

He left the pink Goose at home.

Only a few days until church. If he didn't rid himself of the smell, Sherman would be correct. He'd have the entire pew to himself. Or maybe even be banned from the church altogether.

"Well, Goose, looks like we're both sleeping on the porch tonight."

Goose covered her face with her paws and whined as if she understood she wouldn't be sleeping in her comfortable bed by the fireplace. Timothy brought out of a bedroll and got comfortable beneath the stars. He hated to admit it, but maybe, just maybe, he'd have to use that apple cider vinegar.

Chapter Twenty-Five

"Pew." Albert scrunched his nose and waved his hand in front of his face. "Is that you, Timothy?"

"You know it's me," grumbled Timothy. "Who else recently got sprayed by a skunk?"

Albert chuckled. "Wish I could have been there. I hear the tomato juice turned Goose pink."

"It did." Timothy peered behind him. Folks meandered around the churchyard. Would Albert even let him in for services, considering how he smelled?

"Did you use the apple cider vinegar Mags suggested?"

"How'd you know about that? Of course. Simon and Sherman."

Albert shrugged. "It's part of being a parent to make sure you communicate about the events of your children's day. So. Did you take her advice?"

"I did. Just yesterday, in fact."

"Grew desperate, did you?"

"Would you like to smell like vinegar?"

Albert chuckled. "Look at it this way, little brother. You now smell like skunk *and* vinegar. Might be a repellent for some of those ladies who've set their cap for you."

That was the best thing he'd heard all morning. Wilhelmina, her husband, Hubert, and two other couples approached. "Mind if I go on in and sit a spell?"

Albert's smirk reminded Timothy of the permanent simper Albert had pasted on his face during their growing-up years. A petulant expression he'd well refined. His brother cleared his throat. "All are welcome in God's house, but you might want to sit on the far edge of one of our pews. The far edge against the wall."

Timothy strolled through the aisle. Sheriff Zembrodt and his wife nodded, and his little daughter tapped her mother on the arm. "What's that smell, Mama?"

Thankfully, no one in his family distanced themselves from Timothy. He was pleasantly surprised when Mags perched between him and Ma. It was good to see her in church again. The Lord was certainly answering prayers. "Hello, Mags."

"Hello, Timothy." She lowered her voice and inclined toward him. He caught a pleasing whiff of lavender. "Smells like you used the apple cider vinegar."

"Is it that obvious?"

Her mouth curved into a smile. "Yes, but it's better than the rancid odor of skunk."

Timothy couldn't argue with her about that. He held her gaze a moment longer before focusing his attention on Albert, who'd announced the first hymn.

After announcements, hymns, and the offering, Albert took his place behind the lectern for the sermon. Timothy adjusted his glasses on his nose. He hoped Albert was finished with his series on pride.

"Ladies and gentlemen, thank you for attending on this beautiful summer day. Today, I'm going to preach about recognizing our need for a Savior."

Albert, as he always did, captured the congregants' attention with his powerful sermons. Today was no exception, and Timothy found himself once again in awe of what his Savior had done for Him and filled with gratitude for Jesus' work on the cross. When he was eight, he'd dedicated his life to Christ and hadn't looked back. But never would he take the gift of eternal life for granted.

He glanced at Mags. Tears slid silently down her cheeks. Ma reached over and clasped her hand. Timothy surmised Mags suffered a painful past. Had something Albert said reminded her of what she'd endured. Or...

Could it be that the Lord was drawing her to Him? Emotion welled in his own throat. *Lord, please draw Mags to You. Please let her see her need for her Savior. Heal her pain. Comfort her.*

Albert concluded the sermon and wished everyone a blessed day. Folks filed out of the church. Miss Greta played the final strains on the piano, and Albert took his place at the door to bid the congregants farewell. Children hurried outside to play before their parents took them home.

Mags had closed her eyes. The tears continued to fall, and Ma squeezed her hand. Should Timothy stay? Help Ma comfort Mags?

Mags opened her eyes and stared straight ahead at the wooden cross near the lectern. "It's time," she whispered. "I think I want Jesus to be my Savior."

Timothy feared that if he so much as breathed, it would ruin the moment. He stood and quietly slithered from his seat, a joy so profound emerging in his chest. When he reached the back of the church, he turned to see Ma's and Mags's heads bowed in prayer.

After church, Mrs. Shepherdson invited Mags to a noonday meal at the Shepherdson house. She'd mentioned that today was a day for celebration.

And now, as Mags prepared to retire for the night in her tiny room in the bakery, she opened her brand-new Bible, gifted to her by Mr. and Mrs. Shepherdson. Tabitha had opened the mercantile special just for them.

She thumbed through the pages, the words leaping up at her. She was His now. Forever in His grasp. Mags unfolded the sheet of paper where Mrs. Shepherdson had written down a variety of verses, including the one she'd spoken of in Habakkuk and one reminding Mags that nothing could separate her from the love of God.

But the one she really wanted to read was the one found in the Psalms. The one Cassius had told her that day he'd shared with her about what happened to Ma. She scanned the verses until she came to Psalm 139:14.

"I will praise thee; for I am fearfully and wonderfully made: marvellous are thy works; and that my soul knoweth right well."

It didn't matter that a cruel man she'd never met fathered her. That her aunts had rejected her. That Phoebe's grandmother refused to take her in after Ma and Pa died.

She was fearfully and wonderfully made. Fearfully and wonderfully made by a God who loved her so much, He even sent His Son to die for her.

A ball of emotion clogged her throat, and the blinding tears fell freely.

She was someone to God. Someone so very important.

Chapter Twenty-Six

Timothy tried to slip past the table where Miss Greta sat, handing out envelopes with the gingham ties.

"Timothy Tyler Shepherdson," she said, her voice sounding more like a mother scolding a young child than a friend of the family.

"Yes?"

"You carry yourself back here and choose an envelope."

So much for ambling toward the food choices and getting his fill on cookies and pastries before the ball started.

"Yes, ma'am."

"Before you choose, I must say I'm grateful that noisome stench from the skunk has all but subsided from your person. When you entered the church last Sunday, I caught a whiff of you clear up from where I was plinking on the piano keys."

"My apologies, Miss Greta."

"Did you use apple cider vinegar? Everyone knows that's the best remedy."

It had taken Timothy a while to agree to Mags's suggestion. "Yes, I did."

Miss Greta arched an eyebrow, a look of skepticism on her face. She drummed on the table with a long, pointy fingernail.

"All right. Yes, I did use the apple cider vinegar, but not right away."

"That's what I suspected. You're just fortunate the odor has waned. I want nothing to ruin the Gingham Ball. Now then, make your choice."

He scanned the meager offerings of remaining envelopes. Would he accidentally choose Alma? Someone worse? At least Mary Lou was his friend, but he didn't want to give her any ideas.

Timothy closed his eyes and tapped the table, feeling for an envelope.

"But goodness, Timothy! Open your eyes and choose an envelope."

"Can you choose one for me?" That way, the outcome wouldn't be his fault, he reasoned.

"No, I cannot choose one for you. That is against the rules."

Timothy closed his eyes again and randomly chose an envelope.

"There now. Have a pleasant time at the ball."

He scuttled away to the food table, where snickerdoodles and lemon cakes called his name loud and clear.

And a rolled jelly cake. That particularly called his name. He could still recall the taste of the last one he'd eaten.

His heart sank. Of course, Alma would be here if she were the one who'd make the rolled jelly cake.

Timothy tucked the envelope in his shirt pocket and reached for a slice, then looked up to see a barrage of young women standing facing him.

"Hello, Timothy!" Alma fluttered her lashes.

"Uh, hello."

Soon, the other women barraged him with their questions.

"Where's your envelope?"
"Who did you choose?"
"Was it me?"
"Did you just now arrive?"

He stared at the women. One in blue, one in red, one in green, and Alma dressed in yellow gingham.

Lord, reckon this is an odd request, but could I have received a faulty envelope with no gingham tie at all?

The cost of a ticket was well worth the food offerings. He couldn't risk withering away. He needed his food, even if supper followed dancing.

Mary Lou rubbed her palms together. "Timothy? Might you open the envelope?"

Four pairs of eyes peered at him with expectation. "I was going to open it in a few minutes."

"Please, might you open it now?" He wondered if the optician would diagnose her with an eye condition with the way Alma's lashes blinked so rapidly.

"Yes, please," pleaded a woman named Artemisia.

Timothy wanted to reassure the women that he would, in fact, unseal the envelope in due time in private. But the way they were lurking about watching him, he knew they wouldn't leave until he revealed whose dress matched his tie. He mentally pondered the women's dresses. Mary Lou pressed the pleats of her skirt. "I hope it's green."

"I hope it's yellow," said Alma, her higher-pitched voice drowning out the others.

What color of tie was hidden in his envelope? Would he be relegated to dancing with Alma the entire evening and then sharing the supper meal with her? Not that she was abhorrent, but the woman was an overly dramatic and flirtatious flibbertigibbet.

The two other women, Artemisia and Helen, had followed him around at the church potluck a month ago. They giggled and prattled on like church bells about nonsense while seeking his attention. He'd already said hello to them and bid them a good day. He figured Mary Lou was just waiting for that moment when he asked her for her hand in courtship, although once again, he could never imagine her as anything more than a sister.

There were no good choices, although if he had to pick one, he'd pick Mary Lou.

Miss Greta sashayed over to where they stood. "Who did Timothy choose?"

Alma pooched her bottom lip. "He hasn't chosen anyone yet."

Miss Greta tapped her foot. "Timothy?" Her reprimand could likely be heard all the way to the mercantile.

Timothy could go for the next fifteen years not knowing who his dance partner would be. Miss Greta sent him one last scolding glower before returning to her post at the table.

He reluctantly set down the rolled jelly cake.

Slowly, perhaps slower than he'd ever moved in his entire life, Timothy tore at the corner of the envelope. The women merged closer. His big, awkward fingers ripped another section before tearing the remaining portion. He closed his eyes and withdrew the tie when he heard one of the women gasp. Slowly, ever so slowly, he squinted, then opened one eye fully as he examined the tie in his hand.

"It's lavender," cried Alma. Her bottom lip trembled, and her hand flew to her heart. "I don't see anyone here with lavender."

Mary Lou scanned the immediate area. "Perhaps it's an error.

Perhaps someone should tell Miss Greta so Timothy can choose another envelope."

The four women frantically surveyed the room that had begun to fill with dance-goers. Looking for a lavender gingham dress, perhaps? If Timothy were honest, he was too. What if it was an elderly widow?

Alma's voice wavered. "This is such a travesty."

"I believe I know what happened," said Mary Lou. "I think that a married couple's tie was put in the wrong envelope."

Artemisia, a redhead with numerous freckles, shook her head. "That can't be. It's not possible because the married couples purposely matched their dresses and ties with no envelopes necessary."

"There has to be some mistake," said Helen, a brunette who'd once brought a pot roast to Timothy just before church started. "I see other colors, but I don't see lavender anywhere."

When Timothy perused the room, he saw several other gingham colors, including pink, blue, and white, but no lavender.

Alma held a gloved hand to her mouth. "This is dreadful, positively dreadful."

"I think someone played a cruel joke,"

Alma fiddled around in her reticle and produced a pink handkerchief. "Oh! And to think I waited all year for this." She dabbed at her eyes.

The brunette patted her on the back. "Don't take it so hard. There's always next year."

Mary Lou put an arm around Alma. "It will be interesting to see whose ties match our dresses."

"But it won't be Timothy," moaned Alma.

"You need to calm yourself, Alma. You're causing a scene," Mary Lou whispered.

Timothy wasn't sure what to say, but this was obviously a predicament for the women.

Alma tapped on Mary Lou's arm. "Oh, dear. I think I see the matching dress."

The other women turned in the direction she pointed, and Timothy followed their gazes. He caught a flash of purple gingham.

"It's Magnolia Davenport who matches." Alma's voice trembled, and she began to sob before Mary Lou comforted her and drew her aside. The largest exhale ever escaped Timothy's lips.

Magnolia Davenport's dress matched his tie?

Thank You, Lord!

He watched as Mags spoke with Maribel, Reverend Marshall's wife.

Would she notice that she would be his dancing partner?

Mags had almost been late to the Gingham Ball. She'd barely finished her lavender gingham dress on time and had completed the final stitches just moments before it was time to attend. Thankfully, the Lieutenant and Miss Greta had stopped by to retrieve the rolled jelly cake and cookies she donated. If she had to remember to take those as well, she feared she might have never made it to The Horizon Hotel.

Her hair, of course, had not cooperated, and she ultimately fashioned it into a haphazard chignon. She really had no desire to attend the ball. No desire to dance with some unknown man whose tie matched her dress.

It wasn't that she didn't love to be around people, because she did. It wasn't that she felt awkward and out of place in a new town because she'd discovered that this was the place she belonged, and she couldn't wait to have Phoebe and the baby join her.

So, why the hesitation?

Mags attempted to argue her way out of it due to the cost of a ticket. Miss Greta brushed her concern aside. "An anonymous donor already paid for it." But the way Miss Greta's eyes darted about, Mags wondered if she might be the "anonymous donor". How then could Mags decline when the woman had been so generous?

Now here she was, standing outside The Horizon Hotel, working up the nerve to enter. Maribel, a kindly elderly woman married to Pastor Albert's predecessor, arrived at the front door at the same time with Reverend Marshall pushing her in her wheelchair and offering to make a grand entrance with her.

There was no way Mags could refuse now. She walked through the door, and she and Maribel chatted while Reverend Marshall spoke to Bjorn, the barber. Mags scanned the festively decorated room. Miss Greta handed out envelopes, Timothy stood munching on a cookie at the dessert table, and Mary Lou and Alma moseyed her way.

"Congratulations, Mags." Alma dabbed at her eyes with a handkerchief.

"Yes, you won," added Mary Lou.

"I won?" What had she won?

"Might you consider trading dresses?"

Mary Lou glanced up at the ceiling and shook her head. "Alma, you can't trade dresses with Mags because you aren't the same size."

"Why would you want to trade dresses? Yours is lovely." Alma's yellow gingham dress boasted poofy leg-o'-mutton sleeves and a cinched waist with an oversized bow. Mags's dress paled in comparison.

"It would be even more lovely if it were the one that matched Timothy's tie." The tone of Alma's voice was akin to a histrionic whimper. "How shall I ever recover?" She blinked rapidly and wrapped her arms around herself.

Alma was a highly exaggerated woman. Mags had known women like her in Chicago—such melodramatic connoisseurs belonged in the theater. It was then that Alma's words registered.

"Did you say that my dress matches Timothy's tie?"

"Yes. I can't bear it. It's so dismal. I have been waiting all year for the Gingham Ball for a chance to dance with Timothy, then dine with him at supper. All my dreams are for naught." Alma's lower lip quivered, and she held a splayed hand to her forehead. "This could quite possibly be the worst day of my entire life."

Mary Lou pressed her lips together and patted Alma on the back. "Now, now, Alma. Don't take it so hard. As I previously mentioned, there's always next year."

Alma's expression abruptly brightened, and her eyes widened. She dropped her hand, and enthusiasm transformed her face. "

Or, maybe, Mags, you could ask Timothy if it would be all right if I were the one who danced with him and joined him for supper. Or you could even just trade. I'm sure the man whose tie matches my dress is a congenial fellow."

It certainly meant a lot for Alma to dance with Timothy. Mags had steadily been growing fond of him herself, but if it meant this much, perhaps she could acquiesce. "I suppose if Timothy says it's all right..."

"Hello, Mags. It appears your dress matches my tie."

Mags's heart thumped wildly in her chest. She met his gaze, and all else faded into the background. "Yes, it does appear that way."

"Timothy, if you're amenable, Mags and I could trade partners."

"I'm sorry, Alma, but we must stay with the rules. You know what a stickler Miss Greta can be. She wouldn't condone anything less than us following the proper Gingham Ball directives." Timothy offered his elbow, and Mags slipped her hand through it. "Shall we?" he asked.

Just as if they were attending a royal ball that Mags had read about in books.

Down a short hall and to the right, a prepared room with plenty of room to dance was decorated with festive yellow and green crepe paper streamers hanging from the ceiling and wound around the staircase leading to the upper floor. A circular bench in the center offered folks a rest from the merriment if they so chose. Wallpaper, with purple, turquoise, blue, and green flowers, hung on the walls, and in the corner, a table accommodated pitchers of punch and glasses. An elegant chandelier hung from the ceiling, and an oak grandfather clock stood as a sentinel between two radius windows. Band instruments lined a makeshift stage, and the aroma of cinnamon filled the air.

It was unlike anything Mags had ever seen. And she'd seen some fancy places in Chicago.

Timothy poured a glass of punch for each of them. My, but if he didn't look dapper tonight in his crisp white shirt, blue jeans, and his wire-rimmed spectacles. His dark hair curled at the ends, and he'd recently shaved.

Mags's heart fluttered with several extra beats. "Thank you for the punch." She took a sip and noticed the room filling with familiar faces. "I feel sorry for Alma. She's quite disappointed your tie wasn't yellow."

"She might be disappointed, but I'm rather relieved." Timothy smiled at her, and her knees weakened. "You look beautiful tonight, Mags."

"So do you. Handsome, that is."

"I wasn't going to wear my spectacles."

"I'm glad you did."

He chuckled. "Helps me see much better."

The Lieutenant and Wilhelmina's husband, Hubert, carried a rectangular table and placed it against a vacant wall. Mrs. Shepherdson, Miss Greta, Wilhelmina, and Lucy placed decadent treats on it.

"I wonder if they have any rolled jelly cake. I ate some before the festivities started. It might be my new favorite dessert. I had to stop before I slipped into gluttony."

"Rolled jelly cake?" His compliment meant more to Mags than he could possibly know. She was about to say thank you when he continued.

"Reckon Alma may not be able to cook a lot of things, but she does make a delicious rolled jelly cake."

"Oh." Should she reveal the real baker of the cakes? "I have some rolled jelly cake at my bakery."

"And you didn't tell me?" A teasing glint lit his eyes.

"I had to provide some for the ball."

"You provided the rolled jelly cake and not Alma?"

"Alma may have brought some desserts as well, but I made the jelly cake the women just delivered to the table."

Timothy's eyes widened. "You don't say?" A look of admiration lit his face, warming her heart.

"Care to dance?"

It started with waltzes, and three dances later, the band's tempo increased for a polka. Once the band took an intermission, Mags and Timothy visited the dessert table.

A mother and her daughter of about sixteen, drew Mags's attention. "Ma, could you help me arrange my hair?"

The mother assisted her daughter, and something inside Mags's heart pinched. Unexpected emotion swelled in her lungs, and tears burned her eyes. If Ma were here at the Gingham Ball, she'd be assisting Mags with her hair. They would laugh together and remark about the exquisitely decorated ballroom. They'd join arms and sashay to their respective partners. Pa would take Ma in his arms while they danced, and Timothy would twirl Mags around in time with the music. Phoebe and Larry would join the dance floor soon after.

But such was never to be. Only a fanciful dream that would never come to fruition.

Mags reached for the table as her legs threatened to fold. "I need some fresh air."

Timothy led her outside to the bench just kitty- corner of the hotel. Folks milled about, taking a reprieve from the Gingham Ball.

"Is everything all right?"

The pain of loss struck anew. "Yes. I apologize. I saw a mother assisting her daughter, and it made me think of my own ma and how much I miss her." Before she knew it, she was sharing with him all about her parents and Phoebe. How she'd longed to be raised by Phoebe's grandmother so they wouldn't be separated, but instead had been begrudgingly taken in by her aunts. Until the day she was on her own and expected to carve a life for herself.

Her words carried sorrow like a wound. Timothy figured he had taken for granted the life God had given him. He hadn't suffered the pain Mags revealed had been an integral part of her life. He reached for her hand. "I'm so sorry, Mags."

"I was never good enough for anyone after my parents died." Grief punctuated her every word.

While Timothy usually spoke without giving his words much thought, this time, he prayed that the Lord would give him the words. "Mags, you don't have to be perfect for Jesus to love you."

With her posture bent, she seemed much frailer than she was. She squeezed her eyes shut. "I know that. I know that now."

"My family cares deeply for you."

And I care deeply for you. His unspoken words were true.

"I'm sorry. I don't want to ruin the festivities."

"You're not ruining the festivities. I'm glad you shared that with me, Mags. It helps me to understand."

Timothy welcomed the crisp evening air, a reprieve from the hot temperatures of earlier. He would sit here as long as necessary. Several minutes later, Mags stirred, and Timothy offered his arm. "I think I hear supper being served. Would you like to go in?"

She stood, and they joined several other couples for stuffed beefsteak, potato bread, and Boston baked beans. The supper went well, and the smile soon returned to Mags's face. They discussed a myriad of topics from the bakery to his farm, from his nieces and nephews, to the skunk debacle.

Couples began to filter out of the hotel until they were the last ones there. Timothy surprised himself by wishing it had lasted longer, but he'd truly enjoyed her company. "May I escort you home?"

"Certainly."

They strolled the short distance to the bakery beneath the starry sky. "I had an enjoyable evening."

"I did too."

"And I'm really grateful my tie matched your dress and not Alma's."

Mags's sweet laughter rang through the quiet night. "Me, too. Although she has set her cap for you."

"Yes, well, Alma's fine, but she's not someone I would wish to court."

Silence hung between them for several moments before they said their goodbyes. And as Timothy stood on the boardwalk outside of the bakery, an unannounced thought entered his mind.

For the first time in his life, he might consider courtship.

Chapter Twenty-Seven

Timothy wouldn't consider himself to be a man with a case of the nerves. More of a relaxed sort unless he had reason to be apprehensive.

As was the case today. He tramped through tall weeds to the patch of hidden wildflowers he'd spied while tending to the crops two days ago. Careful not to injure the delicate stems, he picked a whole heap of purple, pink, yellow, and red flowers. As he stalked back through the house to find an old glass jar and fill it with water, his sister's bothersome voice rang in his ears. He'd been coerced into picking dandelions for Ma so she could make some jelly. He'd fervently disagreed with the task, saying that men didn't pick flowers. Rubes, of course, in her typical argumentative way, said, *"Someday you'll pick them for some girl you set your cap for."*

Ha. Well, while he wouldn't admit it, Rubes was correct. He *was* picking flowers for a girl he liked.

"Let's go to town, Goose. We have ourselves an important errand to tend to."

Goose didn't need convincing and happily trotted alongside his horse. Timothy carefully clutched the vase of flowers as he rode to town.

All the while, hoping, *praying* for a good outcome.

"She could say no, Goose."

Goose's tongue lolled.

"Or she could say yes."

Goose bobbed her head and yipped.

"Me, too. I prefer the latter. Now, just act all nonchalant like nothing is amiss." He tethered his horse and dismounted. With his free hand, he removed his hat, smoothed his wayward hair, and adjusted the irksome spectacles on his face.

He hoped no one else was in the bakery. While Timothy appreciated living in Horizon, some mighty nosy folks sniffed around for the scuttlebutt on any given day. He held his hand behind his back. No sense in letting Mags see the flowers before he'd had a chance to say what was on his mind.

Folks greeted him as he passed, and Miss Greta, meddling sort that she was, took an extra glance at him.

"You look suspicious, Timothy Tyler Shepherdson."

"Nope, not suspicious, Miss Greta. Just tending to some tasks."

"Hmm." She scrutinized him. "Why are you walking with a hand behind your back?"

"Comfortable that way."

Goose barked and placed his paws on Miss Greta's skirt. "Oh, yes, I couldn't forget about you, could I? It's a relief to see you're no longer pink." The woman patted Goose on the head, and the dog wagged her tail.

Good old Goose. Always one to save the day.

"Well, I'd like to stay and fritter away the time, but I have a mound of chores to do." She bid him goodbye, and relief flooded Timothy. He exhaled, offered another prayer, then stalked up to the bakery window. He pressed his nose against the glass and peered inside. His irritating spectacles fogged up, obscuring his vision. Timothy pulled the spectacles away, allowing the moisture to subside, then checked again to see if anyone patronized the bakery.

Thankfully, it was void of customers.

He spied Mags behind the counter rolling out some dough. Was she making a pie? Cinnamon rolls? Could he have timed this more perfectly?

At that moment, she lifted her gaze and caught his eye. He waved, and she waved back.

If she didn't say yes, he might just die an early death right there in the middle of the bakery.

You sound like a noodlehead, he admonished himself. He stood up straight. Dogs weren't allowed in the bakery, but he needed the moral support and the fortitude. Hopefully, Mags would understand.

He strolled inside, Goose on his heels.

"Hello, Mags."

"Good afternoon, Timothy. So nice to see you."

"Yes. Nice to see you, too—I mean—it's always nice to see you. Everyday. Well, not every day, because I don't see you every day, although I'd like to see you every day." What a dolt.

"I saw you peering into the window."

"Yes. That was me." This was not going well. Goose peered up at him. Was that pity in her eyes? "Mags?"

"Yes?"

"Might I ask a question?"

"Sure, and before you ask, yes, I'm making lemon raisin pie, and there will be plenty of extra."

"Much appreciated. I have another question." The words spilled out of his mouth so rapidly he hoped Mags understood his garbled dialogue. "Magnolia Davenport, would you do me the honor of courting me?"

Goose barked. "See? Goose agrees."

Mags laughed. "How can I argue with Goose? Yes, Timothy Shepherdson, I will court you."

"You will?" Before he could blabber another incoherent sentence, he set the flowers on the counter. "These are for you."

"They are beautiful. Thank you."

Timothy left the bakery that day with not only a lemon raisin pie, but also a realization he never expected to entertain—he was a courting man.

The days passed quickly, and Mags anticipated the day when Phoebe and her baby would arrive to live in Horizon. Yet, she hadn't received a letter from her sister in some time. Amidst the influx of customers, she penned a missive.

Dearest Phoebe,

I hope this finds you doing well. I haven't heard from you in some time, so I thought I would write to see how you fare. Has the baby been born yet? I am eager to meet my new niece or nephew. How is your health? How is your grandmother?

Mags paused and thought about Phoebe's grandmother. The woman hadn't taken kindly to her, but with the Lord's help, Mags aimed to forgive her. Would the woman be receptive to Phoebe moving to Horizon? Perhaps she could come too.

I have much to tell you. First, I decided to surrender my life to Christ. It wasn't so long ago that I couldn't comprehend why the Lord meant so much to you, Ma, and Pa. Now, after spending time in my brand-new Bible Timothy's mother purchased for me, listening intently to the church sermons, and asking a multitude of questions, I see things differently. It will be some time before I understand even a fraction of the ways of the Lord, but Pastor Albert says that while there are some things we'll never know this side of heaven, we are to always be students of His Word.

A month ago, I attended the Gingham Ball and danced with a man named Timothy Shepherdson. Needless to say, I fear I am losing my heart to him. He loves the Lord and his family, and is kind and thoughtful. He asked me to court him. We have gone for several strolls, a picnic, and have partaken in the noonday meal at Wilhelmina's.

Of course, I was hesitant at first, but after spending time in prayer, I believe Timothy may be the one God has planned for me. I can't wait for you to meet him. His family, too. I know they will welcome you as warmly as they have welcomed me.

As for the bakery, there is abundant business. Remember Ma's lemon raisin pie, rolled jelly cake, and sour cream cookies? Those have been my best-selling items.

Please write soon.

I love and miss you.

Your Sister Mags

Mags checked her image in the new oval mirror hanging on the wall in her room at the bakery. She chewed on her lip and pondered once again whether she was making the right decision. She'd never had a photograph taken before, and the thought caused a round of nervousness to flood her. Hands shaking slightly, Mags removed the hairpins, and her wavy blonde hair tumbled to her shoulders. She attempted once again to wind up her hair into the perfect coiffure and painstakingly fluffed the front portion. She glanced down at the image from the catalog showing a lovely woman with a Gibson girl hairdo. If only she could force her own locks to cooperate.

Heaving a sigh of irritation, she returned her brush to the crate that doubled as a makeshift dresser and pressed the wrinkles from her pink dress. Try as she might, she would not look like the elegant ladies she'd once envied in Chicago.

A glance at the clock warned that if she didn't hasten her steps, she would be late for the taking of the photograph. But indecision weighed heavily on her, and her steps stalled as she exited the apartment. Suddenly, her mouth went dry, and a wave of lightheadedness swirled around her. She gripped the nearby bench and stood for a moment, tilting her head back, her gaze fixed upward. *Lord, do I even belong in this photograph? Help me know if I should even attend.*

A few seconds later, Mags resumed traipsing down the boardwalk. A wagon rumbled nearby, and a dog barked. Mags inhaled a sharp breath, lifted the side of her skirt, and proceeded to her destination. She ought to be inside the bakery preparing bread or mixing a new batch of cookies. Was it even worth closing the bakery for something so frivolous?

Folks traveled up and down the street, laughing and smiling and carrying on about their day. Mags's chest tightened. She veered around to face the bakery, then did an about-face once again. The hesitancy caused her to vacillate between the two options three more times. Just as she was about to decide for certain that avoiding the appointment with the photographer was the best course of action, a familiar voice called out to her.

"Mags? Oh, there you are!"

Mae walked toward her, and Mags inwardly groaned, not because she didn't want to see her newfound friend, but because she felt so woefully inadequate at what Mae would likely convince her to do. "Hello, Mae." In her own ears, her voice shook, and she regretted that for one of the few times in her life, she wasn't brave, stouthearted, and willing to tackle whatever came her way.

"Are you coming to the photograph? Nearly everyone has gathered."

If only she were reassured and confident like Mae. If only she truly belonged in a picture with the Shepherdson family.

"I am actually reconsidering. I really do need to open the bakery and serve my customers."

Mae rested a hand on Mags's arm. "I understand. But we really would like you there."

Mags's throat burned, and she knew the threat of tears was forthcoming. Did they truly want her there, or were they just being kind? From what she knew of the Shepherdson family in her time in Horizon, it was the former. Her mind surely knew that, but to convince her heart was another thing altogether. "I appreciate that, Mae, but I am not a member of your family."

"You may soon be, what with courting Timothy."

The tears that shimmied in her eyes caused Mae's image to blur. Yes, Mags and Timothy were courting, and while courtship wasn't always a promise of an engagement followed by a marriage, she dared hope it would become a reality with the man she was growing to love.

Memories of her youth, when it had been expected that someone would care for her after her parents' death, entered Mags's mind. Hadn't she assumed that she would be cared for, fed, and sheltered by those related to Ma? At any time, Timothy could surely renege on their courtship. At any time, the Shepherdson family could decide she wasn't worth their time, just like her aunts and uncles had all those years ago.

But hadn't she learned that God was the Author of new beginnings?

The warring thoughts tugged at her, and she gulped past the lump in her throat. Mae stepped closer and reached her other hand toward Mags's other arm.

"Please tell me what's wrong."

"I just don't want to ruin this special day for your family."

"Oh, Mags, you won't ruin it at all. Your presence will make it better. My family adores you, and we want you there."

Mags bit back a sob. Her emotions were so close to the surface. When had she allowed those feelings to so easily overwhelm her? She cleared her throat, willing the sorrow to subside. This wasn't like her, and she wasn't sure why she struggled so. "Have you ever felt like you didn't belong?" As soon as she said the words, she wished she could take them back.

"Absolutely, I have. As you know, I was adopted from the orphan train. When I lived in New York, I didn't feel like I belonged. When I first arrived here, I didn't feel like I belonged either. It would take some time before I recognized God's goodness in sending me the parents that He had planned for me all along. The siblings who would embrace me. The family that would love me unconditionally. And most importantly, the Lord, who held me in His firm grasp from the beginning."

Mae's tender words infiltrated Mags's mind and heart. She'd known that some of Timothy's siblings were adopted, but she didn't know their entire stories. "Thank you for sharing that. I just..." She reached up and swiped at a tear.

Her friend's brow furrowed in concern. "We truly want you there, if you'll have us."

The sobs wracked Mags then, and Mae folded her into an embrace and held her. A couple of townsfolk asked if she was all right. Mags now knew it wasn't because of nosiness or spite, but because they likely cared. Or at least that is what she would believe.

Mae took a step back and held Mags at arm's length. "Why don't you go back inside and freshen up? I will return to the location where the photograph is to be taken, and let my family know that something came up, and you will be arriving a few minutes late. And then I will return to retrieve you. Does that sound amenable to you?"

"Yes." Had she ever sounded like such a blubbering fool?

"I do have to warn you that I may not come alone, especially if my sisters think there might be a way they can be helpful."

Such a sentiment caused a tiny smile to tug at Mag's lips. That was one thing about the Shepherdson women—they all sought to be helpful whenever they possibly could. "Yes, you can bring your sisters. I may need more convincing."

Mae nodded and offered her own smile. "I shall return momentarily."

Mags entered the bakery and dashed into the back room. While not completely sure about participating in the photograph, her heart felt much lighter.

True to Mae's word, she, Ruby, Lucy, Velma, and Mrs. Shepherdson arrived about fifteen minutes later with a rap on the bakery door.

Mags had gathered herself together, washed her face, and refixed her hair.

"Is anyone as nervous as I am about this photograph?" asked Ruby. "To think that it will be a permanent rendering of a moment in time for decades to come is quite fascinating."

Mae shook her head. "It's truly not as scary as that."

Ruby inclined her head toward her sister. "Says the one who's had her photograph taken several times."

"Exactly," added Lucy. "What if my eyes are closed?"

Mrs. Shepherdson laughed. "It would be a memorable moment for certain if that were the case."

"Here is the stunning photograph of the Shepherdson family..." Rubes waved an arm in exaggeration. "What started as something so lovely and so encompassing of all of the children and grandchildren and a memento for years to come has been sadly upended due to Lucy falling asleep."

That caused a whole new round of laughter. Lucy shook her head. "Who knew that such an event would cause a case of the nerves?"

"Shall we ask Mags if she has any toothpicks in her bakery in which to ensure your eyes remain wide open?" asked Mae.

Mags watched as the Shepherdson women giggled and carried on about their concerns regarding the photograph. Watching them stirred more emotions. Recollections of her and Ma, laughing and giggling. Remembrances of Pa and his silly antics while driving the milk wagon. Memories of the good days with Phoebe. Oh, but to be a part of something like that again!

As if reading her mind, Mae and Ruby each linked one of their arms through Mags's. "Shall we embark on this adventure?" asked Ruby, always the more theatrical one.

"Adventure, indeed," agreed Velma.

"I believe I am ready."

And, for the most part, she was.

Timothy wasn't sure why everything always took women twenty times longer than it took men. But when he saw Mags sandwiched between Mae and Rubes, and Ma, Lucy, and Velma walking along with them, he realized that however long it needed to take was worth it.

Mags's beauty stole his breath, as it always did, but perhaps even more so today. Something about her face shone. He liked the way she had fixed her hair, and that pink dress she wore was his favorite. Her beauty wasn't the only thing that captivated him. Nor was it the fact that Mags helped feed his insatiable appetite for cakes, cookies, bread, pies, and pastries—although that certainly was helpful. He patted his stomach in response. No one would accuse him of being the skinny little younger brother any longer after consuming more than his share of rolled jelly cake and lemon raisin pie. He now had more girth to him.

Nor was it just her delightful wit or the way she cared for others. It was all of those things, but especially her newfound love for Jesus, her thoughtfulness, and the way she showed her love for others by whipping up a batch of their favorite dessert. Her adventurous spirit and the tender heart she'd once attempted to hide behind a brave façade.

It was all those things that had caused him to fall in love with her. To ask her for her hand in courtship. To consider a future with her. To ponder whether he'd found the one he wanted to spend the rest of his life with, the one whom he would add as the second most important thing in his life after his faith.

He took a step toward her. "You look beautiful today, Mags."

She blushed, the rosy glow in her cheeks competing with the pink of her dress.

"If we could please gather the family together. I do have other appointments today." The photographer, with his top hat, well-pressed suit, and shiny shoes, had been more than patient. Timothy had wanted to ask what had deterred Mags, but figured he could do so later. For now, it was enough just to aid his family in corralling all of the grandchildren into one location. Already, some of his nephews had decided to throw the baseball around and had smudged formerly clean trousers.

Fifteen minutes later, they stood in a formation determined by family sets and enhanced by the photographer's demands so that he could fit them all into the photograph. Mags seemed a bit hesitant when the photographer told her to stand beside Timothy.

Was she unsure about having her photograph taken? Some folks found it eerie or even unsettling to have their image preserved for years to come. He reached down and squeezed her hand before the photographer asked that they prepare for the photograph with a serious expression.

Timothy doubted his nieces and nephews could accommodate the photographer's request. Baby Evelyn was fussing, and Gloria kept holding up her new doll so it could be in the photograph too. L.J., Mae and Landon's youngest, brought along his pet worm, much to the girls' dismay.

"On the count of three," the photographer said.

And Timothy knew however the photograph turned out, it would be just perfect.

Timothy arrived on time, and Mags ushered him to the counter where she'd placed five of her latest concoctions. "I really am eager for your opinion."

"I'm sure I'll like them all."

His irresistible smile lit up the room, and Mags's heart thrummed wildly in her chest. "Please do be honest. I don't wish to sell a dessert that isn't utterly delicious."

Timothy pressed a gentle kiss on her cheek. "You needn't worry. Now, where do I start?"

Mags uncovered the first plate and handed Timothy a chocolate macaroon.

He devoured it in one bite. "Can I have seconds?"

She laughed. "After you try the other four."

Timothy shrugged and playfully lifted the dish towel from the second plate. He lifted a butter jumble and took a bite of the crisp cookie. "Delicious as well."

Perhaps Timothy wasn't the best taste tester. He liked everything. The next two plates held pieces of Providence cake cut into perfect squares and thin slices of rhubarb pie. On the final plate, she'd arranged three pieces of the final confection.

"The cake is good. So is the rhubarb pie. Of course, I've always been fond of rhubarb pie. What's on the final plate?"

"I'm not sure you'll cotton to that one. It isn't as sweet as the others."

"Magnolia Davenport, there is something you ought to know about me. After faith..." heat crept up his face, and he cleared his throat, "you, my family, and my farm, food is a top priority to me. I haven't met a dessert I haven't savored. Unless you consider some of the foods Alma made for me." He cringed. "So I highly doubt I won't like that yellow pie with its perfectly pinched golden crust."

"If you insist." She thought of the ingredients and how the recipe lacked sugar. Nutmeg and lemon extract, but no sugar.

"I insist."

He forked a gargantuan piece. "I think you might want to try a smaller bite."

Timothy shook his head. "No, this is the perfect-sized bite." He consumed the bite, and Mags sharply inhaled.

"Ah!" Timothy gagged, and his eyes watered. "What is this stuff?"

"Vinegar pie," she squeaked.

"I'm sorry, Mags, but it's awful." He gulped and wretched.

"I did warn you."

"After having to bathe in vinegar..." Timothy hurriedly reached for another chocolate macaroon.

Mags laughed. "I—the recipe doesn't call for sugar. But it does contain sorghum."

Timothy ate two more chocolate macaroons and another piece of rhubarb pie. "I should mention there are two things I *don't* eat. Vinegar, and I'm not overly fond of tomatoes."

"But didn't you say you liked all foods?"

"I may have exaggerated slightly." He laughed too, then, before reaching for a second piece of cake.

Chapter Twenty-Eight

Mags was busy rolling dough before the first customers arrived when the bakery door opened and a bowed-backed woman with a basket in her arms entered.

"Hello. Welcome to the bakery. May I help you?"

"Magnolia Davenport?"

"Yes?"

It was only then that Mags realized who the visitor was. "Mrs. Davenport?" Why had Phoebe's grandmother come for a visit? "Where is Phoebe?"

The woman stepped closer. A tiny baby, swaddled in a blanket, slept in the basket. Mags's breath caught in her throat. No, she wouldn't think the worst. "Where is Phoebe?" she repeated.

Phoebe's grandmother blinked. "Magnolia, there is something I need to tell you."

"Oh?" She bit her lip. Surely Phoebe was gathering their trunks. Surely her grandmother had only accompanied her due to the lengthy trip.

"Magnolia..." Mrs. Davenport set the basket on the floor and wrung her hands.

"Please tell me where Phoebe is." Her question echoed in the silence.

The woman reached for Mags's arm, and Mags pulled away. "Why isn't she here?"

"I'm sorry. Phoebe died in childbirth."

"No. That's not true. It's not." Mags clutched the side of the counter, her legs shaking and pain stabbing through her heart.

Mrs. Davenport began to cry. "I hated to have to be the one to tell you." She paused and held a hand to her throat. "Phoebe loved you so much. She spoke often about you and the grand times you shared as children. She told me how you planned to move her and Jenny to Horizon. She missed you every day." Phoebe's grandmother's voice trembled, as tears slid down her wrinkled face.

"I missed her every day." Mags's chest felt hollow, and the rising guilt of not staying in Chicago again returned to her thoughts. "I should have stayed."

"I can't tell you the countless times I've blamed myself. But there was nothing you or I could have done." Mrs. Davenport withdrew a handkerchief from her reticule. "She told me that if anything were to happen, she wanted you to raise Jenny."

"What about you?"

"I'm far too old, child."

"But Jenny knows you. You're her flesh and blood. I'm not sure I can be Jenny's ma."

"Phoebe wouldn't have chosen you if she thought you wouldn't be the best choice."

Mags prayed for God's strength to sustain her.

"Magnolia, there is something else I need to say to you."

It wasn't enough to hear that Phoebe had passed? That Mags no longer had a sister? That the hope of moving her here to Horizon would never happen?

"Please hear what I have to say." The woman's sad eyes pleaded with her. Mags wasn't the only one grieving. Mrs. Davenport had lost her granddaughter. A mournful glistening of tears edged the woman's eyes.

"I regret the way I treated you just because you weren't born to Cassius." She stared at something in the distance. "I had no reason to treat an innocent child the way I treated you. To turn you away." A choked sob escaped her lips, and the baby stirred. "It was wrong of me, and the Lord has convicted me of my grievous error."

"I never understood it," Mags whispered.

"It is among my greatest regrets. I could have taken you in and raised you as my granddaughter. It's what Cassius would have wanted. But I was so selfish. I allowed a disagreement over something so foolish to cause a rift between me and my only child. I..." Her shoulders bowed. "I never got to tell him I loved him before he died."

"I think he knew."

"Well, be that as it may, I have learned the hard way that we are not guaranteed tomorrow."

"I wanted to live with you," she dared say, just in case she had imagined the apology.

"I know you did. I have recalled over and over again in my mind that day at the parsonage. You begged me to take you, but I—I was cold, uncaring, detached, and merciless. Please accept my apology. I hope someday you can forgive me."

Mags didn't want to forgive her. Didn't want to let go of the hurt and the pain and the ache of rejection. She wanted to tell Phoebe's grandmother just what she'd experienced at the hands of the woman's refusal to take her in. "I was all alone."

"I know that, and I am so, so sorry. Words aren't enough to atone for what I did, but please believe me. If I could go back, I would change so many things. My son loved your mother, and he loved you. I regret that I could not show that same love."

Jenny whimpered, and Mags reached for the baby. Jenny peered up at her with dampened eyes, her lip trembling. "It's all right, precious one," she said, holding Jenny close to her, just as Ma had when Mags was a little girl.

Mrs. Davenport backed up a few steps. "I should be on my way. I plan to catch the train back to Cornwall and stay there for the night."

The words Mags needed to say stuck in her throat. The Lord had forgiven her for much. The Bennicks forgave her for hitching a ride on their railway instead of paying for a train ticket. Why was it so arduous to forgive Mrs. Davenport?

"I will raise Jenny as my own. As Phoebe wanted." Not the only words Mags needed to say, but important ones nonetheless.

"Please tell Jenny about Phoebe when she's old enough to understand."

"I will."

"Farewell, then." Mrs. Davenport turned to leave.

"Wait." Mags laid Jenny back in the basket. "I don't want to forgive you. The pain is so deep. The wondering—about—about what might have been if I hadn't had to live with my aunts. If you had taken me in. If I hadn't missed out on all those years with Phoebe."

"Oh, Magnolia. I know. Believe me, I know."

"How could you know? How could you even understand what I went through after my parents died?"

"You're right. I can't know. I just wish I could take it all back. As a woman who professes Christ, I should have done better by you."

The woman's hunched back, shriveled body, and fragile state reminded Mags that life *was* fragile. Mrs. Davenport's red-rimmed eyes and wobbly voice testified that she, too, was grieving. Grieving the loss of her granddaughter. Grieving the fact that her age and health precluded her from raising Jenny.

And the tender mercy that Jesus had shown Mags all these years...the protection He'd put over her while she resided with her aunts and lived alone in a big city. How He'd guided her to Horizon—even though she didn't ask for His guidance. His protection in the stagecoach. His patience in drawing her to Him. The people He'd placed in her path who spoke into her life. The forgiveness He'd shown her for all of her past mistakes.

How could Mags not show forgiveness to Phoebe's grandmother?

It wasn't easy. It wasn't what she wanted to do, but it *was* something she *must* do. She released her firm grip on the counter and took a shaky step forward. "Mrs. Davenport." A fractured whisper escaped her emotion-clogged throat. "I forgive you."

"Thank you." Mrs. Davenport lifted her head, and the tears glistened in her eyes. "Thank you so much." She embraced Mags, and for a moment, Mags pretended Mrs. Davenport was her grandmother as well.

Mags had no idea how she'd care for Jenny on her own, but she did know one thing. God *had* been with her all these years. He wouldn't desert her now. *Lord, please guide me in caring for Jenny. Please let me be the ma my mother was.*

Mags cradled Jenny. She was so tiny. So perfect. A thatch of dark brown hair and her heart-shaped face were so like Phoebe's.

"Lord," she breathed. "I know for so long I disregarded you. I am so sorry. I know now that you had your fingerprints on every detail of my life. But did Phoebe have to die? Jenny needs her. *I* need her."

With one hand, she dragged one of the chairs behind the counter and sat in it, hoping for the first time that no customers would decide to visit the bakery. "Oh, Jenny, I'm so, so sorry about your ma." Unrestrained tears flowed from her eyes and onto Jenny's blanket.

"I don't understand—I don't understand why this has happened." She held the baby tightly in her arms as the emotion flowed from her.

She should lock the door. In a hazy fog, Mags dragged herself to the front of the bakery. But as she was about to bolt the door, she noticed a familiar face on the other side.

"Mags?"

Her mouth opened, but no words came out. Slowly, he opened the door.

Timothy's gaze fell to Jenny. "Who is this? What's going on?"

She collapsed against him, and Timothy
wrapped his arms around her and Jenny. "Let's sit down." He led her back behind the counter, where he pulled another chair beside the one she had placed there. "Tell me what happened."

If there was anyone who could help her—anyone who could help her make sense of it, it would be the man that she had come to love. Mags gently set Jenny back in the basket. Timothy reached for Mags's hands.

"It's Phoebe. She died shortly after childbirth. Her grandmother brought Jenny to me just a few hours ago." Her choked words sounded foreign in her own ears.

"I'm so, so sorry, Mags." He pulled her closer to him. She rested her head on his chest and allowed the tears to flow freely. He said nothing, only stroking her hair and resting his head on hers.

"I don't understand why this would happen. Wasn't it enough to lose my parents?"

A calloused thumb tenderly stroked her cheek. "I don't understand it either."

"And how am I supposed to care for Jenny? I've never been a mother."

"You've cared for your aunt's children."

"But that's not the same."

"It might not be the same, but I do know God will equip you to care for her."

"I didn't get to tell Phoebe goodbye. Maybe if I had been there..."

Timothy framed her face in his hands. "Mags, don't do this to yourself. We don't know what would have happened if you had been there."

"But I feel so guilty I should have stayed. I thought for sure she and Larry and the baby would move to Horizon. But you know what?" Her voice shook. "Larry left before Jenny was even born. He left Phoebe. I never liked him, but she loved him. How could he do that?"

"God in His mercy allowed Larry to leave. If Larry had stayed, he'd be raising Jenny."

The impact of Timothy's words crashed through her mind. He was right. But...

"I just don't know, she's so tiny, and what if something happens to her too?"

"The Lord tells us not to fear. Not to be anxious for anything. To rest in Him. To give Him our burdens. It won't be easy, but God will help you raise Jenny as your own." He kissed her forehead, then took her hands in his. "This didn't catch God unaware. He knew when He created Jenny that you would be the one to raise her. He will be there to guide you as you raise her. As *we* raise her."

Mags lifted her face, the tears clinging to her lashes, causing everything to blur. "We?"

"We, if you'll have me."

Another choked sob escaped Mags, and she nodded. Shouldn't she know by now that God always made a way? This time, that way would be through a stalwart man of faith who would not only love her, but would also raise Jenny as his own.

Epilogue
Spring 1898

"How about we take Papa some rolled jelly cake?" Mags lifted Jenny into the pram. She looked especially adorable today in her pink bonnet and calico apron that matched the one Mags wore while baking.

Mags placed the cake in the pram beside Jenny. The beautiful sunny day, with the fields fresh from plowing and the mountains in the distance, was perfect to share the thrilling news with her husband.

Things were going well. Timothy had started the spring planting. Ozias's father had recovered and was working on a farm in Horizon, and his family no longer lived in a makeshift tent. Mr. Yates secured the job in Ingleville, and reconciliation with his family was a real possibility.

"Papa," Jenny babbled. She reminded Mags so much of Phoebe, and Cassius too, with her curly dark hair and almond-shaped hazel eyes.

"Yes, we'll see Papa soon." Mags spied Timothy mending the fence with Goose, who barked and ran to greet them, placing her front paws on the side of the pram. Jenny giggled when Goose licked her hand. She patted the dog on the head. "Goo."

Timothy started in their direction. His handsome face, work shirt stretched tightly across his muscular shoulders and chest, and his jeans accentuating his slim waist and long legs reminded her just how dapper her husband of five months was. She blushed at the thought.

"How are my two favorite girls doing?" He planted a kiss on Mags's cheek, then bent over to kiss Jenny's head.

"Papa."

"I love to hear her say that." He wrapped his arms around Mags. "I've missed you today."

"And I've missed you. Jenny and I have been busy baking."

"Promise me it's not vinegar pie."

"No, not vinegar pie."

"All right, in that case..." he didn't finish his sentence because his lips met hers in a passionate kiss before they heard a suspicious noise behind them.

Mags turned to see Jenny helping herself to the rolled jelly cake. Goose sat on her haunches, begging for a bite. "Yum." Jenny's face was covered in strawberry jam, smeared all the way from her cheeks to her forehead.

"Oh, Jenny, you silly girl. That's for Papa."

"Papa." She opened her fisted hand to expose a slobbery piece of rolled jelly cake. Timothy opened his mouth, and she plopped it inside, giggling as she did so.

"Yum. You're going to be an amazing baker just like your ma."

"Yum," mimicked Jenny.

Mags teasingly jabbed Timothy in the side. "She'll be an amazing big sister, too."

"An amazing...did you say an amazing big sister?"

"I did."

A glint of wonder showed in his eyes. "Are you saying what I think you're saying?"

"You, Mr. Timothy Tyler Shepherdson, are about to be a father once again. It'll be about eight months from now, but..."

She glanced up at him but didn't have the opportunity to say anything more because he'd lifted her plumb off her feet and swung her around in his arms.

"I love you, Magnolia Cici Shepherdson."

"And I love you, Timothy Tyler Shepherson."

He kissed her again before setting her on her feet. As she surveyed her family, the farm, and even Goose, who still begged for a morsel, Mags couldn't help but fathom at the mercy of the God of second chances...and of new beginnings.

Where Are They Now?

WONDER WHAT YOUR FAVORITE characters are up to? Read on...

Tyler and Paisley reside on their same farm in Horizon and are proud grandparents of numerous grandchildren, whom they dote on and spoil. The once-a-week family supper tradition remains an important part of their lives. Paisley, with their daughter Ruby, has also penned her own cookbook, *Recipes from Paisley Shepherdson's Kitchen*.

Ruby and Jake continue to reside in Horizon. They went on to have four more children, including one they adopted from the orphan train. Ruby writes for *The Horizon Herald* each month and has authored two additional books, including a cookbook co-authored with her mother. Jake secured more acreage and expanded their farm, which is known for its prize potatoes.

Mae and Landon reside in Horizon, but travel frequently to other locales for Landon's job with Bennick Railways. They adopted another child from the Horizon School for the Deaf and are dedicated benefactors of the school.

Timothy and Mags reside on their farm in Horizon. They have four children, including one adopted from the orphan train. Mags is known far and wide for her baking and has won several awards at the county fair. Eventually, Timothy purchased bifocals out of necessity and no longer refuses to wear his spectacles.

Albert continues to pastor the church in Horizon, and over the years, it has grown substantially, in keeping with the uptick in Horizon's population. Velma volunteers her time with the women's ministry, and with her gift of hospitality, hosts a weekly women's Bible study.

Lucy and Hans continue to reside in Horizon, where they enjoy spending time with their passel of grandchildren.

Greta and the Lieutenant continue to own and manage the boardinghouse. They recently became grandparents when their son married. They have one granddaughter.

Polly became a teacher at the Horizon School for the Deaf. She met and fell in love with a fellow teacher, and they live happily ever after with their two children.

Hosea and L.J. carried on the Bennick Railways legacy, surviving downturns in the economy to remain the top transcontinental railroad. Hosea and his wife reside in Horizon with their two children. L.J. has not yet married, but rumor has it that he is fond of a woman who resides in Cornwall.

Simon became a missionary and traveled to other countries before settling in Boise City. He married a fellow missionary, and together, they have two children.

Sherman waited a while before marrying, but finally found the love of his life, Wilhelmenia and Hubert's granddaughter. They are proud parents of twin daughters. Sherman works as a manager for Bennick Railways.

Gus finally achieved his dream by "adopting" a pet skunk. Things did not go well for him, and he was mentored by his Uncle Timothy about the importance of apple cider vinegar. In adulthood, Gus became a farmer like his pa and expanded the Lynton farm. He married a spunky woman from Ingleville, and they have four sons.

Carrie became a teacher and later married the local dentist. They are the parents of three daughters.

Becky married Sherman's best friend after years of declaring him a nuisance. They reside in nearby Ingleville, where they own a hardware store and raise their family of two sons and a daughter.

Pansy married a superintendent for Bennick Railways. They have five children, including three adopted from the orphan train.

Little Hans works with his father in the woodworking business and has served as mayor of Horizon.

Gloria resides on a horse farm outside of Horizon with her husband. They raise, train, and sell horses. Esteemed in horsemanship, Gloria has won numerous awards.

Jenny became a telephone operator for the switchboard in Horizon. She later married a doctor, and they have two daughters.

Ozias became an entrepreneur. After being a salesman and dabbling in farming, trying his hand as a barber, and working for a short time for the railroad, Ozias opened his own shoe store on Main Street in Horizon. He has been successful in convincing folks they need new footwear. He married a frequent customer, and he and his wife have seven children and live above the store. His parents and sisters are doing well.

Gladys and Bertram Bennick, due to their advancing age, no longer travel between their homes and now permanently reside in Horizon, much to Bertram's irritation. They spend plentiful time with their children, grandchildren, and great-grandchildren. Gladys recently made a decision for

Christ and founded a ministry. Bertram has agreed to attend church regularly and, in his older age, has become less cantankerous.

Alma placed an advertisement in the newspaper for a husband and subsequently married a chef who owns a restaurant in Cornwall.

Mary Lou and her husband, a gardener at the Horizon School for the Deaf Botanical Gardens, have one son.

DON'T MISS THIS PREVIEW OF
HEART OF COURAGE

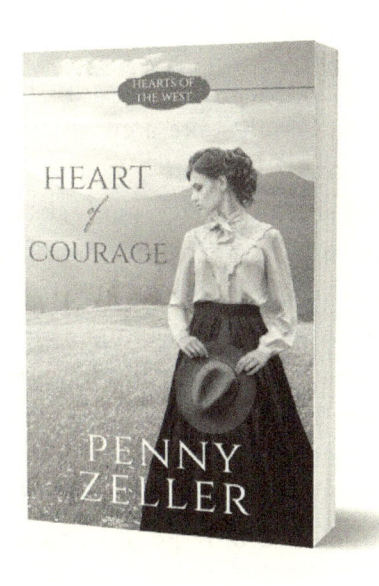

A NEW LIFE AWAITS HER...
IF SHE CAN FIND THE COURAGE.

Heart of Courage
A Preview

Hopes and dreams...gone in an instant.

Funny how life could take a completely different turn than one expected.

LilyBeth Engel leaned back against the train seat and watched the remnants of the city pass her by. Her throat burned as tears threatened.

So much promise. Now for naught.

Her two-year-old son stirred in her arms, his peacefulness reassuring her that somehow, someway, all would be well. She gently patted his swoop of a brown curl that rested on his forehead above pudgy cheeks. Such a precious child. The only good to have come from her marriage.

LilyBeth returned her gaze out the window. When she'd handed the coins allotted for this "adventure" to the ticketmaster, she'd almost turned and changed her mind. *"How far will this get us?"*

He'd arched a fuzzy eyebrow. *"Likely somewhere in the middle of the Montana Territory."*

She wasn't familiar with the Montana Territory, but it would have to do. *"Please, then, a ticket to the Montana Territory."*

He regarded her and hesitated, perhaps attempting to ascertain if she was serious. *"You do realize there are about five people in the entire territory, or so I'm told."*

Five people sounded refreshing after what she'd endured in the city. *"Be that as it may, I'll take a ticket."*

"Don't say I didn't warn you." He traded her coins for a promise of a new adventure. *"The child rides free. Enjoy your new life in Hilltop."*

Hilltop. She liked the sound of it. Wide-open spaces, no cramped buildings on busy city streets. Yes, she would like the Montana Territory.

Wouldn't she?

Apprehension engulfed her for the first time since boarding. What if the ticketmaster was correct and there were but a handful of people? She'd never be able to secure a future for Otis and herself if that was the case.

"Trust in the Lord with all thine heart; and lean not unto thine own understanding. In all thy ways acknowledge him, and he shall direct your paths."

With her new faith brought the unexpected trust LilyBeth needed to have that the Lord would see her through. That she could depend on Someone. That her life was rooted firmly in His hands. Otis's life as well.

Lord, please help me to have courage.

Otis stirred, his eyelids fluttering before his breathing evened again.

She would do whatever it took to care for him. To raise him for the Lord. To ensure his life didn't resemble hers—or the first twenty-three years of it, anyhow.

The train came to a stop, and LilyBeth peered out the window. After several long days, she'd finally arrived in Hilltop in the Montana Territory. She juggled an irritable Otis, her carpetbag, and the trunk, and disembarked. Folks from the train crowded into the train depot. When she finally made her way to the counter, she asked how she might find a place to stay in Hilltop.

The gentleman behind the counter chuckled. "You must be mistaken, ma'am. This isn't Hilltop."

"I'm in the wrong place?" Her breath snagged in her throat. If not Hilltop, then where?

"Yes, ma'am. You're about thirty miles from Hilltop."

"Thirty miles?"

"That's what I said. Now, if you'll scoot on out of the way, there are folks behind you I need to assist."

She stepped to the side, then meandered to the porch. People from the train milled about. Perhaps she needed to re-board and Hilltop was just ahead.

An inspection in every direction indicated nothing but desolation. Even the trees were sparse. Just barren land, a train track, and a nearby stagecoach.

Lord, please guide me.

She set her son down on the weathered porch and clasped his hand. Her arm tingled from having been held in one position for so long. Placing her carpetbag and trunk beside her, she shielded her eyes and again scrutinized the area.

The view hadn't changed.

She tilted her head upward and caught the word, "Walkerville" on the sign above the depot. Taking up her bag and trunk once more, she led Otis inside where she stood in line until it was again her turn to speak with the ticket master.

"Sir, will the train continue to Hilltop?"

"No, ma'am. If you want to go to Hilltop, you'll need to board the stagecoach."

"The stagecoach? Is it an additional fee?"

"Let me see your ticket."

She handed it to him and mentally calculated her meager funds. Would it be enough to purchase a stagecoach ticket to Hilltop? Was there somewhere closer?

"The trip to Hilltop is included in your fare."

Praise God! "Thank you."

"It leaves in ten minutes."

Just enough time to use the privy and give Otis a chance to stretch his legs.

LilyBeth had never ridden on a stagecoach before. She lifted Otis into the coach before climbing the steps and taking a seat on the edge beside an elderly couple. By the time everyone boarded, seven people and Otis, who sat on her lap, crammed into the seats. Thankfully, the early June day was pleasantly mild. LilyBeth could not imagine being wedged in such confined quarters in the heat of the summer.

The driver listed off a multitude of rules, including abstaining from liquor unless one planned to share, men foregoing cigars and uttering foul language, and no discussing stagecoach robberies.

The latter prompted concern among the passengers, especially LilyBeth. She'd heard stories about ne'er-do-wells holding up stages and leaving the riders stranded, injured, or worse.

She attempted not to think of such things. After all, the Lord had brought her and Otis safely this far. He would deliver them without incident to Hilltop, wouldn't He?

Lord, please help me be courageous.

As the horses increased their speed, she stared out the window at the scenery as the stagecoach barreled along. Dirt devils swirled in the breeze, and dust plumed through the windows, causing her and several others to cough. The stage tilted to and fro, jostling its passengers about. A peculiar and unknown scent rode on the wind.

"Nothing like the smell of sagebrush," muttered the stuffy man across from her.

LilyBeth inhaled deeply and eyed the spikey grayish-blue-green plants lining the road. Her heartbeat pounded in tandem with the horses' hooves hammering the earth.

Otis whimpered, his face pale and his body limp and lethargic. LilyBeth situated him into as comfortable of a position as possible given the proximity of the person beside her. He rested his head against her. She prayed he wasn't ill.

"Poor child," clucked the woman beside her. "Likely the swaying of the stage has caused him stomach upset."

LilyBeth smoothed the hair from his forehead. If he was able to hear her, she'd sing a hymn to console him. He fussed again. "Otis walk."

"Not right now, sweet boy. We're going for a ride. Look at the antelope." She pointed out the window to a green meadow in the distance where numerous antelope fed on the grasses.

The crabby man across from her checked his timepiece. "How long on this formidable mode of transport?"

"Hilltop is thirty miles away," offered an elderly man. "Is that your destination?"

He pinched his curly, pencil-thin mustache between his forefinger and thumb. "It is." He narrowed his eyes at LilyBeth. "Best keep the child quiet."

LilyBeth whispered quietly in Otis's ear, attempting to soothe him. His eyes drooped, and she wished she had a cool cloth.

She leaned her head against the back of the stage. If Hilltop was thirty miles away, how long would they be aboard the stage? Several hours?

"If the child is sick, it won't do to endanger the rest of us on the stage," growled the grouchy man.

The woman beside LilyBeth tossed a pointed look across the narrow aisle between the seats. "It's doubtful he's ill. More likely he's just nauseous due to the motion."

The man harumphed and glowered behind his spectacles.

Otis soon fell asleep. LilyBeth attempted to keep him from jouncing about, his weight straining her arms. He had grown much in the past year, a healthy boy despite his sickly beginnings as an infant.

Was traveling to the unknown town of Hilltop a wise decision? Would she be able to support herself and Otis? Would the people be gracious and kind? Should she have chosen another town? Another state or territory?

"Sometimes we can't rest in His peace because we're too busy allowing our minds to wonder about the constant what-ifs and whatnot. Rest assuredly in His arms, and give your thoughts and worries to Him."

Kittie and her husband, Harold, had imparted such wisdom. Such knowledge of the Word of God. Were it not for them...

No, she wouldn't think of it. Instead, LilyBeth attempted to drown out the sounds around her, purge all the worries and thoughts from her mind, and rest in her favorite verse: "*Be of good courage, and he shall strengthen your heart, all ye that hope in the LORD.*"

Two hours later, sporadic ranches came into view. LilyBeth inclined her head out the window. Towering mountains dusted with snow loomed in the distance, their magnificence courtesy of an artistic Creator. Alongside the road, wildflowers in hues of pink, purple, and yellow mixed with green meadows. Cows dotted the landscape, and LilyBeth covered her mouth with her free hand. The beauty before her was unparalleled.

Were they nearing Hilltop?

"Mama?"

Otis peered up at her with sleepy eyes. "Otis's tummy hungwee." He scooted to a sitting position, and she rifled through her carpetbag. Surely there was a soda cracker left in the tin at the bottom of the bag. Surely.

If she could find one, perhaps it would also ease Otis's stomach. Grasping her son tightly, lest he tumble from her lap, she pushed aside clothing until she retrieved the tin. She opened it to find one remaining soda cracker, broken into a few pieces, but a small blessing nonetheless.

Otis ate it within seconds, and she doubted he even took the time to chew it. "More?" he asked.

"Soon, sweet boy, soon."

She prayed she'd be able to keep her promise.

If you want to be among the first to hear about Penny's latest book projects, sign up for her newsletter at www.pennyzeller.com. You will receive book and writing updates, encouragement, notification of current giveaways, occasional freebies, and special offers.

If you enjoyed this glimpse into the lives of Mags and Timothy, please consider leaving a review on your social media, Amazon, Goodreads, Barnes and Noble, or BookBub. Reviews are critical to authors, and those stars you give us are such an encouragement.

Author's Note

Dear Reader,

It's always difficult to leave my characters and the town of Horizon in the rear view mirror. It truly is bittersweet to end a series, and I remember when *Over the Horizon*, the first book, was merely a dream. While I had longed for it to be published sooner, God's timing was (and is) always perfect. A side note: there is an opportunity for a fifth and final book in the series. We'll see what the Lord has in mind.

I charted Mags's course from Chicago to Horizon using a real map from that time. Of course, Horizon is a fictional town, but the journey from Chicago to Boise City was a real route, and some people did ride for free, including reporters and employees of the railroad. Apparently, clergy could ride for half price.

During my research, I discovered that a peddler did, in fact, dupe a customer into purchasing fake crop seeds. People also really did hide loot in strange places, including sugar dishes.

I researched an article that indicated spectacles were a sign of being frail and elderly in years past. There was a stigma surrounding eyeglasses, and on many accounts, it was considered unsightly to wear them. Of course, Timothy, being a strapping young man would not want to be seen as elderly, frail, or "unsightly".

Several things in the book were inspired by true events, and I took fictional liberties in altering those stories for the book. Case in point: Mags's idea to hide her fellow passengers' valuables really did happen, and there was an instance of outlaws wearing beards to conceal their identity. The Gingham Ball was inspired by something called the Calico Ball that took place in Bannack, Montana. Side note: if you've never visited Bannack, add it to your list of must-visits.

A lot of research went into the skunk scene. A skunk with a jar on his head really did happen, as did the suggestion to use oil, which didn't work. There were lots of old remedies for skunk smell removal, including tomato juice and vinegar. Singed whiskers on a dog really did happen as did the tomato juice dyeing a white dog pink.

Some funny errors caught in *Love on the Horizon* before it went to print include:

Threw a bag of *feet* into the back of the wagon instead of *feed*, and Mayor Trabert stood behind the *left turn*, instead of the *lectern*.

Writing historical romances requires hours of research, even if we don't intend to include everything we've discovered. One of the things we authors must be mindful of is word usage at the time. I continue to be surprised by which words were used and which weren't.

Words you wouldn't expect to be in use at the time included the following:

Homebody - 1821

Tug-of-war - 1677

Smattering - 1538

Magnate - 15th century
Faux pas - 1676
Chunky - 1733
Gingersnap - 1805
Crepe paper - 1896

Who was your favorite character in the Horizon Series? As for me, I can't really pinpoint just one. Of course, Paisley and Tyler hold a special place in my heart because they were the first ones whose story came to life. Precious little Mae-Mae, having come from such a difficult place, is one of my favorites, as is Ruby, who reminds me a lot of myself. Lucy, of course, being such a mother hen, was a delight to write. My personal favorites list wouldn't be complete without including our hunky heroes. Jake rates high on the list, as does Timothy. But I certainly can't forget Landon and his more gentle ways or Albert and how he changed so much throughout the years. I would be remiss if I didn't mention Gus and Ozias.

While I also write Christian romantic suspense and Christian rom-coms, I can never stay away from Christian historical romance for long. I'll be taking another trip to Hollow Creek, Montana, with Arrosa's story, and next year, I'll begin a new series set in Wyoming.

Thank you, as always, for spending time within the pages of my books. Your loyalty means so much to me. Until next time, happy reading!

Blessings,
Penny

Acknowledgments

To my family who continually walk with me through this crazy writing gig. I couldn't do it without you!

To my oldest daughter, who helps me brainstorm scenes and is my all-around sounding board for my books. I appreciate you so much!

To my Penny's Peeps Street Team. Thank you for spreading the word about my books, for always being so willing to read and review my stories, and for your steadfast encouragement and support.

To my beta readers. You are the ones who see my project at its beginning stages. Thank you for all of your wonderful suggestions.

To Marie Concannon—what would I do without your amazing research skills? I'm so blessed to have you on "speed dial". Thank you for your continual help in researching trains, railway spurs, passengers, stagecoaches, bake sales, and more. Your assistance has given me so many great ideas for stories and has made current ones come to life with historical richness and accuracy.

To my skunk helpers. When I put out the call for skunk stories, my wonderful readers did not disappoint! I received several awesome suggestions. Joan W., whose white poodle turned pink after being bathed in tomato juice, inspired me to turn Goose in the story pink. Kati Driban gave me the idea for Goose's whiskers to be singed from a true story she told about her own dog's experience with being sprayed by a skunk. Thank you, ladies, for your input!

To my readers, may God bless you and guide you as you grow in your walk with Him.

And, most importantly, thank you to my Lord and Savior, Jesus Christ. It is my deepest desire to glorify You with my writing and help bring others to a knowledge of Your saving grace.

Let the words of my mouth and the meditation of my heart be acceptable in your sight, O Lord, my rock and my redeemer. ~
Psalm 19:14

About the Author

Penny Zeller is known for her heartfelt stories of faith-filled happily ever afters and her passion to impact lives for Christ through fiction. Her books feature tender romance, steady doses of humor, and memorable characters that stay with you long after the last page.

While she has had a love for writing since childhood, Penny began her adult writing career penning articles for national and regional publications on a wide variety of topics. Today Penny is a multi-published author of over three dozen books and is also a fitness instructor, loves the outdoors, and is a flower gardening addict. In her spare time, she enjoys camping, hiking, kayaking, biking, birdwatching, reading, running, and playing volleyball.

Penny resides with her husband and two daughters in small-town America and loves to connect with her readers at her website at www.pennyzeller.com, her blog, www.pennyzeller.wordpress.com, and her Facebook page at www.facebook.com/pennyzellerbooks where she posts faith, funnies, writing updates, and encouragement. All of her socials can be found at https://linktr.ee/pennyzeller.

HORIZON SERIES

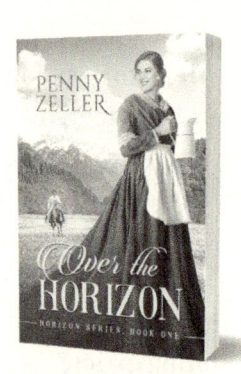

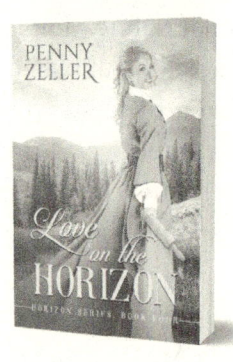

WYOMING SUNRISE

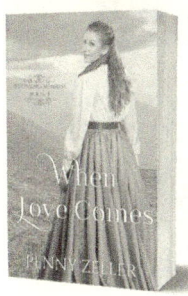

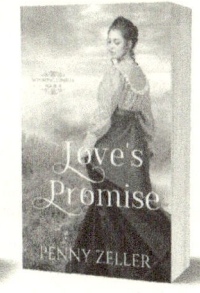

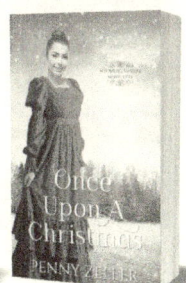

HOLLOW CREEK

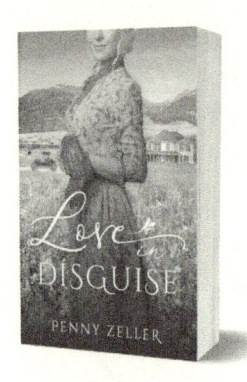

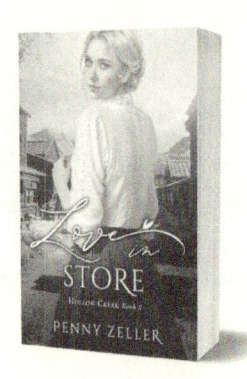

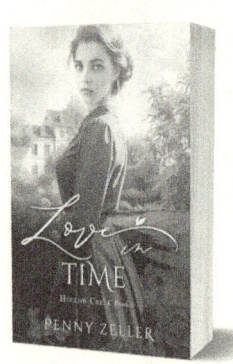

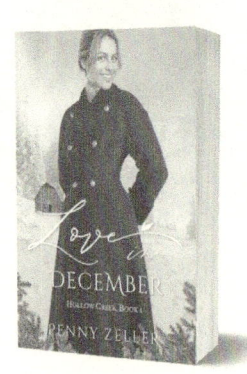

HILLTOP SERIES

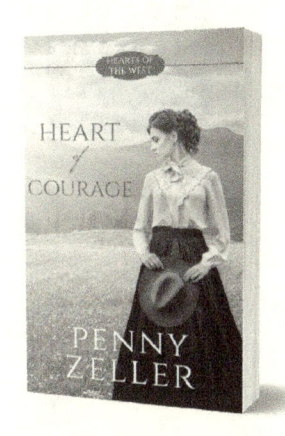

CHRISTIAN ROMANTIC SUSPENSE

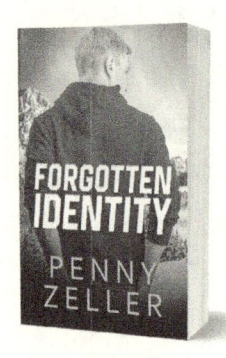

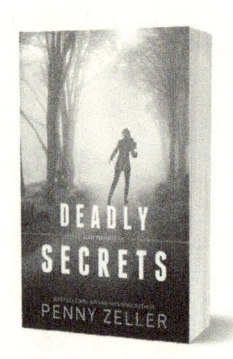

MOUNTAIN JUSTICE SERIES

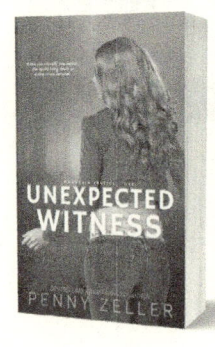

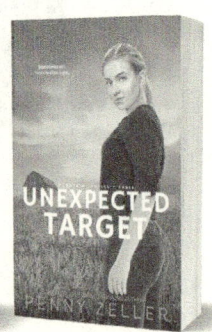

small town shenanigans

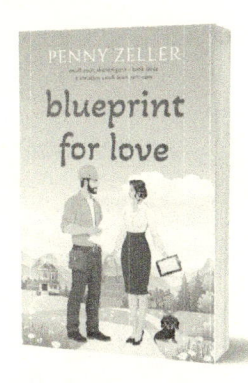

CONTEMPORARY ROMANCES

STANDALONE

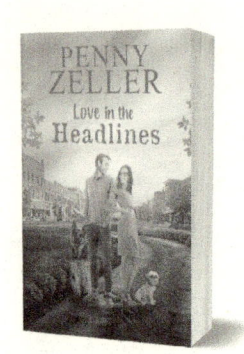

CHOKECHERRY HEIGHTS SERIES

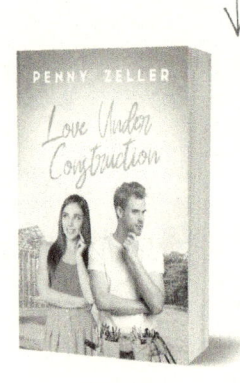

Made in United States
Orlando, FL
29 October 2025